Songbird
UNDER A
GERMAN MOON

Songbird
UNDER A
GERMAN MOON

TRICIA
GOYER

summerside
PRESS

Summerside Press™
Minneapolis 55438
www.summersidepress.com
Songbird under a German Moon
© 2010 by Tricia Goyer

ISBN 978-1-935416-68-5

Scripture references are from the following sources:
The Holy Bible, King James Version (KJV).

All characters are fictional. Any resemblances to
actual people are purely coincidental.

Cover and interior design by Müllerhaus Publishing Group
www.mullerhaus.net.

*Summerside Press™ is an inspirational publisher offering fresh,
irresistible books to uplift the heart and engage the mind.*

Printed in USA.

DEDICATION

To my mom, Linda Martin.
Thank you for being the first to believe in me.

ACKNOWLEDGMENTS

Many thanks to my wonderful husband, John, for being my biggest fan, my loudest supporter, and my rock. And to my kids, Cory, Leslie, and Nathan, who give my life so much joy. And my grandma who is the best laundry fairy ever! Thank you to Colleen Coble and Cara Putman for brainstorming with me. Your ideas made this book so fun to write! Also, thanks to my assistant Amy Lathrop and my friends Cara Putman and Jim Thompson for being great readers. Your comments rocked!

Thank you to Susan Downs, my awesome editor, for helping me and encouraging me in so many ways. This story wouldn't be half as good without your input. Also, Ellen Tarver for your great editorial advice, too!

Finally, special thanks to Janet Grant for being an encouraging agent and mentor. I appreciate you!

We can stand affliction better than we can prosperity, for in prosperity we forget God.

--Dwight L. Moody

PROLOGUE

Dierk scanned the set, taking in every element with a master's eye. Every prop had to be perfectly in place—and it was almost so. The costumes hung with care, waiting for those who would take part in the *Festspielhaus*—Festival House's—final number. The blue and gold gown for Irene, the gold flowing robe for Rienzi's prayer, the white silk dresses for the Messengers of Peace.

The room was dark—hidden in the recesses and tucked behind the stage where the greatest singers in history had brought Richard Wagner's works to life. But Dierk knew it wouldn't remain hidden for long. At the right moment, all would be known. The final act would play.

A poster of the accursed Fuehrer hung on the wall. Dierk rose, paced the room, and then paused. Bending down, he slipped the knife from his ankle sheath. Then he stood. With a flip of his wrist, the knife flew from his hand, striking through Hitler's temple and into the wall with a thud. Dierk's greatest regret was that he hadn't personally killed the Fuehrer when he'd had the opportunity. After all, it was Hitler who'd cost him so much—all Dierk cared about.

Hitler had taken Richard Wagner's work and twisted the message and the music to carry out his own dark plot. Hitler had used Wagner's music in rallies. He'd rewarded Nazi officers with tickets to Wagner's operas. Dierk didn't know which was worse, that the officers cared so little about the great works or that the revered music had rewarded them for killing the innocent along with the guilty. *So many innocent souls.*

As much as Dierk hated how Hitler had used the Festspielhaus for his own gain, at least it had been Wagner's music that had played. Now the Americans, who knew nothing of Wagner—his message or his genius—used the stage for their irreverent song and dance. A disgrace! Anger boiled in Dierk's chest. He must do something to stop them. Who knew how many "singers" and "dancers" would continue to arrive.

They need a warning. They must understand—

As those who'd gone before him, it was now his part to keep Wagner's memory strong—and to destroy those who dared pollute the legacy of such a visionary.

Dierk released a low sigh. His heart ached with the knowledge that destruction and death remained the only way to remind the world of what was lost. If only there were a simpler path. But as Wagner had taught in *Der Ring des Nibelungen,* love and power could not live together.

Now that the war was over, Dierk knew he could choose a new life, a new home. His skills in the opera would be sought after—by those whose minds turned away from war to musical theater once again. But Dierk would not claim such power. Instead, he had chosen love—his love for Wagner. His decision was final.

Footsteps sounded in the hallway on the other side of the wall,

followed by the flutter of women's laughter. The singers had arrived—
or those who claimed to be singers. They would never match the
skill of operatic stars. They could never perform an opera.

Dierk stalked across the room, removing the knife from Hitler's
photo and slipping it back into its sheath. He'd be back later. When
no one would bother him. No one would see.

All would know of this place, this set, soon enough. At the good
and proper time, their final parts would be revealed. The final song
would be sung.

CHAPTER ONE

Thump, thump, thump-thump.

Twenty-year-old Betty Lake gripped her bench seat's front edge, sure the airplane's engine shouldn't sound like that. To her ear, the repeating thrums sounded like a drummer's tempo, warming up for a night of big band. But unlike the drummer's tempo, the thumping didn't stir excitement in its audience's faces.

Sudden silence replaced the joking and laughing of the few dozen soldiers seated around her. The fearful gaze of the soldier sitting across from Betty confirmed her guess. The airplane was having problems. A shudder moved through her even more pronounced than that of the plane.

The twin engine C-47 was a paratrooper transport, certainly not a luxury airliner. Forty passengers sat facing one another against the fuselage on long benches attached to the airframe, with only lumpy, hard-packed parachutes for cushioning. The unheated air nipped at Betty's nose.

That parachute better stay right here—under my rump where it belongs, she thought as the airplane lurched in the air, causing her stomach to drop. She was the only female aboard the utilitarian aircraft. From the attention of the guys as she boarded, Betty could tell they appreciated the company of an American gal. She'd tried to pretend she wasn't afraid, wasn't cold, wasn't tired, but soon the shallow reserves she'd been drawing from would surely run dry. She tightened her jaw and urged herself to stay strong, despite the engine's continued thumping. *Come on, you can make it. Keep chugging along.* She patted the bare aluminum that was her seat.

Just a few months ago, this transport plane ferried soldiers across the English Channel, depositing them to fight on the front lines. The men did their jobs—or died trying—and now she was heading deep into Germany on a different mission—to sing for the remaining soldiers on Occupation Duty. To bring a few moments of joy to the GIs who dreamed of returning home, but instead had to guard the defeated people of a ravaged land.

Trying for a calming deep breath, Betty nearly choked on the odor of fuel, of soldiers' bodies that had been too long without a bath, and on something else—fear. She could imagine the soldiers' thoughts—*I didn't survive the war to die in a transport plane accident.* And she couldn't imagine coming this far and not singing.

It wasn't that she didn't understand the dangers before setting out. Dozens of performers had died "doing their part." Some in airplane accidents, some hit by enemy fire, and others who just happened to be in the wrong place at the wrong time. Still, it hadn't stopped her from coming. Singing for the soldiers was all Betty had wanted since she'd first heard of USO singers and comedians, acts like The Andrews Sisters and Bob Hope. When she'd first seen clips of their performances on the newsreels—entertaining troops, bringing smiles to soldiers' faces, and delivering the good ol' USA to soldiers' foxholes—she daydreamed about being one of them.

I can't die now. I should get to sing at least one song—and I'd rather not have that song be in the angels' choir, if I can help it.

The thumping became a roar. Betty sat erect and cocked her ear. The shake, shimmy, and rumble of the airplane made her wonder how long it would hold together. Her hands searched for the armrest that wasn't there and found the knee of the soldier seated next to her instead. She quickly pulled her hand away and averted her gaze from the soldier's smile.

"It's okay, dollface. You can cling to me for courage," declared the red-haired, freckle-faced man.

"I don't believe my mother would approve, sir. And if this plane goes down, it will do so with my good reputation intact." Betty winked, trying to make light of the situation. Trying to calm the pounding of her heart.

The chuckle of the redheaded soldier, mixed with the hoots of others near enough to hear her remark, told Betty her words did as she intended. She made them smile and found herself smiling too.

"So tell me"—She turned her head and looked directly into the soldier's eyes—"do you have a girl waiting at home?"

The soldier's cheeks reddened. "Well, no one is waiting. I wish there was…"

"From the way you say that, it sounds like you're thinking of someone special? Maybe someone you've been fancy on for a while?"

"How did you know? Are you a mind reader?" His eyes widened.

"No—not quite. I just have a way of getting people to open up to me, that's all. My mother says it's a gift. My father says I need to stop butting into other peoples' business, but I can't help caring." She lifted an eyebrow. "So don't try to hide the truth. There is a girl you care deeply for, isn't there?"

"Yes, I, uh, suppose there is. Her parents live two houses down from my parents' place. We sort of grew up together." Then he leaned closer. "I've never told anyone this before, but I've been thinking about writing her—"

"You should." Betty nodded. "Growing up on the same street, I'm sure you'll have plenty to talk about." She laughed. "And you no doubt already know her address."

"Yeah—right." He looked away, lifting his gaze as if the words were already forming in his mind.

The airplane shimmied some more, and she saw the soldier's smile fade just slightly.

She couldn't do anything about that engine, but maybe she could lighten the mood. *If I can catch my breath first.* After all, her official job as a USO singer was that of a morale booster—she just hadn't realized how soon morale would need to be boosted.

An explosion shook the plane. Betty winced, grabbing the hand of the same redheaded soldier. Her stomach jolted, and she swallowed hard against the rising nausea. This time he didn't say anything, but just squeezed her hand lightly as if to say, *I'll do what I can to protect you.*

One of the guys from down near the tail of the plane—a tall, handsome soldier with light brown hair and a chiseled face—rose and hurried toward the cockpit. Betty supposed he was another pilot, uneasy with the idea of sitting back and waiting to see what happened. He moved through the fuselage with a John Wayne swagger, which she was sure was due to the aircraft's swaying and rocking. As he passed her, he looked down and offered a nervous smile. She hoped the smile meant things would be under control soon. She didn't want to think of the alternative.

They were twenty minutes away from Nuremberg, Germany. Twenty minutes—then an hour-long drive away from her new life and new career in Bayreuth. No, it was more than a career, it was a dream.

"Don't worry, miss," an officer seated across from her said as he leaned forward. "Sounds like a little engine trouble—nothing these pilots haven't handled before."

Letting go of her "friend's" hand, Betty brushed hair from her eyes, where it had fallen during the plane's shimmying. "Thank you, sir. I'm not worried. If these pilots survived Nazi fighter planes and ground artillery, surely they're not gonna let one little ol' engine stop them." She curled her lips into a smile, hoping her grin looked half as confident as her words sounded. In her old job, she'd seen these planes on the production line. She'd spent two days training to work on them before she was given a job that better fitted her skills—singing at the airplane factory's canteen.

Betty dared to glance out the plane's window at the white clouds scattered throughout the sky, thinking of the countless newsreels she'd watched at the Paramount's Saturday matinees. Her mind replayed the black and white images of bombers filling the air as they flew over Germany. Now, unbelievably, she was flying the same route. It was a miracle that she'd come this far, and no doubt it would take a miracle to get them the rest of the way.

Her daddy had said only Hollywood-type girls got picked for the USO, not recent high-school graduates with no formal training and only canteen singing on their resumes. Her older brother had told her the dream was impossible. *Didn't he know that was the last thing he should have said?* More than once Bobby'd tried to squelch her dreams, and more than once she'd proven him wrong. That's why, if anything would get them back on the ground safely, it would be the wings of this plane and her petitions to a faithful God.

She said a quick prayer and then scanned the pasty-faced passengers. Her knee jiggled like it always did when she felt her nerves turning her stomach into knots, and soon her lips began to move with the song "Coming in on a Wing and a Prayer" running through her head.

"Though there's one motor gone, we can still carry on." She sang it once, low enough for only her seatmate to hear. But then she repeated it. Soon everyone sang along.

The thumping, the underlying backbeat to the airplane's loud roaring, accompanied their song perfectly.

* * * *

Even though Army Air Corps photographer Frank Witt had been seated in the fuselage, and even though he hadn't taken one day of flight school in his life, he knew something was wrong as soon as the C-47 climbed out after their last fuel stop.

Please Lord, let us make it there safely. After what happened to Lily— Frank let the thought fade. He couldn't think about losing his sister in a flying accident without the pain cutting deep to his soul. Ever since her death a year ago, he'd thought more of his own life. He wanted it to count. He wanted his assignment on earth to matter. His photographs mattered—but his undercover work mattered more. He just hoped his parents wouldn't lose another child. Although the war in Europe was done, there were many factions who still fought for their place, their power, in the new world. Factions that, no doubt, would rejoice if this plane crashed here and now.

When the Gooney Bird had finally reached its assigned cruising altitude, the vibration, which had been constant, changed noticeably as the engine's speed changed, causing a continuous rise and fall of the engine's roar. His guess was the copilot was working with the mixture controls, looking for the sweet spot where the 1000-hp Pratt & Whitney Twin Row Wasp engines sounded best and the instruments showed normal. These engines were considered bulletproof, and in-flight problems were rare. *Wouldn't you know we'd be the ones to get the trouble—and on the last leg of the flight.*

Before take-off, Frank had been shooting the breeze with the pilot and co-pilot when the ground crew had warned them the area had received four inches of rain overnight and there was concern that water had managed to find its way into the high-octane fuel storage tanks. Frank guessed that was the problem now. At least he hoped it was. He couldn't help but think back to a few of his other flights, when engine trouble had nothing to do with Mother Nature.

His mind raced as he considered those who still wished him dead. There were too many to count—most of whom weren't locked up in Nuremberg awaiting trial. The men and women Frank had ticked off were those who drew as little attention to themselves as possible, just as he had done during the war. Even his closest friends and co-workers didn't understand that the photos he took on bombing runs meant little compared to the ones he took "off duty," during his tours around the English countryside and through London's busy streets. He'd foiled a sufficient number of enemy plots to cause someone to want to see him crash and burn. Frank just hoped that today's trouble had nothing to do with him, especially since the aircraft carried the prettiest girl he'd ever seen, done up in her perfectly fitted USO jacket and skirt.

A loud explosion shook the aircraft, and the cabin brightened as belching flames shot past the right-side windows. Frank glanced around and noticed the faces of the others losing the little color they'd maintained.

Without hesitation, he rose and hurried to the cockpit, feeling as if he were walking the deck of a storm-tossed ship. He stepped into the cockpit doorway, interrupting the co-pilot's words. When they acknowledged his presence, Frank stepped inside and stooped down close enough to the very busy pilots to converse with them.

"Captain, the starboard engine blew a cylinder." The co-pilot's anxious breath sounded hollow. "The cowling is ripped open, and we have flames. I'm killing the fuel supply to that engine."

"Got it." Dewey, the pilot, nodded, his gaze intent on the gauges. "Increase mixture to the port engine to keep it cool, open the cowl flaps, and maintain full throttle. But watch the temps."

"Things okay in here?" Frank leaned back against the bulkhead for support. "Have we been sabotaged?"

Laughter spilled from Dewey's lips, and Frank chuckled too, yet inwardly he knew it wasn't a joke.

"What's wrong, Frank, you scared? Think you've flown ninety missions against the Germans, and now you're gonna buy the farm 'cause of an equipment malfunction?"

"Nah, I trust you and Norm. I just wanted to see if you had anything I could report to our passengers. I saw some of the new guys reaching for their chutes. Suppose this is the scariest thing they've faced since signing up. At least it will give them something to write home about, since they missed the war."

"We'll be fine. There aren't any mountains in our flight path and the weather's good at our destination—except for—"

"Except for what?" Frank asked after a pregnant pause.

"Well, we can make it there on one engine—unless it's a fuel problem." The pilot's eyes remained fixed on the fuel gauge. "If the fuel's contaminated, we're gonna have a situation on our hands."

"Gee, Dewey," Frank smirked. "I think you've seen too many films. 'We've got us a situation on our hands, boys'? You're starting to talk like those bottom-of-the-rung actors in the movies they've been showing lately."

Dewey cracked a smile. "Shh—not so loud. We have a star aboard. She might hear you…"

"Temps going up on the port engine and she's losing RPMs, Captain," Norm said.

The smile on Dewey's face faded.

"Get on the horn with Nuremberg. Inform them we are coming straight in and have them get the emergency crews standing by."

"Captain," Norm's voice rose an octave, "charts show a run of high-tension wires over one hundred feet high on the approach path for the active runway—"

"Keep the wheels up and only drop twenty degrees of flaps until I call clear of wires, got it?"

"Roger." Norm nodded.

Dewey turned back to Frank. "You better head back and belt up. There's nothing you can do, and I have a feeling it's gonna get bumpier before it gets better."

Frank nodded and placed his hand on the door handle. He supposed it didn't matter what had gotten them into this situation. Sabotage or not, all he could do was ride it out.

"And Frank." Dewey's words stopped him.

"Yeah?"

"Don't act like you're scared. Last thing I need is a bunch of new recruits trying to go out the hatch, if you know what I mean?"

"Yeah, of course." Frank tried to ease the tension on his face. Usually he had no problem hiding his emotions, but today it was harder. Especially when he noticed the girl's eyes on his.

She's too young, too pretty, to die today.

CHAPTER TWO

As they sang yet another song, Betty glanced up and noticed Cary Grant—as she'd labeled him in her head—return from the cockpit. He smiled, grabbed a large camera case from where he'd been sitting, and took a seat nearer to her than he'd been in earlier. Then he buckled his seatbelt.

"Just a little engine trouble, nothing to be alarmed about," the man called out. "It'll be a bumpy ride, but we'll make it fine."

The soldiers nodded, but Betty could tell the man hadn't told the whole truth. His words sounded smooth, but his jaw remained tense. Betty watched as he lifted the camera case onto his lap. He looked far too serious as he stared out the window over his shoulder, at the patch-worked German countryside below.

Betty switched to another favorite song. "He wears a pair of silver wings—" She lifted her voice, noticing the vibration of the plane gave it a vibrato. All pilots loved this song, and she hoped that tune would catch the guy's attention and lighten his mood. It didn't work. The man wouldn't even acknowledge her song. As she sang, she stared at his profile, willing him to turn his head and meet her gaze.

C'mon, buddy. Give us a hint. Are we going to die tonight or what?

He continued to stare out the window, and as the plane descended, instead of tightening his seatbelt as the rest of the passengers did, he took his camera from his case, unbuckled his belt, turned in his seat, and focused his lens out the window at the countryside below, draped with yellow light.

Betty's shoulders eased a bit. If he knew they were going to crash, he'd take precautions. Instead, he held up his camera, focused, and snapped a shot. From watching him, she came to the conclusion that he had to be a professional. The type of camera and his confidence gave it away. That meant either he wasn't a pilot after all or was really good at his hobby. *Maybe he was a photographer before the war—before he learned to fly planes.* Or maybe he was a combat photographer, like she'd read about in *LIFE*. Just the thought of him racing into battle with his camera instead of a machine gun caused goose bumps to rise on her arms. It sounded both exciting and dangerous.

After taking a few shots, he turned back around, put the camera away, and buckled up again. "It's pretty out there, don't you think?" he said with a grin to the watching group. "What a beautiful night to be alive." He certainly deserved an Academy Award for his acting.

* * * *

As soon as Frank had seen the pretty singer on the transport plane, he was sure he'd been set up. During his time working with the OSS, he'd learned that no one could be trusted. Everyone had his or her own secret motive and agenda. The beautiful singer on the airplane no doubt believed that she "just happened" to be on this plane with him, but Frank guessed that wasn't the case. He thought about his buddy at headquarters and wondered if Marv really was able to find anything, for anyone, under impossible circumstances, as he'd often bragged. If that were true, Marv had done a fine job serving up Frank's dream girl.

One rained-in day at an English pub six months prior, Marv had asked Frank about his taste in women. Frank had listed a number of qualities off the top of his head, not really thinking much about it. *Petite, dark hair, nice features, a beautiful voice and smile, a warm personality—ya know, someone I could take home to Mom.* From the looks of it, the girl sitting on this airplane fit the bill. Well, at least most of it. Since he really didn't know her, he wasn't sure if she was Mama material or not. Frank shook his head in reluctant resignation, but *boy* was she pretty.

Even though she wore a limp and dirty USO uniform, and her hair had lost its style somewhere between New York and London, the singer looked as if she'd been sculpted under Michelangelo's chisel. But more than that, Frank liked the contented smile that played on her lips, as if she was never bored but looked on everything with interest. And then there was the twinkle in her eye. Or maybe it was more than a twinkle. Maybe it was her whole intelligent, intense gaze that told him if someone asked her a question, they'd get an answer—and most likely one they didn't expect.

I'm not gonna fall for it, Marv. Frank knew other guys in the OSS who had girlfriends, but he didn't want to risk it. When he finally fell in love, he wanted to give all of his heart—not just the half of it that wasn't top secret. Being a combat photographer during the day was danger enough, but the German artillery and fighter planes were the known danger, the known enemy. If an unknown enemy wanted to get to him, they could do it best by getting to someone he loved. Incidents like this airplane's smoking engine were proof that danger could pop up any time, any place.

Frank turned his attention back to the small window and the right engine, watching the swirling, dancing smoke. If it were only an engine problem, he wasn't overly concerned. He'd been on nearly one hundred missions, and minor engine trouble like this wasn't enough to make his heart add too many extra beats. *But what if it was sabotage. Who? Why?*

The singer started in on another song, interrupting his thoughts. Even though her voice was beautiful, intriguing, he looked outside to the engine, because it was easier than looking at her. He'd managed to stick to his vow throughout the war, but this one—this girl could almost make him rethink his vow.

Keep your mind on the job ahead. Focus on that.

Frank wondered what job awaited him in Bayreuth. As a combat photographer, he'd worked hard and his photos had gotten noticed. He'd even had some front-page spots in major newspapers that he was sure his mom had clipped and added to his scrapbook. As an OSS agent, he'd also found success—and his photos had foiled more than one Nazi plot.

With success in both his jobs, he was eager to see what was ahead. An exposé on displaced persons perhaps? Or maybe photos of the rebuilding of an historic German town nearly leveled by the war? Those would be the front-page photos. Then there would be the ones *not* for the public eye. He wondered what that assignment would be about.

His boss, Henry Miller, had told him all the info would be waiting in Bayreuth, and to have his film loaded and his lens shined. Whatever it was, it would most likely distract him from the pretty traveler with the angelic voice, even with the extra vibrato from the plane's vibration as it shuddered through the sky.

Besides, girls like her shouldn't be here. It's too dangerous. She needs to head back—. Enemies lurk where least expected.

Yet, even as Frank thought that, having her here made him hope that one day he would be able to lower his guard and fall in love. One part of him even hoped that Marv had been involved—and that this girl had been sent on this transport plane to catch his attention.

Marv does have a way of getting you what you want even before you realize you need it—

* * * *

The plane bounced as it descended, and the ground seemed to rise toward them faster than normal. The redheaded guy's grip on her hand tightened, and Betty squeezed her eyes shut.

Dear Jesus, thank You for bringing me this far—and if it's in Your plan for me to sing here, then so be it. And if not—save me a spot in that angel choir.

With a hard bump, the landing gear hit the ground. Betty opened her eyes, and the plane bounced two more times—softer than the first—and then smoothed. Cheers rose from the guys, and Betty joined in.

The airplane had barely come to a stop on the runway when all the men stood and gathered their things. All except the handsome photographer, who looked over at her and offered a relieved smile.

When it was time to disembark, the soldiers helped Betty with her bags and insisted she go first. She hurried down the boarding ladder and scanned the crowd for—for whom, she didn't know. Someone in a gray suit and fedora, she supposed. One of those Hollywood types that her father complained about. Instead, there were only a half-dozen soldiers who set to work unloading supplies.

She paused on the tarmac and hesitantly released the handrail.

What now? What if no one shows? What will I do in a foreign country—alone?

From off in the distance, rescue vehicles approached in a single line. Betty's knees grew weak when she spotted them. No doubt their plane had been in far more danger than the handsome photographer had let on.

She followed the group of soldiers toward the small building at the edge of the airfield. As she looked around, Betty realized that this airfield was similar to the one in Santa Monica. She didn't know why that surprised her. For some reason, she still expected to see Nazi soldiers and large swastikas, despite the war here having been over for five months.

Her heeled shoes clicking on the pavement as she walked and her small satchel in hand, she couldn't help but think of all the planes that had taken off from here—bent on Allied destruction. But that was then, this was now—a time of peace—or so she'd convinced her mother and sister.

Mona had been the hardest to convince. Irish twins, their mother called them, since they were less than a year apart. When Mona had learned of Betty's upcoming trip, she'd cried and carried on for days, certain the Germans were just bluffing. Certain that they had hidden arms and men, and would rise up again as soon as the Americans became complacent. It didn't matter that no one but Mona believed it. But the worst of it was over, Betty knew. Even the Japanese had surrendered nearly two months ago.

Betty shook those thoughts from her mind and continued forward with confident steps, even though she was far from confident, striding toward the small building.

The telegram that had awaited her in London this morning had told her to have her pipes prepped. It said that she'd be on stage tonight—and she'd assumed someone would be around to get her to that stage.

Nearing the small airport terminal, she scanned the crowd where a lot of Lookie-Lews—no doubt trying to figure out what this broad was doing here—awaited processing in or out. But no one stepped forward to whisk her away.

Up ahead she saw the man who looked like Cary Grant standing near a jeep, obviously waiting for someone. Betty's stomach tightened. He was so handsome, so mature. He was different from all the guys she knew in school. Even different from the other soldiers on the plane. She had a feeling he was important just by the way he carried himself.

"Excuse me, sir." Betty approached the photographer. "Are you waiting for a ride to the opera house in Bayreuth?"

"I believe you're talking about Festspielhaus, ma'am. I understand that's where this jeep is headed. Let me guess, you've come to sing— to spread your vocal sunshine across the rows and rows of soldiers in a packed-out house?" His face was kind and his eyes were intense as they focused on her, as if he was trying to look deep within her.

Betty felt warmth filling her. "Yes, well, that's the idea—"

The man nodded. "Your singing was nice. I can see why the USO sent you." He winked. "There are no artillery shells and bullets to keep the soldiers distracted, so the army's trying to keep the men's minds occupied with a pretty voice and an even prettier face."

"Well, if I'm able to help—"

The photographer's gaze narrowed. "No offense, ma'am, but this is no place for a lady. It might feel as if Hitler's forces have dissipated into thin air, but does anyone really think that five months ago the people who were giving their lives for the Fuehrer are now good Germans who embrace the Americans occupying their homes?"

The warm feelings Betty had a moment before instantly cooled. She could see concern in his gaze, and she didn't know whether to be flattered or annoyed. Didn't he know she'd considered the danger and had still come? Besides, it didn't matter what he said. It's not like she was going to get back on that plane and head home. Her temper flared.

"Listen, mister." Her voice shook. "I didn't come here because I thought it would be a nice vacation. I haven't spent nearly one full week on trains and planes just so I can write a postcard back home to Santa Monica saying I've traveled the world. I'm not a man, so I couldn't sign up to fight. I can't do much, but I can sing. And if, by whiskers, that's what my country's asking me to do, then I'm going to do it. I've been waiting to sing from the first moment I heard about the bombing of Pearl Harbor as I washed my daddy's car—getting it ready for church—that Sunday morning, ages ago. So, if you'll excuse me, I think this is my ride. It was nice meeting you—"

"Frank." He tipped his hat. "Frank Witt, ma'am."

She offered a forced smile as she saw a short and stocky military police officer with blond curly hair approach with her luggage. He wore the same uniform as regular military, but also wore a black armband with **MP** in white letters. "Yes, well, it was nice to meet you, Frank."

The MP neared the jeep, placing her luggage in the back. His eyes widened as he looked at her. "Are you Hedy Lamarr?"

"No, sir."

"Well, you sure look like her."

"Thank you, soldier, that's a huge honor." She extended her hand, ignoring the photographer's gaze.

The man placed his hand in her gloved one, and she shook it enthusiastically.

"Really, it's an honor." She climbed into the front seat of the jeep. "And what is your name?"

"You can just call me Mac. My mother named me that, so I guess it's a good choice." He chuckled. "I'll be driving you today."

Betty placed a hand over her heart. "Sir, I told you I'm not Hedy Lamarr. I'm not certain why the USO sent an MP to chauffeur me. I'm sure a regular driver would have done just fine."

"Didn't you hear how things are run now in Europe?" Mac chuckled. "Of course you didn't." He chuckled again. "Bob Hope was in Nuremberg not too long ago, and he said one thing he noticed was that each soldier was protected by his own MP. That's not the case, of course, but sometimes it feels that way. Sometimes the only thing we have to do is watch out for each other—in the pubs, on drives around the countryside, on double dates—" His eyes twinkled as he shot her a glance.

"Which is why I'm here to sing for you." She smiled.

"So are you nervous—singing on the stage over here? It's a real fancy place. Famous too."

"Oh no. It doesn't matter if it's a huge stage or a table in the cafeteria, I'll sing. My mother says it's always been that way. I sang in church, at school, and I'd sing myself to sleep. At the factory, I sang for lunch crowds and for big celebrations."

Betty settled in. Then, with one smooth motion, the photographer climbed in and settled into the seat behind her. Betty turned, surprised. "So you *are* coming to Bayreuth?"

"Yes, ma'am. I'm on special assignment—or so I'm told. And if I'm not too busy, I might even have time to catch your show. Maybe tonight even."

"Ah, man, some guys have all the luck," Mac complained. "I mean, I'd love to listen to the singing. But the opera house isn't my favorite place."

Betty's stomach flipped, just as it did when the airplane had made an especially large dip. *Frank's coming. He's going to see me perform on stage?*

For the first time, she realized that when she'd planned for Germany, she'd thought about the singing, which was to be expected. She'd also thought about the "soldiers" as a collective group. But it never crossed her mind that there'd be someone like him here. Someone who could spark a rant and a smile from her in less than one minute.

Suddenly, she was more nervous about tonight—about performing—than she had been in a very long time.

CHAPTER THREE

It was an hour drive to Bayreuth, and Frank knew there was nothing to do but sit back and enjoy the ride—and the view. He especially liked the way Betty's dark hair bounced on her shoulders as the jeep jounced over potholes, and the way she tilted her head back as she laughed. And it wasn't a girly laugh either, but one that came from her belly and poured out, a musical laugh, carrying on the fall air blowing through the jeep.

They drove off the airbase and down a country road that looked as if it had seen better days. Beyond the airfield, he scanned what was once the stately city of Nuremberg. Derelict buildings' jagged remains clawed the skyline, suggesting Roman ruins or some warped impression of church spires. From the vantage of rumbling B-17s during the war, he'd often photographed Allied bombs reducing the once-beautiful, classical architecture to the mockery that remained today.

It was not far from here, in fact, where he'd taken some of his best photos. That day was clear—too clear—with the German anti-aircraft batteries targeting them like ducks in a shooting gallery, blasting shards of flak within twenty yards of their planes. He'd never seen the Germans so accurate with their gunfire, yet he'd done his best to focus on his task—to take photos of what happened in the sky outside the window without worrying if the next hit would be a direct one.

On film, he'd caught the ground artillery exploding in the sky all around—and in the middle of the B-17 formation—yet the black puffs of smoke that appeared in the photos gave no hint of their destructive powers. The flak hitting the plane sounded like metal baseballs batted at them by Babe Ruth. Despite the near misses, all of the planes had made it back, and only one guy—a waist gunner in the lead plane—had been lost.

Of course, later missions had received far worse damage.

Frank shook his head, willing the memories to dissipate. He didn't need to think about that. Not now. Not here. There were more beautiful things to focus on. Take in.

As they neared the wooded countryside, the afternoon sunlight brightened the fall colors that made their appearance in full array. The trees were concentrated in the hills, leaving the valley bare and open, perfect for farming. Frank sniffed the air. The strong sent of manure told him the Germans were already preparing their fields for the spring. If nothing else, they were efficient.

"So what are you doing in Nuremberg? Is this your typical work—driving around very important singers and their tagalongs?" Frank asked the MP.

"Oh no, I'm usually stationed over at the Palace of Justice. Or at least I will be. The trials are supposed to start in a few weeks. I'll be one of the lucky jokers who'll be transporting prisoners back and forth from their cells to the courtroom each day."

Frank felt a slight wind blow in through the side of the jeep. A cold chill climbed up his arms, and he wondered how many of those guys he'd helped to put in prison. A number of them, he supposed. But it wasn't the ones who were locked up that frightened him.

"Do you mean Hitler's key men?" Betty asked. "I read about that. I heard they were being held there."

"Yes, ma'am. And the Nazis involved with all the death camps."

"Are you guarding them so they don't escape?" she asked.

"Well, less of that and more for protection from those who would want to hurt them."

"It sounds dangerous," Frank commented, leaning forward in his seat. His face was close to Betty's shoulder, and he noticed she smelled of some fancy perfume that reminded him of his mother's rose garden. "I'm sure there are those who'd like to assassinate those guys themselves instead of having them go through the process of a fair trial."

"Yes, it seems strange to me. You know, to protect the guys who killed millions so we can see that they pay for their crimes—"

"It doesn't sound like my cup of tea at all." Betty shivered. "I'm glad I'm here to sing no danger in that."

The MP turned and glanced at Betty, and Frank noticed Mac had a wary look on his face—as if he disagreed with her words.

"You know, sometimes it's easier to work with the Germans than the GIs," Mac said with a chuckle. "I've been patrolling the Occupation Zone since the war ended, and I feel like a tattletale, or worse, a goody-two-shoes, always trying to keep the guys in line."

"Yeah, it was the same way in France," Frank said. "It's hard for the guys to obey a set of rules when they can hardly believe they're alive and want to really live." Images of the GIs loose on the Paris streets flipped through Frank's mind—the champagne, the girls. He'd kept far away from both.

"In Germany, we're telling them who not to date, where not to go, what not to do. I've heard GIs say they feel as if the Germans are free, and they're the ones locked up by all these rules. We like to think we're here for protection, but sometimes we're viewed as babysitters." Mac shrugged. "And then there are those who love that role—being the boss, putting everyone else in their place, being the final say because they wear this." He patted his MP armband. "It might as well be a swastika."

"But enough of that talk. Have either of you been to the Festspielhaus?" Mac asked, briefly looking over his shoulder toward Frank. The MP's eyes were wide, almost fearful.

"Can't say I have," Frank answered, "Opera really isn't my favorite thing."

"I like opera—or I think I would if I ever had a chance to go to a real one," Betty said, "but this is my first time in Germany. My first time away from home, in fact."

Frank noted color rising on Betty's cheeks.

"Listen to me, I sound like a country bumpkin." She clasped her gloved hands on her lap and turned her attentions to the Bavarian landscape.

"Oh, you're going to love Bayreuth. It's an interesting place to visit for your first trip." The driver jutted his chin and took on the tone of a tour guide. "It's formerly part of Bavaria—the Saxon region. It was favored by the royals, and around the turn of the century, a lot of people flocked there. You'll see their influence in town. It's royal, Baroque, and basically gaudy."

"It sounds great." Betty smiled.

"Yes, the town is," Mac said. "Of course you couldn't get me within a mile of the Festspielhaus. It's too close to evil if you ask me."

"And this from a man who guards the men who designed and manned the death camps." Frank smirked as the wind whipped his words.

"The enemies I guard are men—disillusioned men who invested their souls in the wrong religion, the wrong cause. It's the forces I can't see that I'm more worried about."

Frank eyed the driver and felt the muscles in his stomach tightening.

"What do you mean?" Betty turned in her seat. "I can see from the look on your face there's a story behind those words. An interesting story, perhaps?"

"I'm not sure how interesting it is—"

"Well, you can tell us, and then we can judge. 'Unseen forces' have to make a good tale," Betty said.

Frank eyed Betty, and he couldn't tell if she was just being nosey or if she truly was interested in the story behind Mac's words.

"Well, I've never told anyone before—mostly because no one seemed to care or ask—but my mother was an opera singer. She used to travel Europe before things got bad. I must have been twelve or thirteen, and I remember waking up one night and hearing the sound of paper tearing. I went into the kitchen, and there on the table in front of her were bits of paper. She wouldn't speak of it at first, but I saw that they were the music sheets for Wagner's operas.

"After one of her concerts, she had met a man who'd been a childhood friend of Hitler. The man, August, had attended an opera with Hitler when they were both in their teens. It was Wagner's opera *Rienzi*. It's the story of a man who wrests authority from a corrupt, Roman ruler. After the performance—so August told my mother—it was as if young Hitler had been overwhelmed by something beyond himself. He spouted his plans under the stars. He wanted to do something to make Germany great again. He claimed he would be the one to wrestle it from the oppression placed on it after the Great War. It was as if Hitler had transferred Rienzi's complete mission onto his own shoulders."

"And what was Rienzi's complete mission?" Frank dared to ask.

"To lead his people out of servitude to the heights of freedom, which Rienzi did, until nobles and the church schemed and conspired against him. Every time my mother read about another horrible thing Hitler did, she reminded me of the opera, especially when Hitler used the *Rienzi* overture as the musical theme for all Nazi Party rallies. Yet while Rienzi had good motives, Hitler's were far from that."

"So did Rienzi achieve what he desired?" Betty asked.

"No, in the opera's finale the conquering Rienzi—the historical hero—is overthrown by the mob."

"Maybe Hitler should have taken note of that." Frank chuckled.

"I wouldn't laugh too hard if I were you. And I'd keep a watchful eye. My mother doesn't think it's over yet."

"What do you mean?" Betty's face paled at Mac's words. "Hitler is dead, and all the guys who can cause trouble are locked up. You, more than anyone, should know that."

Frank tried not to react to her words. Tried not to reveal that he believed nothing could be more wrong. He wouldn't still be around if that were the case—if all the bad guys were locked up. He'd be home, preparing for his future and looking for a girl to spend his life with.

"I don't know enough about these things to make heads or tails of it, but I received a letter from my mother just a few weeks ago. She warned me to stay away from the Festspielhaus, especially in the month of October."

"Why would your mother warn you of the month of October? What does she know, what has she heard?" Frank rubbed his jaw, wondering if Mac was making the whole thing up to get Betty's attention. He wouldn't put it past him. She was nice, and pretty too.

"I'm not sure. She didn't say, but she still has a lot of friends in that circle. I just assume she's passing the warning on from something she's heard."

"But it's the fourth of October now," Betty said.

"Exactly, and I've decided to break my own rule not to go within a mile of the place. I'll slow enough for you two to jump out." Mac chuckled, but Frank could see from the look in his eye he was partially serious. "Then, as soon as I drop you off, I'm heading back to Goering and Hess, where it's safe."

"Well, I have to say, I've never had a tour guide quite like you before. I would tell you that your horror stories are going to keep me up all night, but after this long trip I don't think that'll be the case." Betty's voice sounded tired, and Frank could see she was trying to suppress a yawn. "Still it was a great story. I'm glad I asked." She winked.

"I imagine you're exhausted, miss. Do you want me to drive you to your quarters first?"

"No, no, straight to the opera house, please. I know you're trying to get out of going there, but it's not going to work. I'm supposed to perform tonight, and I'll barely get there in enough time to get ready."

"Can you give me a preview, seeing as I'll most likely never get brave enough to attend and see it for myself?"

"Sure, soldier—I mean Mac," and then without batting an eye she broke into "That Lovely Weekend" by Vera Lynn. "—I haven't said thanks for that lovely weekend, those two days of heaven you helped me spend—"

Mac asked her to sing song after song: "I'll Walk Alone," "The White Cliffs of Dover," "Long Ago and Far Away." Appearing glad for this chance to warm up before her performance in a few hours, she sang until they approached Bayreuth. Then Betty paused as the driver stopped the jeep at the bottom of a hill. From the look on her face, Frank could see she was enraptured. He couldn't help but be too, but not entirely because of the view outside the jeep.

Sloping gardens swept upward, and a large building rose—seemingly from the top of the hill—like a modern castle ready to lift into the sky.

It was a colossal structure. It was far from beautiful, but beautiful didn't matter any longer. It stood, and realizing that impressed him.

"Much of the town was bombed," Mac explained. "Over a thousand people from Bayreuth were killed. Half of the buildings were destroyed, but not her. She still stands. It's as if she has supernatural protection, or something."

"Or maybe bombing an opera house wasn't the Air Corps's main priority," Frank quipped.

The jeep drove up to the Festspielhaus, and to Frank it looked like a giant turtle on the hill with stucco and wood finish. His favorite part, he supposed, was the green arbor and patio off the front entrance. He could almost imagine the horse-drawn carriages lined up there as they dropped off their important passengers. There were no fancy carriages around here, but there was a long line of jeeps driving up from town, and a group of GIs already lining up at the door.

"I can't believe it." Betty's voice was no more than a whisper from the front seat. "Pinch me, Mac, pinch me hard. This has to be a dream. Some of the most famous singers in history have sung here—I can't believe I will too."

"Sorry, miss, but I won't pinch you. That's not gentlemanly. I will say, though, that this isn't a dream. I mean, if you were going to dream something up, you most likely wouldn't include someone like me in it." Mac pointed his thumb behind him toward Frank. "Him maybe, but not me."

Mac drove around back and parked the jeep by the back door. Mac jumped out. But before he could walk around and help Betty from the seat, Frank climbed over the wheel-well and offered a hand.

"Miss, watch your step."

Tears of joy rimmed her eyes, and she looked at him and smiled. It was a lovely smile, sincere.

"Thank you." She placed her hand on his. "It looks like a perfectly safe and wonderful place, no matter what your mother says, Mac." She chuckled. "I never expected this. I still think I must be dreaming."

She scanned the huge opera house behind Frank, and he knew she was talking about the building, but he didn't mind. His heartbeat hammered at the touch of her hand, and he wondered if he should reconsider his stance on waiting to find a girl.

I never expected this either, sweetheart, not in a million years.

CHAPTER FOUR

Had her dreams come true?

One look at the immense, beautiful Festspielhaus—even while wearing a droopy uniform—made Betty feel like a princess. She held her breath as she entered the back doors. *I can't believe it, they've invited me to sing—here.*

She followed the festive sounds of voices down a long hall. Mac and Frank followed with her luggage, setting it down as soon as they entered the backstage area. Around them, people fluttered in motion and sounds—musicians tuning their instruments, singers chatting and adding last-minute touches to their costumes, dancers stretching out long limbs. Betty turned to the guys, noticing their wide-eyed gazes, and knew hers matched.

A man approached in a gray suit and red tie, with brownish gray hair slicked back, and a wide grin. Betty could tell he was the stage manager from his commanding style. He glanced at his gold watch. "Listen here, my little chickadee, I wish we had time for you to rehearse, but we have some very important guests tonight—all of them. These GIs have seen the last show a few times, so I'd like to work in some new acts. The stuff around here is as stale as day-old bread. You got anything for me?"

"Are you—?" She scrambled through her memories trying to recall the name her recruiter had given to her, but came up blank.

"Mickey. Mickey Bench at your service." He took her hand and kissed her middle knuckle and then swept his arm around the room. "I'll introduce you to the rest of the crew later. So you got some songs, kid?"

Betty straightened her shoulders and took in a deep breath. A dozen songs spun through her mind, and she tried to remember which ones the crowds back home requested most. "I can sing Lena Horne's 'Stormy Weather' and 'Silver Wings in the Moonlight.' Does the orchestra know those?" She turned to a man standing next to Mickey. He wore a light blue suit and held a baton in his hand. She guessed he was the conductor.

"Know them? My orchestra plays those numbers better than you've ever heard, kid."

"Great. You're gonna sing those numbers after the Johnson sisters do their little dance act."

"But that's my spot. I always sing after the Johnsons' jiggle." A woman with jet black hair done up in a tall pile stepped forward.

"Irene, Irene, don't spin yourself into a tizzy. Tonight I'm putting you with Esther and Trudy. The duo is now a trio."

Irene's gaze widened. "She took my spot? What are you going to do, give her the shirt off my back too?" She crossed her arms over her chest.

"No, but now that you mention it, I think the dress will work. You two look about the same size."

"I don't think—" Betty started, but Mickey's sharp look silenced her.

"Sure, Mick, but you better have this thing worked out tomorrow. I'm my own act—not a trio." Irene turned, stomped two steps, and then paused. "You coming, kid, or are you going to strip right here?"

"I'm coming." Betty bit her lip.

"Hey, either of you Captain Frank Witt?" Mickey called to the driver and photographer who still stood there, as if waiting to be dismissed.

"Yeah, I'm Frank." The handsome photographer removed his cap and stepped forward.

"Great. Ready to go? I'd recommend finding a seat front and center—best place in the house, if you ask me. There's a media box, but I thought you'd like to be with the soldiers. Maybe to be part of the experience."

"Excuse me, I don't understand." Frank took a step forward.

"Didn't Marv tell you? It's your assignment, kid."

"This?" Frank's face scrunched up as if he'd been sucker punched in the gut. "This is my assignment?"

"Sure is. Got your equipment? The doors open in fifteen. You'd better get your spot while the gettin's good."

"You coming?" Irene approached and tugged Betty's arm. "Mickey's a stickler about the show starting on time. The last thing you want to do is hold him up. That wouldn't be a good way to start your 'opera' career."

Betty blinked, confused, but turned and followed Irene with quickened steps. Her new pumps pinched her toes as she hurried along. They didn't fit like they had when she tried them on in McMillan's

Department Store in Hollywood last week. Maybe the fact that she'd worn them for three days straight had something to do with it.

They entered a dressing room with lighted mirrors, where three other women were in various stages of suiting up. The room was clean and bright, with chairs scattered around and a lounging couch against one wall.

"I don't mind that you're wearing my dress, really." Irene turned her back to Betty. "Can you unzip me?"

"Yes—uh—sure." She unzipped Irene's dress and then made quick work of getting out of her USO uniform. From the way the other girls were dressed up around her, she doubted she'd be wearing the uniform much. While everyone at the canteen wore the drab USO suits, here the singers dressed like starlets in the movies.

"I bet you're beat." Irene handed her the dress, holding up the shimmery pink gown between two fingers. "I think I slept two days when I first arrived. I can't believe Mickey's making you go on tonight."

"I'm tired, but the idea of singing energizes me. I'll be fine once I get on stage."

"Oh, you must be one of *those* girls."

"What do you mean, 'one of those girls'?" She took the dress and put it on over her head. It was silky and smooth and slid over her body like butter on hot corn.

"Oh, we all love to sing, don't get me wrong. It just starts to feel like work after a while. There's always a new song to practice or a new show to get right. Not to mention all of the impromptu shows. We can't go to the mess or even walk around town without being stopped and asked to sing. That's not even taking into account the stuff that happens after the show." Irene hurried to a large wardrobe filled with gowns and pulled out a simple black dress, slipping it over her head without messing up her hair one bit.

"After the show?" Betty straightened the pink gown and turned her back to be zipped.

"Yes, you don't think our work ends when the show's done, do you?"

"Ladies, ladies, save your chatting until after the show." Mickey poked his head into the room. "We're on in ten, and I still need to give Songbird a rundown of the show." Seeing that everyone was dressed, he walked in, writing something on a clipboard in his hand.

"Songbird?" Betty gazed at her image in the tall mirror, pleased by how the gown fit.

"That's you, kid. That's what Mickey calls all the new girls. Eventually he'll learn your name."

"That's okay. I sort of like Songbird."

"The dress looks good, but we have to do something with your hair," one woman with white-blond hair chirped.

"And your makeup too. Kat, can you hand me the rouge?" A redhead in an emerald green dress brushed some type of powder all over Betty's face. Betty held her breath and tried not to sneeze.

A beautiful woman she assumed to be Kat, with blond hair and perfect curls framing her face, glanced over. Betty sucked in a short breath. She knew that woman from somewhere—from the pictures. She just couldn't remember which ones.

One of the women pulled up a chair behind Betty, and she

obediently sat. The motion of the brush through her hair and the powder-puff caused her heartbeat to quicken. *This is really happening. I'm really here.*

When Betty was finally ready, she followed the others from the dressing room to the backstage rehearsal area where members of the band eagerly introduced themselves. Betty shook each person's hand, but her smile faded when she turned to Kat, who glared at her with a narrow-eyed gaze.

"Funny—don't you think it's strange that everyone's all aflutter, but we've yet to hear this one sing?" Even though Kat was looking at Betty, it was clear she was speaking to Mickey, who was scribbling something on the schedule.

Betty felt her own smile fading, and all heads turned to Mickey, waiting for his response.

"My buddy Marv promises she has the voice of an angel. Think I got time for this business, Kat, when them soldiers are already filling their seats?" Mickey pointed to the stage area and then stalked up to Betty. "Don't worry about her, kid. You'll do great. The band's prepped for your numbers. Just know that after the Johnson Sisters do their little kick-dance, you'll be on next."

Betty nodded, watching as Mickey headed out with purposeful strides to announce the performances scheduled for tonight's variety show.

"Don't mind her. Kat's always a little sharp with her words. I think she wants to make it clear she's not one of us. C'mon." Irene grabbed Betty's arm, pulling her to the side of the stage. "This is the best place in the house to watch."

Betty patted her hair, realizing that in less than one minute they had twisted her dark hair up in a chignon at the base of her neck. She also realized that she hadn't even checked her makeup, but she trusted she was in good hands. It was clear that it was a top-notch show, and everyone did their part to make all the other members look good.

"By your special request," Mickey started as he leaned close to the microphone, "a night that will take you home. More than that, a night that will bring the stars of home to life—performing the best numbers of the decade, just for you."

Applause exploded, and Mickey strode off, pausing briefly at Betty's side. "Don't mess up, kid. If you don't nail it tonight, you'll be on tomorrow's plane home."

Betty reached for Irene's hand.

"Don't worry about him, Betty. He was a studio czar back in Hollywood," Irene explained. "I don't want to spread any rumors now, but there's a reason why he's here, you catch my meaning? There were problems. Mr. Nice Guy one minute and then—"

Loud music interrupted Irene's words.

The evening started with an accordionist unlike anyone Betty had ever heard. She tried to enjoy herself without getting too worked up about Mickey's words. She couldn't go home tomorrow. She had to do well. The alternative was unacceptable.

Dear God, since I know You're around to help—now's a great time.

After that, a tap-dancer took the stage with feet that didn't stop moving and a smile that was wide and pearly white. Betty stood just to the side of the curtain, which allowed her to watch the dancer without being seen. When the woman added cartwheels to her tapping, flipping around the stage like a tumbleweed caught in the wind, the crowd cheered with approval so loud it would put the roar of the Douglas C-47 to shame.

"How many men are out there?" she mumbled to herself. She dared to take a step forward, peeking out. The first dozen rows were so packed she sucked in a breath. Beyond them, there was an olive-drab sea of smiling faces.

"Oh, my goodness." She placed a hand on her stomach. "I think there are more men out there than people in my hometown."

"Have you ever performed before a crowd this large?" Irene asked, leaning close to her ear.

Betty shook her head, no. "Not even close."

"I have a tip for you. It's something my mother taught me." Irene guided her farther behind the stage, talking loudly, close to her ear. "She said whenever I went to a party, I needed to wait by the door until I spotted the hostess, and then I was supposed to go to her, and she would introduce me to the rest of the room."

Betty furrowed her brow, unsure of how this advice would help, but she listened intently, trying not to fret over the fact that three girls who looked like sisters in matching red dresses and white bloomers waited in the wings. *The Johnson Sisters, I suppose.*

"So what you do when you go on stage is scan the crowd and find your hostess—or in this case your host. Find someone with a friendly face you can turn back to time and time again, especially when you feel overwhelmed and lost. Feel free to look around, but it helps to know that he's got your back. Helps even more if he's hand-some." Irene winked.

Betty nodded, and she supposed it was good advice, but she wasn't sure she would remember that bit of wisdom once the panic of being on stage set in. Right now, she was having a hard enough time remembering the songs she'd told Mickey she wanted to sing. *I thought this would be easy—but this is big. Real big. And really important too—nothing like the canteen.*

She felt her leg jiggle as she watched the Johnson sisters do a high kicking act. She couldn't help but laugh when the sisters picked two soldiers from the audience and encouraged the guys to kick along with them. The laughter eased her nerves, but only slightly.

Finally, they kicked their way off stage, and it was her turn.

Just when she was about to step out, Mickey beat her, rushing onto the stage. He'd changed during the high-kicking act and now wore a canary yellow suit with a blue tie.

"And now, just flapping her wings and flying in from Santa Monica, California, we have a new performer tonight—I like to call her Songbird. Flutter on out and sing us a song or two!" Mickey wiped his brow with a blue handkerchief that matched his tie, and hurried off stage. Applause rose from the soldiers.

Betty's breath caught in her throat as she strode onto the stage. The ceiling rose above her nearly to the clouds—or so it seemed. Tall white columns lined the side walls, as tall as trees. Round globe lights lit the columns' tops, like dozens of stars that had dared to drop down from the heavens to take a listen.

Below her was the orchestra pit, now empty. Instead of using the pit, a small orchestra sat behind her, stage right. In front of her were row upon row of seats filled with smiling, cheering, clapping GIs.

Above and behind the regular seats more GIs sat in theater boxes. For the briefest moment, she remembered hearing that one of the boxes used to belong to Hitler. But that thought was pushed away as she glanced to the orchestra and the music began.

The opening chords started for "Stormy Weather," and she widened her eyes and stretched a smile over her face.

So many faces, smiles, eyes directed on her. She wasn't easily scared, but suddenly her stomach felt as if it were filled with a hundred little bubbles, bouncing against each other and trying to get out. And then, at the right moment, Betty opened her mouth and the words came out clear, sweet, and beautiful, surprising even herself.

CHAPTER FIVE

The singer dressed in pink waltzed to center stage as if she were an angel. She glanced to the orchestra for the briefest moment and then the music began.

Frank lifted his camera, feeling the anger release from his neck, sliding down his back as she smiled into the crowd. He couldn't believe Marv. How could he dare give him *this* assignment? He was a combat photographer. He'd flown nearly a hundred missions, getting shots of the land, the destruction, the battles in enemy territory, and now they wanted him to take photos of singing, dancing girls, of evening gowns and bloomers?

He couldn't wait until he made it into HQ tomorrow. Only one thing made him halfway okay with this assignment—surely the real reason he was here didn't have to do with snapping shots of singing and dancing girls. Surely something else was going on behind the scenes. From the relaxed smiles on the faces of everyone behind stage earlier, he also guessed it was something none of the performers knew about.

He watched as Betty scanned the crowds at her feet, of men in olive drab uniforms. He lowered his camera as her gaze found his. When she reached the center where he was seated, she paused on him, focusing on his gaze, and her smile widened.

Frank swallowed hard and smiled back. Then he lifted his hand and waved. He felt like a schoolboy with a crush, but at that moment, with the music and her in that dress—he didn't care.

Okay, maybe there were two things he didn't mind about this assignment.

How could you, Marv? Frank didn't know if this rush of anxiety was focused on Marv or himself. *Don't give in. If you get involved with a girl, she'll be pulled into your work. You never know what trouble's around here—what trouble you'll get someone into.*

"Stormy weather, since my man and I ain't together," she sang, swaying slightly, with her captivating eyes glancing back at him.

Hearing the song's lyrics, Frank felt as if his lungs filled with lead.

She probably has a guy out there somewhere. He lifted his camera to take a shot of Betty, while trying to hide his look of disappointment. The flash from his camera brightened the room.

She's a pretty girl. He thought about the way she'd engaged the soldiers on the airplane too. *Maybe she's already promised her heart away or is engaged. Not that she'd be interested in me even if I could pursue her.*

Then again—she hadn't mentioned any guy when they, or mostly Betty and Mac, had chatted on the hour-long drive from Nuremberg to Bayreuth. *She would have mentioned a boyfriend if she had one, right?*

New hopes buoyed Frank's heart, even though his mind reminded him not to go there. He took a few more shots of Betty—or Songbird as she was now called. She *was* a songbird too. Her velvet voice filled the room, and the men around her went silent, entranced by her song.

If Frank hadn't been around her all day—hadn't experienced it—he wouldn't have guessed she'd been singing all day—first on the plane and then on the drive. The song was so pure, so sweet, it seemed as if she'd saved it deep inside, just for this night and these guys.

Betty finished her second song, and the guys rose to their feet, cheering wildly.

Frank couldn't help but join them. He let the camera hang from its strap on his neck, placed two fingers into his mouth, and whistled.

Betty curtsied and then scanned the crowd, her eyes pausing on his.

Frank's heart pounded in his chest in tune to the next song the orchestra started up. He knew the first thing he'd do when he got to his quarters would be to write Marv a note.

How dare you—? Thank you. How could you?

Marv had picked a keeper, all right. And Frank had a feeling he'd like to pursue this one—if only he could.

* * * *

Even though the music had stopped, sweet melodies continued to replay in Betty's mind.

After her performance, she'd stood on the side stage and watched the monologue, the specialty dancer, the comedy skit, and even listened to the cheers and boos as Mickey related the most current sports scores. Last of all, Kat ended the night with an amazing performance of Vera Lynn's "We'll Meet Again." Yet, Betty'd been so tired, so overwhelmed with where she was and what was happening, that she'd hardly taken in any of it.

"Heading over to the soldiers' canteen with us, Songbird?" the trumpet player asked, wrapping an arm around Betty's shoulder. He was her height and thin. So thin, it looked like a heavy wind could blow him away.

"No, I don't think so. Not tonight. Thanks for the invitation, though." Betty moved toward the dressing room.

Irene strode to Betty's side, slipping her hand around Betty's elbow. "Our job isn't over. Every evening we have our usual post-show appearance at the canteen. All the girls head over there with Wally and the band."

Betty blinked twice, struggling to keep her eyes open. "I'm sorry—"

The woman smiled. "My name's Irene. Did you forget already?"

Betty forced a smile. "I'm sorry, Irene. I'm afraid my brain has turned to mush. I've been traveling for the last three days straight, and I haven't laid down that whole time. You should have seen my head bob when I tried to sleep on those airplanes." She reached up and rubbed the back of her neck. "It's gonna take awhile for me to recover."

"Of course you need your rest. I'm getting carried away with myself. You're right. I'll go back with you—show you around. But I think..." Irene paused. "I think the only bed left, though, is in Kat's room."

"Is that a problem?"

"Oh no. Maybe not." The words spilled out of Irene's mouth a little too quickly for Betty's comfort. "I suppose it'll be fine."

"You don't sound very confident."

"Yes, well, Kat does like her own room," Irene said. "She's a professional after all, which is to say she insists on her own wardrobe, her own room, but seeing as she's leaving in a few days I'm sure she'll understand. She'll have to. We can't have you sleeping on the floor now, can we?"

"I hope not, although if it meant I could lay down..." Betty stepped from foot to foot, suddenly realizing how much her feet ached. She looked down, noticing they were swollen. Her ankles too. And she wondered if she'd be able to pry off her shoes.

"Oh." Irene covered her mouth with her hand. "The only problem is that we don't have someone who can drive you back. They're taking all the jeeps to the canteen, which is in the opposite direction—"

"I can give the two of you a ride," a man's voice said from behind her. A voice she recognized.

Betty turned and saw Frank.

"Sorry to interrupt. I was just coming to congratulate you on your first international performance. You did swell, Betty. More than swell."

Betty placed a hand over her heart, her fingers trembling. "It is my first international concert, isn't it—I mean, wasn't it? Wow, it really happened." She studied Frank's face, appreciating again how handsome he was. Remembering how comforting it had been to scan the audience and see him there, smiling up at her.

"Yes, you did it, and I have to say that I never would have guessed you'd just arrived in Bayreuth thirty minutes before you took stage, but since I was riding with you, I know better."

"You can give us a ride? You have a jeep?" Betty asked.

"I don't have one, but I can find one. Give me five minutes. I'll ask around. There's a whole pool of drivers out there, and I have a feeling any of them would think it would be a special privilege to give a ride to the star of the night."

"Sure." Betty forced a smile despite her weariness. "That will give me time to change."

Frank offered a small wave. "Be right back."

Betty hobbled to the dressing room. She hated getting back into her rumpled uniform, but she had little choice. At least her hair looked great, and her makeup too, even if it was hard to hide her exhausted eyes.

When she emerged from the dressing room, Mickey and Frank waited.

"Got a ride, Betty, whenever you're ready."

"Thanks, Frank." She turned to Mickey and shrugged. "Well?"

"Great job, kid. You really shined tonight. You were like Cinderella at the ball. And your voice is as pure as a crystal sea. I wasn't worried one bit. My buddy Marv always comes through."

Frank looked sharply at Mickey. "Marv? From HQ?"

"Yup, said he saw this little songbird when he was back stateside. Called me right away and told me to sign her. Gave his word that I wouldn't regret it." Mickey pulled a cigarette out of his pocket. "Also told me about you, kid. I told him I needed someone great to shoot my girls, and he said he had someone in mind."

Frank nodded. "Did he now?"

Mickey placed the cigarette between his lips and was preparing to light up when a man rushed toward him.

"No light up in opera house, Mr. Mickey. You know the rules." The man wore slacks and a button-up shirt that looked two sizes too large. His pants were held up with a belt, and he nodded and smiled as he spoke.

"Yeah, right, Oskar. A habit, you see." Mickey tucked the cigarette back into his pocket. "Songbird, I'd like to introduce you to Oskar, our prop manager. He runs the place. Knows it inside and out."

Oskar brushed his graying brown hair back from his wide forehead and then extended his hand. Betty liked him immediately. He reminded her of a younger version of her grandfather. Thin but strong, with large hands that looked like they were used to work. He seemed like someone you could count on to get the job done.

"Beautiful music tonight, yes. Great crowd." Oskar nodded again.

"I agree. It was." Betty looked around. "Oskar, I'd love a tour of the Festspielhaus. Not tonight of course—but this place looks amazing."

"More amazing than anyone realizes." He pointed a finger in the air. "We will make sure and see that this happens."

"Yes, wonderful." Betty blinked her eyes.

"Let's get you home, Betty. You need some rest." Frank gently took her arm and led her down the hall, outside to the jeep.

"Is—Irene coming?"

Frank shook his head. "No, she told me to tell you she'd catch up with you in the morning, but I asked Jimmy here and his date to chaperone. Even though I'm a gentleman, I didn't want to do anything to make you uncomfortable. You know, an 'appearance of evil'? Got a reputation to protect—I mean—not just mine."

"Thank you." Betty raised her eyebrows, made a mental note of Frank's scriptural reference. She noticed her luggage was already loaded in the back of the jeep. In the front sat a soldier, and next to him was a beautiful blond woman. She nodded and smiled, and Betty wondered if she spoke English. By her guess, she was one of the locals—despite the non-fraternization policy. What she'd heard before she left the States was that even though the policy was still in place, no one really did much about it, except try to occupy the soldiers' free time with activities and performances. Basically, the more often she sang, the less often the guys in the occupation zone would get into trouble. Or so she'd been told.

Betty settled into the back seat next to Frank, noticing he was still lugging around his duffle bag and camera bag.

How nice of him to see me home. Surely he's tired.

The jeep rolled down a winding hill, away from town, through a park that the bombs had somehow missed. The park was like a fairytale land with tall trees, endless lawns, and a large golden moon that hung over it all. As they drove, she tried to imagine what it would have been like, living here a hundred years ago. Nothing much had changed, she supposed, except for her mode of transportation. Now she had a motorized carriage instead of a horse-drawn surrey.

"So what did you like most about singing the canteens?" Frank's words interrupted her thoughts.

"The people, I suppose. Some came from nearly a hundred miles to help in the canteen. There was a stream of volunteers always coming and going, always making sure there were smiling faces to greet and feed the soldiers on leave or on their way to foreign locations. The guys were great—from all over the U.S.—but the best part was meeting folks from down the street that I'd somehow never become acquainted with. Everyone pitched in and did his part. Washing sheets, making beds, serving up meals—"

"And singing?" Frank said.

"Yes, and most of the time I felt bad because I had the easiest job. I just opened my mouth instead of rolling up my sleeves." Betty yawned. "It was nice. The people were nice."

"The complete opposite from here, huh?" Frank grinned.

"Well, I wouldn't say that—"

"The rest of the troupe will warm up to you. Well, except for Kat. I think she's too high on her horse to notice how rude she is." He snickered. "I bet it's hard to have so many egos in the same room. I suppose everyone's threatened by the new girl at first, thinking she's prettier or more talented."

Betty laughed. "Is that right?" She shook her head. "*That* is far from the truth. I mean—"

"Actually, I disagree. Both are true. And for the others, well, they'll have to get used to it."

Betty turned to him. He was sitting just as close to her as that soldier on the airplane, but somehow this felt different. She cleared her throat, hoping he wouldn't notice how unsettling his nearness was. "Well, sir, those are flattering words. You're just the type of handsome soldier my mother warned me about."

"I can say the same about my mother. I received plenty of warnings myself." Frank snickered.

The jeep turned onto a circular driveway and up to a house. Betty couldn't believe her eyes.

The house was a large rectangle with six steps leading up to the front door. It was stately and beautiful—more like a museum than a bunkhouse for traveling singers.

"Most of the main house was destroyed by bombs," the driver explained. "But I hear the USO girls are in the annex that Hitler stayed in when he visited. It's still intact."

Betty placed a hand to her throat. "I'm sorry. Can you repeat that?"

"Oh, your rooms are in good shape. The bombed part has been blocked off. There's only one entrance—the front door—but as long as you don't mind that half the house is open to the night air, the rest is good," the driver said.

"No, not that part. The other part. Did you say *Hitler* stayed here?"

"He sure did. He'd come here often. A great fan of Wagner and friends with Winifred Wagner, Richard's daughter-in-law. It's because of Winifred's pro-Nazi stance that she had to turn over her home to us. But Hitler's not the only one who stayed in this home. All the Nazi bigwigs did. There are spas nearby, and when they came here, it seemed the war was far off. They came to relax and not think about the war for a while."

Betty scoffed. "Sounds nice. Wish the rest of the world could have done the same."

The driver parked the jeep near the front door. The German girl still sat by his side, quiet, smiling.

"Do you know which room was Hitler's? Which bed?" Betty's eyes widened and she was suddenly more awake than she had been since her performance. The thought of sleeping in the same room Hitler had once occupied made her skin crawl.

"I heard the old beds are gone—they took out the larger ones for simpler cots," the driver said.

"We could find out which room," Frank said, "but do you really want to ask? If I were you, I don't think I'd want to know. It's frightening, don't you think?"

"My father would keel over dead if I told him. My mother would insist I take the next airplane home."

Frank chuckled and patted her hand. "If you tried, there'd be two hundred GIs blocking that plane."

Would you be there too? She wished she had the nerve to ask. She looked into his eyes, seeking an answer in his gaze—but Frank quickly looked away.

CHAPTER SIX

Betty was thankful Frank had offered to walk her in. They'd made it just inside the door when the light switched on, startling her. Standing by the light switch was the beautiful blond singer named Kat.

"Hey, *Songbird*, didn't expect you here so soon. Thought you'd be out with the others, living it up." Kat held a long silver cigarette holder in her hand and, with the grace of a ballerina, lifted it to her lips and drew the smoke deeply into her lungs. Her hand shook slightly, and Betty assumed it was from the cold.

"You can set that luggage there. No guys allowed farther than the doorway. Mickey's rules." Kat flipped her hand toward Frank as if he were a vagrant she wanted to shoo away.

"Yeah, sure. Good rule." Frank set down the luggage and took a step back. Betty's heart warmed to see him eyeing the place, as if he was concerned for her safety.

Betty offered him a parting smile. "Thank you. For everything. I think I'm all set now. Glad we survived the flight and my first performance. What a day." She blew out a low whistle.

"You can say that again. See you tomorrow most likely." He snapped his fingers. "Gotta make sure I don't miss any of this *very important* assignment."

"Not tomorrow. Tomorrow's a rehearsal day. Friday is our next performance. Maybe that will give you time to rest up. I know you worked *so very hard* tonight. I can imagine keeping up with us performers was nearly as hard as your work in the combat zones." She jutted her chin, letting him know she was all too happy to play along.

"Okay, you got me." Frank chuckled. "See you Friday then." He offered Betty the same cute wave he'd given her when she was on stage.

"'Bye." She gingerly closed the door, almost afraid to be alone with this woman. Even though Kat reminded her of one of the China dolls in Haggin's Toy Store, Betty guessed there was more going on beneath the beautiful exterior. Irene had said Kat acted this way because she was a star, and Frank had implied the same thing. Betty wasn't sure she agreed. Kat had a hard look on her face, but there was something else Betty saw in her eyes. It was as if Kat had been hurt too many times, and she made it clear she didn't want anyone too close.

Well, Mama, here's my chance to exercise that "gift" you've always said I have. I just hope Kat doesn't end up agreeing with Dad.

Trying not to show how intimidated she was, Betty turned and smiled. "So how did you get here? Maybe I should have caught a ride with you."

Kat shook her head and exhaled the smoke from her cigarette, blowing it toward the ceiling. "I walked. It's only ten minutes at the most." She looked away and Betty could see something in her eyes that resembled fear, but when Kat glanced back at Betty it was gone.

"It would have been trouble, with all you packed. Did you think you were moving in for good or something?"

"You walked at night? In the dark? Alone?"

"C'mon, kid. The Nazis are gone. The trail's mostly quiet. It's no problem, really." Kat rubbed her brow, and it sounded to Betty as if Kat was trying to convince herself with her own words. *Something happened out there on the trail, something Kat's not telling me.*

"Are you sure—"

"So you want to see the room?" Kat picked up a suitcase and started down the hall. "Mickey says you're bunking with me." Betty picked up the other two suitcases and followed.

Then, as the woman sauntered away in front of her, an image came to Betty's mind. It was that of an actress in one of those Saturday afternoon romantic films she caught once in a while in town. She'd carried a suitcase like that. Walking just like that. Suddenly, Betty knew where she'd seen Kat before and excitement pumped through her.

"Excuse me, are you Katherine Wiseman?"

The woman didn't pause. "Do I look like Katherine Wiseman?" she called back over her shoulder.

"Yes."

"Do I sound like her?" Kat asked, opening the last door at the end of the hall, stepping inside.

Betty followed her in, setting her suitcases down near the bed that was unruffled. "Yes, well, you do."

"I sure hope I am." Kat placed the suitcase on the floor by Betty.

"Did you dream of becoming an actress when you were a little girl?" Betty ignored the room, the tapestry on the wall, and the tall window. Instead she focused on Kat's face.

Kat's eyes widened and her forehead folded into a scowl. "I—I don't know. No, actually I never thought of it when I was younger. I never really went to the picture shows."

"Didn't you have a theater in your town? I was lucky, there was one just down the street from my house."

"It wasn't that. We didn't have much money." Kat crossed her arms over her chest, but her face softened into a wistful look. "I'd always thought I would become a secretary like my mother. I never thought—well, that I'd make movies and sing."

Betty nodded. "My mom never worked outside the home—until the war, that is. I wish I could have brought her here with me. She always dreamed of traveling. She would have loved to meet you, too, Katherine."

"You can call me Kat. Especially since we're roommates now."

"Are you okay with that—with me being your roommate?" Betty sat on the bed and lifted her foot. Then she wiggled the shoe to pry it off.

"Do I have a choice?"

"Well, I can sleep in the hall—as long as I can take a pillow and blanket."

"Are you kidding?" Kat smiled, and Betty hoped it was the beginning of a new friendship. "Honestly, I don't mind. I just want Mickey to think I do. I can't let him think I'm too happy, now can I?"

Betty didn't understand that last statement, but she nodded as if she had. "Gee, I never thought I'd have a famous movie star as my roommate."

"I'm *not* your roommate, kid, you're mine. Until I head back for the States."

"You're leaving?"

"Got a contract with my studio to fulfill. Don't have a choice. They need me for a new picture. Wonder who's going to be my leading man this time? I hope he kisses better than Cary Grant. Kissing that man was like kissing a sponge."

"Doesn't your husband get jealous? I mean, of you kissing other men. I read about you getting married last year. He—what is his name?"

"Edward."

"Yes, I saw a photo of the two of you in the newspaper. Edward is very handsome."

"I agree. I wouldn't have married him if he wasn't." Kat crossed to her side of the room. She unbuttoned her dress and slid out of it, putting on a silky robe over her slip. "He has other wonderful qualities too. There are a lot of handsome men out there. Edward's the only one I've met who's as kind as he is beautiful." Kat flopped onto the bed, propped her pillow against the wall, and leaned against it. She looked relaxed, yet also introspective. She rolled her eyes upward, and Betty guessed Kat was thinking about her husband.

Betty put on her pajamas, then sat cross-legged on her bed.

"Is it hard, being away?"

"It's been hard for everyone, not only me. War is war."

"Are you excited about seeing him soon? I bet it's been a long time."

"I saw him two months ago—" Kat's voice trailed off. She shrugged. "Considering the way this world is, that's not too long ago." Her voice softened, and the hard set of her jaw did too. "It was only for one night. He was stationed in Paris." She smiled. "But sometimes one night is enough." She placed a hand on her stomach and glanced down.

"I don't mean to meddle, but are you—in the motherly way? I mean are you expecting?"

Kat glanced over. Her eyes widened in surprise. "Why would you ask that? I mean we just met. That really isn't something you ask someone you just met." Betty put her hands up in defense, as if she was blocking Kat's wrath.

"You're right. I'm so sorry. How rude of me. It's only, well, because of your comment—and the look in your eyes. I've seen that look a lot lately. Most of my friends back home are already married and have babies."

Kat glared at Betty for a moment, as if sizing her up. Then she flipped over onto her stomach, rested her chin on her hands, and kicked her feet up behind her as if she were twelve and enjoying a slumber party with a friend. It was a different Kat than the nose-in-the-air-actress she'd met earlier that day. "Do you promise not to tell? I'm hoping the next picture will wrap up quickly, before I show. I have to finish this last film. After that, I'll be done with my contract and will be a free agent—no one will be able to tell me what to do anymore."

"Of course."

Then as quickly as the fanciful mood caught Kat, it left. She pushed her pillows back into their rightful place and reached over to the nightstand for her brush and sat up.

The moonlight cast yellow rays into the room as Kat sat at the edge of the bed, running a brush through her long hair. Betty could tell from the look on her face that Kat was done talking about Edward and the baby. Obviously, whatever was happening with her movie contract was enough to put Kat in a sour mood.

"Don't you wonder who slept in this room before—before, you know, we took control?" Betty lay down, tucking her pillow under her chin.

"I've thought of that, but I don't like to ponder it long."

"Hitler could have slept in here. This very room." Betty sat up slightly, leaning on her elbow.

Kat again placed a hand over her stomach. "Don't say that. I'm feeling ill as it is. I've been all over Europe, and we've been in some harrowing situations, but every time I'm in this house, I have a bad feeling. Evil lived here too long, I suppose. It worries me—"

"What worries you?"

"Well, like something bad's going to happen. I can feel it." Kat stopped brushing her hair. "You know what they say, don't you?"

"No, what?"

"This place is haunted. Some of the other girls say they can hear footsteps at night. They say they hear someone—or some*thing*—walking in the rafters…and below us too."

"How do you know it's not just hoodlums trying to find hidden treasure?"

Kat lifted a thin, penciled eyebrow. "Could be, but I wouldn't put it past those Jerries to stick around—to haunt us even after they're dead. There're lots of rumors going around. Sometimes I can feel it too. It's as if someone is here, in this house, watching us."

"Really?" Betty sat up, planted her feet on the floor, and curled her hands into fists, trying to lighten Kat's doomsday mood. "I'd be willing to go toe-to-toe with any Nazi ghost."

Kat didn't answer. She didn't smile. Instead, she placed her brush on the nightstand and got into bed.

Betty padded over to the dressing table, poured fresh water into a basin, and brushed her teeth and washed her face. Just talking about ghosts gave her a sick feeling. Her stomach rumbled and she realized part of the reason she didn't feel well was the fact she hadn't eaten since they took off in London. The other part, though, was because Kat was right. Being in this house brought an icky feeling, and joking about it didn't help. Betty turned off the light and hurried to her bed, thankful for the moonlight that brightened the room so it wasn't completely dark.

Even though she was exhausted, Betty lay awake awhile, trying to comprehend everything the day had served up. It was unlike any day she'd ever experienced. She also had to admit she was sad that Kat would leave soon. Betty could tell that most of the other girls in the troupe gave Kat a wide berth, but she had a feeling that if they spent enough time together, Kat could become a friend.

Betty rolled to her side. "Kat?" she whispered.

"What?"

"Can I ask you a question?"

"Are you sure it's only one? All you've done is talk. I'm glad I'm leaving in a few days. If not, I'd request a different roommate. A girl needs her beauty sleep, you know." Even though Kat's words were sharp, her tone was gentle.

"Just one. I promise." Betty took a deep breath. "How do you know if you've found the right guy? With all of them out there—"

"Do you like someone, kid? Heaven knows you have a good shot of winning his heart if you do. There's a one-to-a-thousand ratio of American girls to soldiers around these parts. And as you know, the soldiers aren't supposed to fraternize with the German girls—"

"I sort of like someone. But I'm not sure. He's so mature, so professional. And he's a soldier. My mother told me soldiers are bad news."

"Edward's a soldier, and I don't mean any harm by this, but I think your mother is wrong. The fact that a man signs up to fight is commendable. The ones you should watch out for are those who were too chicken to join, who hid back home with 'safe' government or production jobs."

"Yes, that's true, but this guy's really great and—well, do you think I'd have a chance of him liking me back?"

Kat was silent for a moment, as if she was thinking. "Well, you're not Betty Grable beautiful, but you're not hard on the eyes either. So if some soldier around here isn't interested, he's either married or he's devoted to some broad back home who's good at writing sappy letters."

"Yeah, well, I promised my mother I wouldn't lose my heart to a guy too quickly. She says if I want to make something out of myself and get more than bit parts and walk-ons in Hollywood that I'll need to be married to my work."

"It's true. Hollywood has its demands. When I told my boss that I wasn't renewing my contract, he about blew his top. My agent told me he didn't invest so much in me for me to walk away. But I'm not concerned anymore with what he thinks." Kat sighed. "I'm ready to be with Edward, to live like a family for once. I couldn't have been happier when I heard the war ended. To me it meant Edward was going to make it through. And that, to me, is better than any applause or seeing my name in lights—guaranteed." Kat's voice began to fade. "Still, you shouldn't jump into things too hastily. You're young, give yourself time. If I were you I wouldn't even consider dating until my job with the USO was up. Enjoy what you have. Enjoy the music."

"Yeah." Betty snuggled down in her blankets. "You're right—I'll wait. I'll give myself time."

CHAPTER SEVEN

"So, where now, Bub?" the driver asked when Frank got back to the jeep.

"Well..." Frank took off his cap, ran a hand through his hair, and then returned it. "I'm supposed to room with my friend Art Spotts. He's a photographer like me. But I don't have much more info than that."

The driver nodded as the German woman snuggled closer under his arm.

"Ah, yes, I think I know where to start. There's a house where all the artsy types hang out. If they don't know who your Spotts friend is, I don't know what to tell you."

The driver took them into the town of Bayreuth, and for the first time Frank understood the magnitude of the war's destruction. Half of the buildings, at least, lay in rubble. The other half looked as if they were damaged in some way. It was strange, seeing up close what he'd photographed from above. He'd seen the bombs they'd dropped and their explosions, and he was more surprised by what still stood than by what had crumbled.

They turned onto a side street, and as the jeep's headlights swung around the corner, the light reflected off the eyes of a small group of people—men, women, and children—huddled under a makeshift tent in the middle of the rubble in what appeared to be the shopping district. A little bit down the road, another group slept inside a building in which the front had crumbled away— most likely from a near-miss by an American bomb.

"What's going on? Who are these people? Why are they sleeping outside?" Frank asked, even though he knew the answer. He'd seen many displaced persons all over Europe. He also knew, though, that one of the best ways to get information about any area is to play dumb tourist. People often liked sharing what they knew. He'd gotten more than one bad guy to spill key information in his or her role as tour guide. Not that he thought his driver had anything to hide—Frank was just warming up. Getting ready for the assignment he still didn't understand completely.

Surely there has to be more to this thing than just shooting photos of pretty girls. They wouldn't have brought him in if there weren't.

"Who are they?" The driver shook his head. "'Who aren't they' would be an easier question. Some are Germans who've been kicked out of their homes to make room for the American troops. Some are families who lost their homes in the bombing. There are former prisoners from Hitler's concentration camps—those are the saddest cases. There are also Germans from the Sudetenland—the ones who poured into Czechoslovakia after Hitler invaded and then were kicked out again."

"Things were similar in Paris. I hung out there the last few months, but it was nothing like this." Frank sighed. "It's been months now, and these people are still out of their homes. It just doesn't seem right to me. I wonder what will happen next. I hope the government does something before winter sets in."

The jeep stopped beside a tall house, and the driver pointed. "They use the bottom as an officer's mess. Upstairs is a little restaurant, but lately there's been more music than food. I can almost bet your buddy Art is up there—or at least someone who knows him."

"And if not?" Frank asked.

"Bayreuth headquarters will be open in the morning. I'm sure you can crash here until then."

From the look in the guy's eyes, he was done driving Frank around. It seemed like he had other things in mind, like getting to know his date better. Frank couldn't help but eye her with suspicion. She most likely was a simple German girl looking for companionship after the war, but one never knew.

Frank jumped out, grabbed his duffle bag, and thanked the driver. Then he headed upstairs, via the outside stairway. He was only five steps up when he heard the music. It was a woman's voice, and in a strange way, it reminded him of Songbird. *What in the world?* Frank knew it couldn't be her, yet he took the steps two at a time. On the landing at the top of the stairs, two GIs were smoking cigarettes with another couple of young German girls. He nodded to them and moved inside.

The room looked almost gray from the swirls of smoke that curled in the air. Soldiers sat on worn-out sofas, at small tables, and even on the floor. The woman stood in the corner. Her head was tilted up as she sang. It was as though she serenaded a balcony that wasn't there. Frank scanned the room and there, in the far back corner, sat Art at

a small table. Frank moved in Art's direction, for the first time realizing how quiet the audience was—all of the soldiers focused on the
woman's song.

Frank was halfway to Art when his friend stood, motioning him
the rest of the way over. As he neared, Art shook his hand.

"Was wondering when you were coming. Have a seat, your duffle
bag will make a great chair," he said in a low voice, and before Frank
could respond, Art had already turned his attention back to the singer.

Frank set his duffle bag on end and sat. He didn't ask Art about
the empty chair at the table. He guessed it was for the singer. Art
always had the most beautiful girlfriends wherever he was stationed.
The only thing that would surprise him was if Art *didn't* have a date.

The woman sang her last note, and the room erupted in applause.

"Don't you think she's great? She's a star—or at least she used to
be. Magdalena used to sing in the opera house, back when they still
performed Wagner's *Siegfried*, and not the jazzy rubbish that's playing there now."

"I'm offended by that." Frank straightened his shoulders. "It's
good music. I was there tonight."

"Oh, yes." Art half-smiled. "We're giving the GIs real culture—
variety shows and revues—put on in the same building where last
summer Nazi officers and invalid troops watched *Goterdammerung*."

Frank rubbed his eyes. "Are you saying we don't have any culture?"

"Not saying that at all, but it's not Wagner. Don't you know this
town is what it is now because of him and that opera house? No
works by any other composer had ever been performed there until
we showed up—"

"You seem to know a lot about music, Art. Last time I saw you in Paris a couple of months ago, you couldn't have cared less about German culture." Frank's head started to ache, and he didn't understand why he was arguing. Yesterday he most likely would have agreed with Art, but today things were different. Mainly because when he thought of the USO singers, he thought of *her.* Yesterday Frank would have taken Art's comments as just observation, but now they seemed to be an insult to someone who had strangely managed to wiggle through a crevasse in the wall he'd built up around his heart.

I have to stop thinking about Betty. It's better for me—and for her. Don't want her wrapped up in the business I'm in—

"Yes, well, that's what two months here will do for you, when you come to care for someone, I suppose. Your world gets turned upside down overnight."

The woman looked in their direction and met Art's eye. He lifted his hand and signaled her over.

"So, is that your girl?" Frank asked.

"I wish. She's still looking for her husband. Magdalena is Czechoslovakian—an international star who is now penniless. The Czechs sent her back to Germany because of her connection to Bayreuth and all her luggage was stolen, including valuable jewelry. So sad. But I'll stick around, just in case. It's horrible to say, but if her husband doesn't show up, I want to be first in line."

Frank wanted to be outraged by what the Czechs had done to the woman, but he couldn't help siding with them. Their land had been overrun by the Germans and now they were ready to be rid of any German influences and reminders. Still, as with so many people he'd met who were now displaced, the question wasn't "Where should I go?" but "Where are the ones I love?" Seeing their desperation at learning the fate of family members they'd lost track of during the war made him realize even more how important family was.

The woman approached. She was plain-looking, but in a beautiful way—like a statue of Mary, without adornment. She sat in the chair next to Art and smiled.

"Dis a friend?" She pointed to Frank.

"Yes, my old buddy—a photographer like me."

The woman extended her hand and Frank took it in his, shaking it gently. Her hand was cold and frail, and he was almost certain that if he shook it too hard it would break.

"So you are a singer?" Frank asked, even though it was obvious.

"*Ja*. Or I used to be such."

"Sweetest soprano you ever heard," Art said.

"Did you sing in some of Wagner's operas?"

"Ja." The woman nodded. Her face appeared weary. "That was many lifetimes yet."

"Your English is good." Frank felt a weariness coming over him and he smiled, wondering when it would be polite to ask Art about their accommodations so he could head out.

"I worked with many Americans. I've traveled there also, debuting—" She shook her head and looked around. "It doesn't matter now. I've had good life. A good career."

"Maybe it's not over yet. You never know." Art patted her hand.

Magdalena smiled at Art, but it was obvious she didn't believe his words.

"I know some of the singers who are at the opera house now. I'm sure they would like to meet you—to hear about your career," Frank said.

Magdalena's eyes widened and her lips pressed into a thin line. "I think I would like that," she finally said. But even as she said the words, Frank could see it was far from the truth. The woman's forced smile said one thing—but her eyes said something else completely.

* * * *

Dierk's footsteps were light as he walked down the narrow alley. Rays from a yellow moon lit his way, yet he knew that even if there were no moonlight he'd still walk unhindered. He'd made this same trek nearly every night since the Americans had moved in and the Germans had abandoned their labors. The warehouse at the end of his path stood in the midst of a larger factory complex. Thankfully, the Americans had yet to explore thoroughly the treasure hidden within the boxes and piled in dusty corners. The foreign invaders believed the war had ended—Dierk knew this was not the case. The war would never end. Evil would rise again. And what Americans didn't understand *would* hurt them. Their death cries would be part of the final act.

The warehouse was only one place he looted, although Dierk liked to think of it as gathering only what had already been prepared for him. The Nazi death forces had done their work, used their weapons as long as their time allowed. And now it was his turn.

Even though Wagner's focus had been musical drama, the work of Wagner's family spun off in other weighty pursuits. Dierk had co-labored with Wieland Wagner at the opera house and with Wagner's brother-in-law, Lafferentz, on more technical matters. Lafferentz was a man Dierk admired greatly—especially his work with the "sighted bomb," an effort to improve the accuracy of rockets launched from planes or submarines. They'd been so close to achieving success. If only they'd had more time. He would have liked to see the rocket finished to help the German people, but not for Hitler. The madman didn't deserve such a reward.

Time caused us defeat once, but not twice.

Again the ticking clock sounded in his ear—his performance must happen at the appointed hour. He didn't have a minute to waste.

Dierk's steps quickened as he walked toward the trees at the back of the factory. Years ago they had made thread here, but during '44 they had made death—or rather the type of rockets that had carried death into England and France.

He strode toward the sign that read NEW COTTON MILLS. It was here that specialist workers—electricians, engineers, technicians, and physicists—had worked on the *wunder* weapon.

If Dierk continued down this road, he'd come to a gate where two American MP officers stood, but they wouldn't have the pleasure of meeting him tonight.

They guarded a main building—the former thread factory—that stood idle for want of raw materials. The former rocket factory also stood idle since wunder weapons were no longer needed. And the large concentration camp beside it, where forced laborers had worked, stood empty too.

It had been a little over a year ago when all German theaters had closed as Goebbels appealed for "total war." All exemptions from military service were cancelled—even all the artists in the Berlin State Opera company and the singers to the *corps de ballet* had gone off to war. Only his opera—Wagner's *Mastersingers* being performed at the *Festspielhaus*—was allowed to finish the season. But after its final performance on August 9, Dierk had also found work inside these gates. Not as a prisoner, but as a well-respected laborer. And since then, his labors had not ceased.

Even though he was far out of view, Dierk gave a mock salute to the American military police and chuckled. It amused him how the Americans considered themselves safe. Didn't they understand that those who wish to do harm don't come announced? They don't plead for entry? He'd always found other ways to get what he wanted. He always found the unseen paths.

Cutting off from the main road, his footsteps barely made a sound as he moved under the trees. The leaves pressed under his feet in submission. The air smelled of dirt and decay. The decay of the leaves and the scent of death also lingered in the scattered ashes of the nearby camp. Though the gates had been opened and the prisoners freed, the stench remained. The Americans had tried to clean up the camp—as they did with everything—but evil clung. It stuck to all that had life, assuring that those who still breathed would not forget.

If a million nights passed, Dierk would not forget.

He approached the opening to the fence and glanced around, just in case some poor beggar saw him enter the woods and followed, hoping for a companion and maybe a little food. Seeing no one, he slipped through the opening and stayed crouched as he hurried to the warehouse's back door. He entered and noticed the moon's rays streamed through the high windows. He didn't need to use his flashlight tonight, which was fine. Dierk felt more comfortable in darkness.

He went through three boxes, pulling out the parts he needed, and made a pile. These parts were designed for rockets, but he had different plans. The explosives were marked for the enemy of the Reich, but he'd use them against the enemy of the town—those who trampled their heritage. Dierk could not change how Bayreuth and Wagner, its most famous citizen, were disgraced, but he could ensure the abuse didn't continue.

When he found all he needed, he put it into a sack and tucked it under his shirt. Then he buttoned his shirt and his jacket over it.

He wasn't greedy. He only took what he needed for this night's work.

He had enough time for the task set before him. A limited number of days to work—until his masterpiece was complete. Until the chosen date of the final show.

CHAPTER EIGHT

The sound of footsteps in the hall pulled Betty from her fitful sleep. Her first thought was that Kat was right—this place was haunted. But as Betty opened her eyes, she was amazed to find that it was morning. And as she sat up and listened closer, she could tell the footsteps were mixed with the voices of women preparing for the day.

Betty rose and stretched. She noticed Kat still sleeping, with her silk eye mask in place. As quietly as she could, Betty padded across the room to the window where she got her first real look at the place.

Villa Wahnfried was a beautiful estate. Their bedroom window faced the front of the house. A long driveway lined with trees led to the front door. Expansive lawns stretched in all directions, and Betty was sure that at one time they'd been well cared for. Now the lawns were brown and scraggly. The shrubbery was unkempt, and some of the trees nearest to the main roadway had been blown down—not by high winds, but by bombs. *It must have been the same bombing raid that hit the house.* To her right, she could see the piles of rubble where the rest of the house used to stand.

She tried to imagine what it would have been like to be here when that raid took place. *It must have been so frightening.*

She quickly pushed those thoughts out of her mind. It was war, and the bombers did what had to be done. If they hadn't bombed—who knew what would be happening now? Who knew how many more American lives would have been lost? Who knew how many more prisoners would have died in the death camps?

Last spring, right before the end of the war, the newsreels had shown why they'd fought. Even now, her stomach ached, thinking of the images of thin prisoners and stacks of bodies in Hitler's death camps. It was all more real to her. The fighting wasn't something that happened "over there." She would now walk the streets where it had taken place. She had sung in the auditorium where Hitler had been entertained. She might even be sleeping in the room—*No, don't think of that. Don't dwell on those things.* But despite her attempt to push those thoughts from her mind, a shiver traveled up her spine.

Outside on the front lawn, three girls she recognized as the dancing sisters were busy washing their clothes in a large tub placed near the front door. They'd strung a line between the porch handrail and a nearby tree and now hung their garments out to dry.

Betty chuckled as she noticed how they hung their dresses with the same uniformity that characterized their act. Three blue dresses, three scarlet dresses, and then three black gowns glimmered in the morning sun. The wind whipped the women's hair, and the dresses swayed as if warming up for their act.

Seeing the women work together made Betty think of her friends back home. Even simple tasks like knitting or bandage-rolling parties had become fun when they worked together. Would she find that kind of friendship and camaraderie here? She unpacked her suitcase into the small bureau, organizing all the items the USO Camp Show advisor had told her to bring—hosiery, dresses, theatrical makeup, cold cream, sewing kits, and bobby pins. She also pulled out her Bible, and a yearning filled her chest. She pulled it to herself, thankful she'd remembered to pack it. She sat down on her bed, with her Bible opened on her lap, but a call from one of the women interrupted her.

"Twenty minutes, girls, until we leave for breakfast!"

Betty's eyes widened. She didn't have time to read. Not today. She set her Bible in the top drawer of the dresser and closed it. If she didn't join the others, she had no idea where to get food, or how to get to the Festspielhaus.

Tomorrow. I promise.

Grabbing up her things, she opened the door as quietly as she could and hurried to the bathroom that Kat had pointed out last night. Betty soon found that the bath was almost as uncivilized as their laundry facilities. She filled the basin with cool water, washed, and then dressed in the olive trousers and jacket provided by the USO.

Her stomach rumbled, and she was eager for breakfast.

When she returned to her room Kat was still sleeping.

"Kat," Betty whispered.

"Hm?" Kat mumbled.

"Are you coming to breakfast?"

"No. I—I feel awful. Tell the others to go ahead. I'll catch up."

Within two minutes, the whole foyer was filled with women, dressed and ready to head out to the mess hall.

Betty followed the rest of her troupe as they walked down the road to the mess and lined up for breakfast chow. The mess hall was an old, brick building that looked as if it had previously served as a dance hall on the property of a wealthy family. The GIs around them laughed and joked, yet they all seemed to quiet and brush their fingers through their hair as the performers entered the building. Betty scanned the faces looking for Frank. She tried to hide her disappointment when he was nowhere to be seen. *Maybe later, during rehearsal. He knows I'm going to be there—maybe he'll stop by.*

The room smelled of burnt toast and bacon. Her stomach growled, and she hoped there was plenty of food to go around. She was sure she could eat any soldier under the table.

"If we wanted, we could eat in the officers' mess, but things are often more interesting in the mess halls with the GIs," Irene explained. "We follow their schedule and use their tins. I've actually learned to like dehydrated eggs and Spam—although the food has gotten a bit better lately."

Betty got her food and sat down. As she did, she looked for Kat, but still didn't see her. *Most likely doesn't feel like eating, with her condition and all.* Betty wondered what Irene and the others would think about Kat's big news. But she was determined not to betray Kat. It was Kat's news to share, in her own good time.

Betty chatted with a group of GIs, but couldn't truly enjoy the conversation because she was wondering about Frank and where he was. Even though they'd agreed they'd see each other tomorrow at the performance, she hoped he'd come around today.

Betty was pleased to find Kat waiting outside the mess hall when they were finished, even though her face looked pale and her hair hung limp on her shoulders. Dark circles ringed her eyes, and she gripped her stomach.

"Is everything okay, Kat?" Irene said, rushing to her side.

"I'm feeling a little under the weather, that's all." Kat waved a hand toward them.

"Should we run ahead and have Mickey send down a jeep and driver?"

"No, I need exercise. I'm sure the fresh air will do me good." Kat looked to her feet and kicked at a rock. Betty wondered if she was going to tell her news, but Kat quickly changed the subject. "Just thought I'd like some company, no big deal. Maybe it isn't too wise after all to be walking alone in these parts."

"Did something happen?" Dolly took Kat's hand.

"Yes, Kat, spill it. We know you aren't telling the truth. Something happened, and I think you should tell us. You've never wanted our company before." Irene's words spilled out. "I mean, not that you've been rude or anything, just independent." She placed a hand on her hips. "And if there is something going on, you better tell us. We walk that path too, you know."

"Well, last night…" Kat paused. Then she lifted her eyes, peering up from under her eyelashes. "I think there were some kids trying to play games with me. I thought I heard footsteps following me from the opera house to Wahnfried, but I never saw anyone behind me."

"I told you not to walk alone," Irene said.

"I thought you said it was perfectly safe." Betty crossed her arms over her chest. "You should have said something last night."

"It *is* safe." Kat attempted a light-hearted laugh. "Personally, I think it was the Nazi ghost. He'd gone up to watch our show and needed directions getting back."

All the girls laughed, but Betty could see they were still concerned. With cautious steps, they headed up the tall hill. And even though she couldn't see it through the trees, Betty knew the opera house was waiting, as it had waited for its singers for the last sixty or so years.

They were halfway up the hillside when the trees opened up to a beautiful garden area with a pond. Betty paused her steps, taking it in. The pond was light green and nearly as big as the swimming pool at her old high school. Lush bushes ringed half its shore and tall trees shaded the waters. In her mind's eye, she could almost picture Snow White's cottage beyond the trees. She'd taken her niece Hazel to watch that show and wished she could get a photo of this place to send back to her.

Maybe I can ask Frank later. It would be a good excuse to come back and enjoy the spot—and the company.

"This is so beautiful. Oh, I wish it were warm, I'd love to take a swim," Betty said, reluctantly hurrying to catch up with the others who'd continued ahead.

"It is a good swimming hole, and we tried it out a few times this summer. It was fun until word got out and all the soldiers thought us flopping around in our swimsuits was a show of its own. When one guy brought a movie camera, we stopped coming. The last thing we wanted was movies of us to be sent home," Irene said.

"Not that *we'd* be recognized." Dolly brushed her red hair back from her forehead. "Still, it's the idea."

"Kat would be recognized." Betty turned to her friend, who was starting to get a little color in her cheeks. "They'd like that, wouldn't they? I'm sure it would have shown up in the newsreels." Betty laughed.

"Oh no, not me." Kat held up her hands. "I didn't go near that death trap." She continued to look ahead, as if she was afraid to so much as look at the pond.

"Kat told us the story once, after we begged her to join us taking a dip. It turns out her cousin drowned when she was a little kid and Kat almost drowned trying to rescue her."

"How sad." Betty covered her mouth with her hand.

"And that," Kat said, marching forward, "is why I only wear my bathing suit for photo opportunities."

Laughter carried up the hill and through the trees. Betty had only been here one day, and she already enjoyed getting to know the other women. She wished she had more time to get to know Kat. She found it hard to believe Kat was leaving so soon. Only one more performance, Kat had told her, and she'd fly away.

* * * *

Mickey was working with the band on a jazz number when they arrived. The band sat on the practice stage, on the other side of the dressing room wall. They all wore slacks and white shirts, and their eyes were focused on the metal music stands in front of them. They were practicing a jazzy number, and Mickey stood to the side of the conductor's stand with one hand on his chin and his eyes closed, nodding along as he listened.

Betty followed the others into the large dressing area, with the heavy scent of talcum powder mixed with dust. Bright lights ringed a row of mirrors and reflected light around the room, brightening the faces of the singers and dancers.

"Well, I guess this will be as good a time as any to pack up my things." Kat moved to a rack of dresses. "I'll only leave out two gowns. Which do you think I should wear?"

"Depends on what Mickey asks you to sing," Shirlee, one of the sisters, commented.

"I think she should pick what looks best." Irene pulled out a white gown with layers of thin, light fabric. "This is my favorite, with the wide black belt."

"Or what about the red dress with flowers? I have a hat that will go perfect with it," one of the other sisters piped up.

"You don't have room for all these dresses to go back with you, do you?" Dolly asked. "I mean, it's so hard to get anything decent around here—don't you think you should leave some?"

The other singers were busy trying to convince Kat to leave some of her little-used gowns behind when Betty looked through the doorway and noticed Oskar working on a beautiful landscape set in the back corner of the rehearsal area. The curtain was open, yet he wasn't giving the women, or their fashion chatter, any mind. Instead, he studied the large wooden-backed set as intently as a Van Gogh.

Betty left the others and approached him. He looked sad, and Betty wondered why. Then she noticed the paint can on the floor and the paintbrush in his hand.

"Hey, Oskar, how are you doing today? Busy at work?" She attempted to sound chipper.

Oskar's head jerked up as if surprised by Betty's approach. "Oh, well. I have these old sets and Mickey wants me to—change them." Oskar's gaze was narrow, and Betty could tell he wasn't happy about it.

"Were these sets used before? For the operas?"

"Ja, Wagner designed them himself. They were for his great *Ring* opera trilogy."

"Maybe you can talk to Mickey—explain the importance of them?"

"No." Oskar lowered his head. "It is no use. Wagner is banned, and I see no hope of things changing. Wagner existed before Hitler, but no one remembers. I am afraid there will be no Wagner operas performed here again." He sighed, and his shoulders trembled slightly. "What is the use of saving what will only become rubbish?"

"How do you know that? Maybe someday in the future Wagner's operas—" Betty's voice trailed off, and she crossed her arms over her chest. She didn't know why she was saying anything at all. She knew very little about Wagner, his music, or this opera house. The one thing she had heard is that Hitler had first gotten some of his ideas from Wagner's work, and he also used Wagner's music in his big rallies and propaganda events.

Oskar opened the can of paint, dipped the brush, and painted a large white stripe down the center of the forest scene with a quick stroke. Betty cringed. If she knew Mickey better, she'd consider talking to him herself, but who was she? She was new—to this place, to this show. What did she know?

"Betty, come over here and look at this white dress with black polka-dots. Kat's leaving it and I think it will look perfect on you."

"Be there in a minute," Betty called over her shoulder. Then she turned back to Oskar.

"I'm sure the Germans wouldn't be happy if they knew what will happen to these sets," she said.

"My father would weep. My neighbors—no, I cannot tell them."

"Wait, you're German?" Betty took a step back. "But your English is spoken so well. I thought you came with Mickey—from Hollywood or something. I never would have guessed you're—" She didn't know how to say it—that he used to be one of the enemy.

Irene strode up and Betty noticed a belt in her hands.

Oskar offered Betty a soft smile. "Ja, yes. Many tell me I have good English." He winked at Irene. "I do not know as much as I used to."

"Go ahead, Oskar, tell Betty the story," Irene pleaded. She turned to Betty. "He has the most amazing story."

Oskar waved a hand in the air. "You have work to do. I have work to do."

Betty looked to Mickey and saw he was still working with the band. "Just a short version then?"

Oskar nodded, put down his brush, and wiped his hands on a paint cloth. "I have lived in this town my entire life. My father worked with Wagner himself—was a carpenter on the original sets. He also worked on building Wahnfried—the mansion you are staying in. He would be heartbroken to see it in this state."

"Wahnfried, that's a strange name—at least to me. What does it mean?" Betty asked.

"In German it means 'Peace from Delusions.'" Oskar rubbed his chin, and though he was looking at Betty, she could tell he wasn't focused on her. His mind was in another place. "*Hier wo mein Wähnen Frieden fand—Wahnfried—sei dieses Haus von mir benannt*," he said. "Here where my delusions have found peace, let this place be named Wahnfried."

Betty thought about that for a minute. When she thought about peace, she didn't think about a building. To her, peace was the oak tree in the meadow behind her house. It was there she often took her Bible. Those were her favorite moments, sitting in the sunshine, listening to the birds, reading and praying.

"Yes, things are different now. Our world will never be the same." Oskar swept his arm toward the band. "The music will never be the same."

"Did you learn English from your father?" Betty asked.

"Oh no, my father was a good German. He wouldn't think of speaking anything other than his mother tongue. My mother was deaf, you see. She became deaf from an illness right after she was married. She did her best to care for me, but my father didn't think she could take care of me alone. He hired a nanny. She was American, the daughter of one of the American opera singers who lived here for many years. Her native tongue was English—and so mine became."

"Fascinating. What did your father say…"

"Ladies, ladies, enough of your chatter. We have work to do." Mickey clapped his hands as he approached Betty and Irene. "Oskar has work to do too. That new set must be ready by tomorrow night."

Betty excused herself, thinking she needed to pick up their conversation where they'd left off. Then she hurried to where the others were circled. She stood next to Kat. In her hands, Kat held the black and white dress that Irene had mentioned.

"First of all"—Mickey turned to Kat—"I have an idea for your last number. We're going to send you away big, see. Imagine the room goes dark. You move onto the stage, quiet-like, and then you start— just one note—clear, strong. Pretty soon, a single spotlight shines on the stage, lighting your face, and then the orchestra kicks in. It's going to take their breath away. I can see it now."

"What song, Mickey? What's Kat going to sing?" Irene leaned closer.

"I was thinking of 'America the Beautiful'—something to really get them feeling all those emotions of patriotism and home."

Kat didn't look impressed.

"But what about 'Boogie-Woogie Bugle Boy'?" Kat softly stamped her foot. "I've been practicing that for weeks."

"No problem, kid. That will be in the show. I just wanted something strong for the end."

"Okay, that'll work, I suppose. But I wish you would have told me sooner, Mick; I need time to prepare. In fact, I'll need some practice time on stage this afternoon. I'd hate to make you look bad by blowing the last big number."

"Whatever you need, Kat, let me know." Mickey walked over and placed an arm around her shoulders. "Maybe you should get some rest too—you're looking a little pale."

Kat glanced at Betty and then back at Mickey. "I'm feeling a little under the weather, that's all." She stepped out of his one-armed hug. "Thanks for telling me how horrible I look, Mick. I'll make sure I put extra makeup on tomorrow night so I don't look like the walking dead."

Kat turned to Betty. "Here you go. Irene's right, this will look great on you." She placed the dress in Betty's hands. Then she turned and stomped to the dressing room.

"Did I say something wrong?" Mickey scanned the faces. "Did I, Dolly?"

Dolly twirled a strand of red hair around her finger. "I don't think so, Mickey. You know how Kat is. I think she's tired, that's all."

"I don't think that's it." Irene took the dress from Betty's hand and held it up in front of Betty, nodding her approval. "When Kat planned on leaving, she figured she'd leave a big hole. She didn't think anyone could step in and take her place. But now we have Betty here—and Kat sees that the show's going on without her. I think that's what's bothering her."

"I don't think so. Maybe it's something else entirely." Betty took the dress and held it behind her back. All eyes turned her direction, and she felt heat rising to her cheeks, suddenly embarrassed to be pushed into the center of this conversation. "I know I just got here, and I know I've only known Kat one day but—" She glanced around.

"Maybe Kat's a little sad about leaving and she doesn't want to show it. I mean if she gets all of you mad at her before she goes, then there'll be no emotional good-byes."

"Who do you think you are, kid, Sigmund Freud?" Mickey's voice was sharp, and Betty flinched. But then as she watched, his scowl turned into a smile. "Actually, I like the idea, even if you don't know what you're talking about. I like that idea that we'll be missed—even by someone as famous as Kat. There's only one Mickey, right? Kat's gonna miss me when she's gone. She's gonna appreciate me when she gets around those Hollywood-types. You'll see."

CHAPTER NINE

Frank opened the window and sucked in a breath of cool, fall air. It smelled like rain, and he had no doubt that by this afternoon—or maybe tonight—showers would fall on the town.

At least I have a warm place to lay my head, he thought, pushing out the realization that hundreds of others around the town didn't.

If there was one benefit to being transferred to Bayreuth, it had to be the house he shared in the nice residential area across from a pretty, walled park. Frank knew the residents who used to live here had vacated their homes for the army's use, but every time he started feeling bad, all he had to do was think of the friends he'd lost, including the crew of the Klassy Lassie. It was war. People died. People were injured. Others were left with memories—and some had to sleep out in the cold for a while.

Frank had already been to breakfast and then to headquarters, only to find the officer he had to report to was out for the day and wouldn't be back until tomorrow. *Maybe I should head back to the opera house—to make plans for tomorrow's shoot.* The sound of footsteps coming down the hall to his shared room interrupted his thoughts.

"How do you like our digs?" Art entered their room carrying two mugs. He handed one to Frank. Frank took in a whiff and realized there was coffee in those mugs. Honest-to-goodness coffee, not the ersatz stuff that most of the rest of the continent choked down. Frank didn't have to ask to know Art most likely got it off the black market.

"This place isn't bad. Better than the freezing tent back in England."

Art sat down and patted his mattress. "It's warmer and softer—and I'm not just talking about the beds. The German girls have been purdy friendly with the guys. Not me, of course, nonfraternization and all." Art chuckled. "I set my sights high—like Magdalena—isn't she a peach? And a girl like that isn't one to lower herself to becoming someone's girlfriend for a can of Spam."

"Well, at least you have your standards." Frank glanced out the window at a woman pushing a baby carriage and a small girl walking by her side. There wasn't a baby in the carriage, though. Instead, it held bedding and a few books. He wondered if that was all they owned in the world. He wouldn't be surprised if it was. Again, he thought of the guys—his best friends who lost their lives. It helped to ease his conscience. He grabbed his shoulder holster from his bed and put it on. Then slid his pistol inside. As a soldier, he was ordered to wear a weapon at all times, and now that he was on the ground, the pistol had become his weapon of choice. Not that he wanted to use it, but it was good to have, just in case. They were living in enemy territory after all. And who knew what his true assignment was about? He hoped he would soon find out.

Art took a sip of his coffee. "The way I see it, it serves the Germans right. First we take their country, then we take their girls.

And then—then they'll think twice about trying to pull a stunt like that again. Of course, like I said, you're not going to see me with a German girlfriend anytime soon."

Frank cocked an eyebrow.

Art cleared his throat. "Magdalena's Czech, remember? I'm not sure I'd trust the Germans. I guarantee most of them were in the Nazi Youth. Not that they'd admit it. Now that the U.S. soldiers are here, involved with the local population, you'd think there wasn't a Nazi in Germany. The people blame the Nazis for their problems, their defeat. Maybe those soldiers were just ghosts, you know. Since they didn't come from these parts. Since no one around here supported them or liked them much—or so they say."

Frank nodded. "Yeah? Well, I, for one refuse to swallow that line." He sipped his coffee, feeling the warmth carry down his throat and fill him. Through his time under cover, he'd learned there were few people you could take at their word. Everyone had something he or she was trying to hide. Some of the secrets were small. Others affected many, many lives. The hard part wasn't being fooled by the enemy. The hard part was remembering you could trust your friends.

Art chuckled as he put down his mug and began to pack his camera equipment. "Of course, you don't need to worry about whether or not to get a German girl, you get to spend your time with those beautiful American singers. You should have heard the guys coming back from the concert last night. They went on and on about the show, especially about that new singer—what's her name?"

"Mickey, the stage manager, just calls her Songbird."

"Yes, well, from what I hear she's a looker—and she sings great too. One guy said he thought his heart was gonna jump out of his chest."

Frank's heart did a double beat recalling Betty up on the stage, yet he tried not to show it. Since pursuing a relationship wasn't in his immediate plans, it shouldn't bother him—but it did.

The thing was, even if he did decide to risk his heart, she most likely wouldn't feel the same way. Also, from what he could tell, Betty seemed far less enthralled by him than he was by her. To her, he was probably just another Joe. Another reason not to let the spark of feelings run away with him.

"Yes, the show was something all right. All the girls were great," he said, steering the conversation away from Betty. "I hear they have a show tomorrow night. You should go."

"I will." Art swung his camera bag over his shoulder. "Only if you promise you'll introduce me to Songbird."

Frank eyed his friend. "I know you—too well. You'll want more than an introduction."

Art's eyes sparkled, and Frank could tell his friend was teasing him. "Yeah, well, if she's as pretty as everyone says she is, I might ask her out on a date. Do you think she'd say yes?"

"Doubt it. What does a lousy cuss like you have to offer? Besides, how would I know? I don't know the singers that well. Our relationship is limited to the lens of a camera. I'm sure Bet—Songbird is already in a relationship or something."

"Wait a minute—" Art punched Frank's shoulder, causing some of his coffee to splash over the mug's rim. "You're sweet on her."

A grin spread across Art's face. "Out of all the years I've known you, I've never seen you sweet on a girl. She must be as wonderful as everyone says."

"I don't know why you'd think that."

"Is she beautiful?"

"Yes."

"Does she sing well?"

"Of course."

"Is she kind—nice to talk to?"

"We talked for quite a while—"

"Then what's not to like?"

"You're right, what's not to like?" Frank's mind scrambled for an excuse. He'd come up with many of them over the years—he had a girl back home. He was recovering from a broken heart. He'd sworn to his dear mother not to marry until after the war.... But none of those would work now. He was sure that Art could see through him. For the first time, he told the truth—or at least half of the truth.

"The question is, do I have anything to offer in return," Frank said with a sigh. "Shoot, all I know how to do is take photos. It's not as if I've won a Pulitzer—and there's no chance for that now, especially with this new assignment—taking shots of singing girls. Not exactly important subject matter. I don't even have my high-school diploma. What type of job can I get back home? I also have to think what my parents would say—"

"Man, you think too much." Art strode to the door. He placed his hand on the knob. "You'd be a fool to get this great assignment and not take advantage of it. Especially when there's a girl like that around. In fact, I don't know what you're doing standing here talking to me." Art ran a hand down his face. "I'm not nearly as pretty."

Frank finished his coffee and set his mug down. He scanned the roadway outside the window that was starting to fill with more people, and he felt a grin curling his lips upward. "Maybe you're right. Maybe I should head over to the opera house and check things out—you know, scope out the place to make sure I get the best shots tomorrow night."

"You have all the dumb luck, that's for sure." Art opened the door. "Here I am taking photos of destruction and reconstruction. You get to take photos of pretty girls with pipes, and I get to take photos of—"

"Sewer pipes?" Frank hid his grin.

"Exactly. How did you know?"

"I saw some of your prints drying in that darkroom you've got set up."

"Jealous, aren't you? Bet you've never photographed a sewer." Art smirked, and then he slapped his leg. "Hey, I got an idea. I'll make extra copies of my photos and trade them for extra copies of yours—"

"What are you trying to do, get me sent home?" Frank began packing his own camera equipment. "You know we can't make extra copies for other people. These photos are property of the US military—although I have a feeling *if* I considered breaking that rule, it would be to keep photos of these girls, not give them away. Or at least one in particular."

"That's my friend. Man, I thought you'd never loosen up." Art slapped Frank's back. "Welcome to the real army."

* * * *

Everything seemed different in the daylight. As he walked along the road to the opera house, Frank snapped shots of the rolling hills and fields that bordered the buildings and park. The opera house itself was one of a complex of buildings—workshops, rehearsal areas, storage facilities—that had all been constructed behind the theater. He took photos of it all, noticing there was also a painting studio and two rickety refreshment halls.

Frank walked around to the front door of the opera house and was surprised to find it open. Inside it smelled of wood and cold. Paintings of composers hung on the walls. He could hear music coming from the auditorium, American jazz, and it struck him how out of place it sounded bouncing off the composers' smiles.

He focused his camera on the large painting of Wagner and took a shot. He couldn't help but think about Art's words last night about the "culture" of the Americans on stage. The difference was probably most clear to those who'd seen how things used to be. Of course, the German citizens hadn't been allowed to attend the new shows, and most of the Nazi high-ranking officers were now in prison in Nuremberg, awaiting trial for their crimes. Who was gonna speak up and complain that the Americans were replacing important German culture with jazz? No one, that's who.

Movement caught his eye, and Frank turned to see who was

there. The door to the auditorium swung slightly as a fleeting shadow passed by, but when he stepped forward, he didn't see anyone. Frank rubbed his eyes.

"Hello," he called. He walked into the auditorium, and the only person he saw was Kat on the stage, warming up. He walked down the aisles and scanned the rows of wooden seats. They, too, were empty.

Frank walked back to the lobby, wondering how someone had slipped by him. From where he stood, it would have been impossible. He finally looked around one more time and decided to check on the singers in the back. A chilling sensation ran up his arms. Someone had been watching Kat. For the briefest second he was sure he saw a figure in a long, black cloak. And whoever it was either didn't exist—or didn't want to be seen.

* * * *

Dierk tightened his fists, wishing today were the day when it all would end. When Wagner could be reborn. He didn't know how he could face the humiliation any longer. He was glad the great master had not lived to see this day.

Soon—

It had been disgraceful enough to know that the local commander of the American troops had moved into Richard Wagner's son Siegfried's house. And who knew what the Americans had pilfered when they snooped thorough Winifred's abandoned study?

Even worse was listening to the Americans play jazz—music that had so exasperated Siegfried. Thankfully, Wagner had died before hearing such "music." How it pained Dierk to hear such noise being played on Wagner's sacred pianos. *This should never be so.*

For a time, Dierk had regretted what he must do to ensure that Wagner's work, his stage, and his instruments were remembered in their purest form, but now he knew it was his sacrifice. He must destroy what was worth the most in the world to him, a sacrifice to ensure that all Richard Wagner loved would not continue under such disgrace.

His head pounded. His chest ached, and he needed freedom from the music that vexed his soul. With hurried steps, he left the lower quarters of the Festspielhaus and made his way, heart thumping, to the old set-painting workshop nearby.

Dierk stepped inside, shut the door behind him, and smiled. He felt most comfortable here, among boxes filled with things he'd managed to hide from the Americans—letters written in an old German gothic script, busts of long-dead composers, and an old painting of Hitler and a menacing. Alsatian dog. They weren't things he treasured, but if he had them they were a few less things for the Americans to pilfer.

He did have one treasure amongst the piles—the plaster model of what seemed to be the Festspielhaus transformed. The grandiose design, produced at the Fuehrer's wish, appeared like the Parthenon in miniature. He knew Hitler's plan was to rebuild the opera house to this new design as soon as Nazi Germany had won the war, but fate did not allow it. If all worked as Dierk planned, a second Festspielhaus would arise—but without Hitler's name attached. Even though Dierk couldn't imagine such a thing—how something new could be even greater than the old, his dreams told him it would happen. But first, he had to play his part. The part designed for him. One that would make his name greater than that of any musician or singer who'd performed within these walls.

With his mind once again focused on his task, Dierk stepped from the building and peered down at the valley below. Each time he walked into town, he discovered more people had arrived: soldiers and other conscripts, freed political prisoners, prisoners of war, disabled men discharged from the military hospitals, and evacuees.

A growing audience for the show.

CHAPTER TEN

They practiced all day and even worked through lunch. Betty was pleased that she knew most of the songs, and she worked especially hard on an Andrews Sisters number with Dolly and Irene.

The day was almost over when Betty spotted Kat turning down a side hall, disappearing around a corner.

"Where you going, Kat?" Betty called after her.

"Stage right. I thought it would be easiest to sneak onto stage from there for the last number," Kat's voice called back, echoing down the hall.

"You're heading the wrong direction." Irene snickered. "You need to go down the first hall, not the second, and then take the first right. It will lead you to the back of the stage."

They watched as Kat retraced her steps, re-emerged, found the right hall, and stomped down it with her hands balled into fists at her sides. "I'm so glad to leave this place. All these halls, rooms— whoever designed such a place should be taken out and shot."

"Richard Wagner's been dead for quite a while," Dolly called after her. "I don't think it'll do any good!"

"Is it really hard to get around?" Betty asked Irene.

"If you're just in the dressing room and going to the side stage it's no big deal," Irene explained. "It's the other rooms that are the problem. More than once, we've been practicing in a room and then someone shows up through a door we hadn't even noticed was there. Even Mickey's gotten lost a time or two. Oskar's the only one who really knows the ins and outs of everything."

"Remind me to never go wandering around the place without one of you." Betty pointed to her new friends. "I don't even want to think how horrible it would be if I was supposed to be on stage for a number and ended up in some dark closet instead. I wonder if the opera house has ghosts too."

Irene smirked. "I wouldn't put it past this place."

"Speaking of our number—and not of ghosts—we really should go over this one more time." Dolly held up the song sheets in her hand. "We nailed the song, but Betty, you really need to add some moves."

"I don't understand."

"Sure you do." Irene moved her hips from side to side. "Shake, jiggle, dance."

"But aren't we here to sing?"

Dolly laughed. "Sweetheart, if those boys aren't whistling, you aren't doing your job correctly."

Betty bit her lip. "I'm not sure—"

"Come on, we're not asking you to be Carmen Miranda. Just add a little sway."

They practiced awhile longer, until Betty had jiggled enough to make gelatin jealous, and then she talked Irene into heading into the auditorium with her. She wanted to hear Kat sing without the distraction of the noise and commotion from behind the stage. Betty was also curious to see how the music—and Kat's voice—sounded from the seats.

Betty knew there was something different about this place from the first note she'd sung from the middle of the stage. In Santa Monica, her singing had mostly taken place in the canteen of the Douglas airplane factory. To her, "canteen" was a fancy way of saying cafeteria, just fixed up a little, and her voice had sounded the way it always did. But on the stage of the Festspielhaus, her voice sounded prettier than she'd ever heard it. At the canteen, it had dissipated in the air, but here it came back, filling the air, wrapping around her, even without the benefit of a microphone. If she hadn't heard it for herself, she'd have never believed it.

They made their way to the middle of the third row and watched as Kat finished warming up. Soon the band joined her, and they launched into "Boogie-Woogie Bugle Boy."

Kat was nearly done with her first time through when Betty noticed movement beside her. She jumped slightly, and then relaxed when she saw Frank walking toward her. He took a seat without saying a word and then clapped along as Kat finished the catchy number. As she sang, Kat stepped side to side and swayed her hips with so much energy that Betty looked behind her, sure that a large crowd had snuck in unaware. Never had she seen anyone practice with so much gusto.

"See," Irene whispered in her ear. "You need to spice it up a little."

After Kat had gone through her two numbers a few times, Betty turned to Frank. She'd felt his presence the whole time, as evidenced by the goose bumps on her arms, and when she looked into his dark eyes, she was reminded again how handsome he was. How kind his smile made him appear.

"I wondered if you ladies wanted to walk into town? If your practice is over, that is."

"Yes, we're done." Irene stood to her feet. "But I have to wash my hair." She gave Betty an exaggerated wink.

"How about you?" Frank's eyebrows lifted as he turned to Betty. "Are you hungry?"

"Starved. We missed lunch."

"I think if we hurry we might be able to get something in the canteen."

Betty nodded, trying not to be disappointed. Then again, her guess was there weren't too many restaurants around here, so perhaps it was sort of a date.

She waved good-bye to Irene, and they walked toward the front door. She hadn't been out this way before and was surprised by the elegance of the foyer. From outside, the Festspielhaus looked more like a big warehouse, but inside was a different story. She could see how high-ranking Nazis and other people who thought they were important could be drawn to such a place.

When they got to the middle of the foyer, Frank paused, and then he turned around quickly.

"Are you okay? Did you forget something inside?" Betty asked.

"No, I—didn't you see that?" He hurried to a hallway that led to a side door. "I was sure I saw someone walking that direction out of the corner of my eye. And earlier—" He paused, pressing his lips tight.

"What?"

"Never mind." He shook his head.

"No, tell me."

"You'll think I'm crazy, Betty."

"No, I won't. At least, I don't think I will." She winked.

"Just a little while ago, I was sure I saw someone walking into the auditorium, but when I followed, no one was there." He placed a hand on the small of her back and then continued walking, quicker than before, almost as if he was eager to get her out of the building.

"I don't think you're crazy." Betty quickened her steps too. "Maybe there are just weird shadows from the windows or something. Or"— she touched his arm—"Earlier today Irene said she felt Wagner's presence in this place. I don't know what she meant by that, but sometimes it does feel as if I'm being watched—almost as if all the other people who performed here are watching from the sidelines, seeing how we measure up compared to them. It made me think of what that MP said—that there are things to be afraid of around this place."

Frank snickered. "Personally, I think Mac's mom was taking things too far. Who knows why Hitler did what he did? I think Wagner's music had less to do with Hitler's madness than we think. Lots of other people listen, and they don't turn into crazed rulers." Frank's arms swung at his sides as he strode down the hill. "Besides, I believe God is with me, watching over me, but—Wagner, nah." He tucked his hands into his pockets. "Then again, it would make a good story, wouldn't it? One needs to do what he can to make the papers, right?"

Betty couldn't help but smile at Frank's comment concerning God. She always pictured herself spending her life with someone who loved God as much as she did. She glanced over at Frank, wondering how fortunate she was to meet such a man, to spend time with him, to get to know him. Frank glanced at her, his eyes meeting hers, and then he quickly looked away.

The air was cooler than it had been before and smelled of wood burning and of manure, most likely from the fields. The sky above them was more gray than blue, and two birds fluttered from tree to tree, chirping, as if sending them down the hill to the village with an afternoon song.

"Yeah, I know what you mean about everyone's fears. I think most of them are self-inflicted. Kat was trying to get me scared last night, talking about Nazi ghosts roaming the place. If you ask me, I think Wahnfried is just old and falling down, so the floors creak. Besides— my mom's worried enough about having me here. She can worry enough for the both of us. Creaking floors and disappearing figures is something I won't be writing home about. My family has enough concerns as it is."

"So your family didn't support your coming?"

"Well…" She glanced at Frank, wondering how much she should confess to him. He looked at her intently, and she felt she could tell him the truth. If he liked her half as much as she was starting to like him, she should tell him. It would be worse if it came out later. If she remembered anything her mother told her, it had to be that honesty was the best policy.

"You're hesitating, Betty. You don't have to tell me if you don't want to."

"I do want to tell you, but I'm trying to think of the best way to say it. You see, some people back home say I ran away from my duties, but I like to think I just found a new job—a better one."

"And what job did you have?"

"I *had* a job at the Douglas factory. I was gonna be one of those Rosie the Riveters making airplanes. My dad's been disabled ever since he fell from a ladder two years ago, and my mom worked at the factory. I knew the extra money would be welcome so I applied at the factory. The only thing is, I got fired after the second day."

"You don't say—that bad, eh?" Frank tucked his hands deep in his pockets and chuckled.

"Actually, one of the foremen told me they were looking for a singer at the canteen. Singing for the war effort sounded better than riveting all day. My boss fired me so that I'd be free to apply for the job as a singer."

"Well, it doesn't sound like you ran away to me."

"Actually, that's not the end of the story. I was happy singing there for a while, until I read in the paper that there would be auditions for a troupe of singers going to the South Pacific. One day I called in sick at work, and then I borrowed my friend Elizabeth's car and headed to Hollywood. My parents were worried sick when I called them from LA that night, and Elizabeth wasn't happy when she had to catch a bus to come for her car, since I told her I was staying…"

"Auditions must have gone well," Frank said, "except if you look around, this isn't the South Pacific."

"There were three other girls besides me in the final round of auditions. The other three were cast as a trio, and I thought for sure my walking papers were coming. Instead, they said they needed someone in Germany as soon as possible, and I was the one they wanted. That was two weeks ago—"

"Two weeks?" Frank slapped his leg. "Two weeks from canteen singer to Songbird. You better not tell the other girls that. I'm sure they didn't catch this gig quite as easily. I still don't understand, Betty, why people say you ran from your duties. You're serving your country and helping the morale of the occupational troops." Frank had an easy, relaxed gait, and Betty couldn't help but enjoy walking by his side.

"My brother and his wife think I should have stayed at home and helped my mom. We used to work opposite shifts so we could take turns caring for my father. My sister's still there—but, well, she needs her own care. She's extremely sensitive. We can't let her watch newsreels or read the newspapers—it's too much for her. Everyone thinks my leaving was too much for her too. My mom is the only one who thinks I have a chance in Hollywood—although sometimes she even changes her mind."

"Also—" Her voice trailed off. She'd said a lot, but she still hadn't said the most important part. "I have many regrets about how I handled things. I took advantage of my parents' trust. I acted like I was going to work, knowing full well I wasn't. And, when I got the job, I should have figured out how to get the car back to Santa Monica, instead of inconveniencing Elizabeth like that. My biggest regret, though, is that I didn't get home to say good-bye to my parents. Since I only had a few days, I stayed with a lady I met at the USO office. I bought my suitcases and packed the few things I'd brought with me to LA—a change of clothes and my Bible. I also bought all the items on the USO's 'to pack' list, and some other things—too many things—with my paycheck that I usually turned over to my mom. I think I overdid it, as my luggage showed. After that, I got fitted for my USO officer's uniform, a few pairs of new shoes and some stage dresses, and by then it was time to catch the plane."

"And what do your parents think now?"

"I haven't heard, and I'm not sure I want to know. My family knew this is what I wanted to do—I had bigger dreams than the canteen—and they all said it wasn't possible. Yet now that it's happened, I haven't heard a word. I haven't received any response from them. I've sent four letters and I haven't heard back—which I didn't really expect with me being over here, but the silence is hard—you know? I'm afraid everyone's upset."

"But you said your mom thought you had a chance in Hollywood?"

"Hollywood, yes, but this is far from Hollywood. I only got to speak with my parents a few minutes on the telephone before I left. They were quiet, shocked, and worried. Perhaps angry too."

"Maybe your family's disapproval is like those footsteps we thought we heard when no one was there—or the figures we imagined seeing out of the corner of our eye," Frank responded. "We think something scary is there, but it turns out to be nothing but our imagination. Maybe you're more worried than they are upset. Like you said, the mail just hasn't caught up to you yet. It was a fast trip."

Betty turned to him and studied his face. "Who are you? Are you my guardian angel in disguise, Frank? First, you tried to calm the fears of those on the plane. Then you helped me find a ride to Wahnfried last night. Now you're easing my conscience concerning my family—which is not an easy task."

Frank smiled, lifted his camera, and shrugged. "I like to think I see things that others miss. Or maybe I'm just making up some crazy ideas in order to impress you." Then he paused and snapped a shot of the town.

"Really?" Betty paused and turned to him. "Well, if that's your motive—"

"Did it work?"

Betty shrugged. "Maybe, maybe not." She quickened her step, thankful she wore more sensible shoes today. "You'll just have to watch me closely and tell me what you think. I don't get impressed easy, but I have to say, you're not doing too bad."

CHAPTER ELEVEN

Betty had just settled onto her bed after being dropped off by Frank and an MP that he'd talked into giving her a ride, when Irene's face peeked around the door.

"Okay, spill it. I want to hear about your romantic date with Frank." Before Betty had a chance to respond, six more women hurried into the room, including Kat.

Betty scooted back across her bed and leaned against the wall. "There's not much to say. We ate at the canteen, and then we walked around town. It was too depressing though." She shook her head. "There are so many displaced people. Then, he took me to his friend's darkroom, and he showed me how he developed film. I saw some great photos of the Festspielhaus and some good ones of all of you. Especially you, Kat."

"Yes, of course, what a surprise. Kat always looks good. Even when she's ill, the camera loves her," Pearl, Shirlee's sister, complained.

"So do you think we can see them? Can we get copies?" Dolly asked.

Betty shrugged. "Frank has to ask his boss. He says it's against the rules—but since we're not a top-secret project or anything, his boss might agree."

"It's not fair, you know." Shirlee sat next to Betty on the bed. "We've been here nearly two months, and I haven't found anyone like that photographer. You're here one day and—*poof*, there he is."

"Yeah, that's because we flew in on the same airplane, which is a story all its own." Betty launched into the story of how they lost an engine, and how Frank had gone to check on things and then calmed everyone down.

"It helps that our photographer is handsome," Irene said. "It makes it easy to look his way and smile."

"I agree, but I bet he thinks we're trying to get a lot of good shots for the newspaper. If he had any idea we all were sweet on him—" Dolly fanned her face with her hand.

"Personally, I think he's just using you, Betty," Kat groused, easing onto her bed and pulling her knees to her chest. "He knows that those photos are going to make the papers. He's trying to advance his career. And he's being nice to all of you so that when you're finally famous, he'll publish these shots and make a buck."

Betty felt her smile fade as she listened to Kat's words. She didn't want to believe them, yet a small pain struck her heart. Kat had been around. She most likely knew about these things.

"But you're already famous," Irene put in.

"Exactly, and I've never had a shot taken of me that wasn't used to line the photographer's pocket. It's part of this business. If you stick around, you'll learn all about it." Kat rested her chin on her knees and let out a low sigh. "He's not interested in you, Betty. All he's interested in is the dough that the photos of your face can bring him. I bet even now he's making extra copies and selling them to the

GIs on the black market. Mark my words, as soon as this Frank guy gets what he wants, he'll be on the road."

Betty's chin dropped, and her stomach felt sick. She'd tried to be understanding with Kat. Tried to be a friend. *Why is she saying this? Doing this? She's deliberately trying to hurt me.*

"Hey, Betty." Irene patted her leg. "Why don't you come and sleep in our room tonight? We can help you carry the mattress upstairs if you'd like."

Betty appraised Kat. Even though she didn't feel like hanging around and getting the cold shoulder, she didn't want to add any more regrets to the ones she already carried. She didn't need to run away anymore.

"Thanks, Irene, but I'll hang out here tonight."

Kat looked over at her, and Betty couldn't help seeing the surprise in her eyes.

"Okay, kid. Get some sleep." Irene gave her a hug. "We're supposed to be there early for rehearsal." Then she stepped back and swept her arms around the room, mimicking Mickey. "Girls. Girls. Come on, work with me, we got a big show tomorrow."

Betty laughed along with the others, but deep down her heart still ached from Kat's words. She shut the door behind her retreating friends and then hurried to her bed, refusing to look at Kat. Refusing to let Kat see her tears.

Maybe she knows what she's talking about. She's been in this business a long time. Maybe Frank doesn't like me as much as he's letting on. Maybe he's just using me to get to the other girls—to get their photos. To get closer to Kat.

* * * *

Frank finished up his breakfast and then carried his dirty tin to the scullery, adding it to a pile of others. Then he hurried toward the exit, eager to finish developing his rolls of film and get them to HQ. After his work was done, he could head up to the opera house to see Betty. His steps paused, though, when he noticed a sign posted at the door that he hadn't seen yesterday.

Need your high school diploma? Classes every afternoon. Sign-up at HQ. Don't head home a dummy.

Frank scratched his chin.

"Thinking about signing up?" A soldier stood beside him.

"Yeah, I'm thinking about it. I dropped out my senior year to join up."

"So did a lot of us. My bunkmate says a hundred and seventy guys have already signed up. There aren't many spots left."

"A hundred and seventy? You kidding?"

"Nope."

"I guess that makes me feel better. Shows I'm not the only dope around here."

The man pointed to Frank's uniform. "Well, from those two Battle Stars and the Purple Heart, I doubt anyone would think you're a dope."

"Thanks, but you don't have to be smart to get shot at." Frank chuckled. "While I'd love to get back to the States, I don't want to go before I can get a good job."

The man nodded in agreement. "For the last two years, I've lived in overcrowded barracks. Here, it's an overcrowded house. I can't even imagine going back home and moving in with my parents and all my brothers and sisters and their spouses. Know what I mean?"

"Yeah." Frank nodded and smiled, even if that wasn't his case at all. His mom and dad were the only ones left, and he knew they'd be heartbroken if he didn't want to move home—for at least a while. A sadness washed over him as he thought of Lily. He couldn't imagine being back home without his sister. Lily had always been the sunshine in their family. The passionate, laughing one. The one that took a joke and gave it back. *Sort of like Betty.*

He looked at the poster again. *I need to start thinking of what type of life I can offer a wife someday.* The thought both scared and excited him. It scared him because he'd always questioned if his work in the war would bring danger to those he cared about. It excited him because now he had a chance to work toward that independence. Signing up for these classes would be a good thing, even if his future missus wasn't the pretty songbird who'd recently caught his interest.

The other guy left, and Frank headed into the street with a lighter step. He knew he only had an hour's worth of developing work, and he would sign up for the classes when he dropped the film off—since they were in the same building. He just hoped he didn't miss a spot on the roster.

Back at his place, he finished developing the film in Art's darkroom. He waited for the photos to dry, and then he packaged them up for Henry. He couldn't figure out why the country needed to use his talents to take pictures of singing girls, but that wasn't his call. He figured Marv had another assignment that he'd had to keep from everyone else, including Art.

Headquarters, he discovered, had taken over a large building that used to be the mayor's office. He found the right office and knocked at the door.

"Come in!"

Frank was only partially surprised when he saw Denzel Bailey, Marv's right-hand man, sitting behind the desk. Frank had spent a lot of time with Denzel in England. They'd been assigned to the same base, and both favored walking around, seeing the city, and touring the countryside, rather than picking up girls, which meant they'd hung out together a lot. Denzel had tagged along on a number of Frank's assignments when he'd photographed suspicious people in and around London. Of course, Denzel hadn't a clue as to what Frank had really been up to.

"Hey, Frank. Didn't expect you to be in so early. You had all day to get those photos in."

"Yeah, well, I thought I'd get a head start—gives me time to get back to the Festspielhaus. I didn't know you were in Bayreuth."

Denzel shrugged. "For the time being. Who knows how long I'll be here. This is my fourth German town in the same number of months. Seems like the American public is still hungry for news and photos of what Germany's like after the war." He shrugged. "Maybe it helps them feel better to see things worse off over here, especially when so many have sacrificed so much."

"Well, if you talk to Marv, tell him thanks a lot for the assignment. How am I ever going to find a serious job after telling my future employers that while the trials were going on in Nuremberg, and the Russians were being bullies in Berlin, I was shooting girls in evening gowns? Man, the most exciting thing I've seen so far was when our transport plane almost went down coming in to Nuremberg."

"Are you kidding? It's big news that Katherine Wiseman's over here singing for the troops. Everyone likes to see photos of stars in combat boots, even if there's no combat going on."

"That might be true, but she's leaving tomorrow. Then what?"

"Well—then you need to start grooming some new stars. Treat the other girls like they're the hottest thing coming down the pipeline and to the American public, they will be." Denzel opened the large envelope and started glancing through the images that Frank had taken. "Pretty girls, all of them. Not one of them looks like they've been hit with an ugly stick—speaking of which, Marv wanted to know how you like that new singer."

"Do you mean Betty?"

"Yeah, sure, Betty sounds right. I don't remember. All I know is that when Marv came back from USO tryouts in Los Angles he was all talk about some young thing that was going to capture ol' Frank's heart."

Frank crossed his arms over his chest and grinned. "I guessed that. But I don't understand. Why has Marv taken such an interest in my case? I'm just one photographer in a thousand; what does my happiness mean to him?"

Denzel's face dropped. "You're kidding, right? Don't you know?"

"Know what?"

Denzel motioned to the chair in front of his desk. "You better sit." He rubbed his temples with his fingertips.

"Sit? Denzel, what's going on?"

Denzel pointed to the chair again, and Frank had no choice but to sit.

Denzel leaned forward, resting his elbows on the desk, no longer interested in the photos.

"I don't know why Marv didn't tell you himself, maybe it hurt too bad to talk about it. But personally I think you have a right to know." Denzel took in a deep breath and then released it slowly. "Marv made a promise to Lily, see."

"Lily?" Frank furrowed his brow. "My sister?"

"Marv was sweet on her—had been since they first met at an airbase in New York. They wrote often, and over the years their friendship grew into something more."

"You have to be joking. I'm sure Lily would have told me—" Frank's voice trailed off, and he swallowed hard. "Then again, my sister kept her personal life personal. She never did tell me what guys she was sweet on—said she was always afraid I would try to butt in."

"Yeah, that's my guess too. Since you knew Marv—worked with him—maybe she wanted things to happen natural-like, and not because her kid brother gave the thumbs up. Or didn't happen because he gave the thumbs down."

"I still don't understand." Frank's throat felt raw. He could see his sister's face in his mind. She'd been too young to die. She'd had so much potential. "What was the promise about?"

"Well, Lily was worried about what you'd experienced—mostly that you'd seen a lot of war, lost a lot of friends, and didn't have anyone to turn to. She told Marv that if he met anyone she'd approve of to make sure you got a proper introduction—or at least that's what Marv told me."

"So Marv put us on a plane together—and gave me this assignment?"

Frank furrowed his brow. Denzel didn't know how many dangerous situations Frank had been in—and would no doubt continue to get himself into—but Marv did. *Why would he try to set us up? Doesn't he realize that Betty's life could be in danger by just being around me?* It made no sense.

Frank turned his attention back to Denzel, who shuffled through the photos. "It could be worse, Frank. You could have Art's job. I hear he's been taking photos of bombed basements."

"Yeah." Frank chuckled softly, but deep inside, his heart still ached with thoughts of his deceased sister. For his parents too. No one should lose a child. Even though it had happened to hundreds of thousands of families, their pain was unique to each of them.

Frank stood. "Well, thanks for letting me know. It makes me feel good that Marv thinks Betty is someone Lily would have approved of."

Denzel glanced down at the photos again then lifted one from the stack. "Is this Betty?" he asked, examining a photo of Betty in the pink silk dress. Her arms were spread open as if she were embracing the troops, but her eyes had been looking directly into the shot.

"Yeah," Frank nodded. "How did you know?"

"From the way she's looking into the camera. Or more accurately, looking at the photographer holding the camera."

Frank eyed Denzel but didn't respond. "Yes, well, did Marv send anything for me? Uh, there were some things I left back in England and he promised to send them over."

Denzel pursed his lips and then his eyes lit up. "Oh, yes, there's a box with your name on it. I would have forgotten." Denzel turned in his chair and ruffled through stacks of files on the shelf behind him. Underneath one of the stacks, there was a box.

Denzel handed it to Frank. "This came last week, before I even knew you were coming. I wonder how Marv could send things that you forgot when you hadn't even left yet..."

Frank shrugged. "That's why he's the boss—always thinking ahead." He smiled and then turned, making his exit before he could get in any more trouble.

"Have a great day. See you later."

Frank nodded and smiled back, but from the look in his eye, Denzel didn't fall for Frank's poor excuse.

You're slipping, buddy. You need to watch that. You never know who you can trust—

CHAPTER TWELVE

Frank took the box back to his house, thankful Art wasn't there. He entered their shared bedroom and locked the door. Then he took a small knife from his pocket and opened the box. The first thing on top was a typewritten letter from Marv.

> *Hey buddy, looks like you made it to Bayreuth okay. It's a nice place, don't you think? I hope you're enjoying your assignment. I won't ask you about one special girl. All I can say is that I hope you open up and don't let the events of the last year close your heart to finding love.*
>
> *Okay, down to business.*
>
> *I brought you here because of some letters that have been showing up at HQ. We passed the first few off as meaningless threats, maybe from someone who doesn't like the Americans hanging around. But the more we got, the more I decided to take them seriously. Perhaps you can discover who wrote them, but even more important, why.*

Frank turned Marv's note over, but the other side was blank. It was just like Marv not to sign it. Not to sign anything that could be traced back to him.

Frank set the paper on the bed. Then he pulled out six white envelopes. All of them had been opened. All of them bore the same careful, neat script that read: *to American offices*. Frank opened the first one.

> *This message is very urgent matter. Trouble will come in next month. There are some who wish to destroy Festspielhaus. Danger is possible for those whose music plays there.*

Frank read the words a second time, wishing there was more to go on.

He opened the next letter.

> *There are some who wish to bring much harm to Americans in Festspielhaus. Please take these threats as real. I would speak to you myself if my life were not in danger for this very reason.*

What reason? He continued reading and soon realized the rest of the letters were basically the same message. There just wasn't much to go on.

> *There is trouble at Festspielhaus.*
> *People wish to do Americans harm.*
> *I cannot come and tell you myself.*

Frank put the letters back in the envelopes, and his various thoughts fought for pre-eminence in his mind.

Could Betty be in danger? Someone is trying to get his point across. This is a serious warning, not a joke. Someone is worried about the Americans.

The same person wasn't worried about the soldiers in town, but only those at the Festspielhaus. The musicians? The singers? Who would want to do them harm? A wary smile curled on his lips as he wondered what threat women in pretty gowns and men in suits with instruments could be. The only reason he could think of that someone would try to hurt them would be to send a message—but to whom? *Maybe a message that danger still lurks, and that this is still a war zone and no place for civilians?*

Or the trouble comes from one of them. Someone among their ranks. Someone with a grudge.

Frank took the box and tucked it in the back of his duffle bag. He'd come back to the letters later. Then he stuck the bag under his bed, far in the back. He needed time to ponder the words, to try to make sense of the messages.

No wonder Marv wanted me here—wanted me close.

Frank's assignment was clear—he'd have to spend more time around the Festspielhaus. More time than just during the shows when he was taking photos. While he was at HQ he had signed up for high school courses, and he hoped spending time there wouldn't hinder his investigative work. He'd do the best he could for Marv, but he also had to think of his own future. He was ready to take a break from undercover work. Tired of keeping secrets. If he were ever going to become serious with someone, he'd have to have something to offer.

Until then, he couldn't think of just one girl. He'd have to get to know everyone. No one was beyond suspicion.

No one was beyond suspicion—except Betty. His contradictory thoughts unsettled him, and he found himself ticking off a mental balance sheet:

The letters were delivered to HQ before Betty arrived, so she couldn't have sent them. Then there was Marv's approval of her. That had to be a good sign. Marv was aware of his undercover work and surely would have done a background check on her.

Since he was sure she wasn't a suspect, it was a good reason to stick closest to her.

He could also use Betty to get close to the others.

But there was one most important factor Frank had to focus on—*I just have to find out what's going on before anyone gets hurt.* Betty's smiling face filled his mind. *Especially her.*

* * * *

Even though they'd slept in the same room, sat at the same table at the mess hall, and walked up the hill together to the Festspielhaus, Kat hadn't said one word to Betty since the previous evening.

Kat's face looked as pale as it had the day before, and after their rehearsal was over, she asked Mickey if she could head back to the house to rest before the evening's performance.

"Sure thing, Kat, just make sure you're here an hour before curtain.

I don't want to have to send the hounds out looking for you or none of that business."

Most of the girls stayed in the back prepping their hair and makeup and trying on the dresses Kat had agreed to leave behind. Betty was more interested in walking down to the town center. Partly because she needed some fresh air, but mostly because she wondered if Frank happened to be around. She hadn't heard from him since he'd dropped her off the night before, and each hour that passed without his showing up at rehearsal drilled Kat's words deeper into her heart. *He's just using you, Betty.*

It was a short walk to town—in the opposite direction from their estate. The day was partly cloudy, and it was only when she was halfway down the hill that Betty started to worry it would rain. She had washed her hair last night and slept in curlers. Even though it meant she didn't sleep as well as usual, her hair was full, with soft curls framing her face. She'd be in real trouble if rain messed up her hairdo. According to Mickey, tonight needed to be perfect.

The sun peeked out from the clouds, and Betty walked around town a little, but nothing had changed since she was there yesterday. The people were just as desperate. The buildings hadn't magically rebuilt themselves overnight. Frank wasn't around, and misty rain indeed started to fall.

Disappointed, she'd started to head back up the hill when a jeep filled with young GIs pulled over. She waved to them and smiled.

"Songbird!" the driver called. "Look, guys, it's her." He waved her over to the jeep.

Betty shyly approached. "Hi there."

"Hey, Songbird."

"Great singing the other night."

"You were the best of the show, hands down."

"Thanks, guys, I'm glad you liked it." She lifted her palm and held it up as bigger raindrops started to fall. "I forgot my umbrella—do you think you could give me a ride up the hill?"

"Sure thing. Of course." The driver pointed to the guy in the passenger's seat. "Hit the back, Fred."

Trying not to let her worries about Frank's intentions sink her spirits, Betty chatted with the guys about that night's show as they drove up the hill. The open-air jeep blew rain into her hair. She held her hands over it, trying to protect it as best she could, fully expecting that it was going to be a rat's nest by the time she made it backstage.

"Although all the songs are good, I think you'll especially enjoy Kat's farewell number." She turned in her seat, looking into the guys' faces as she spoke.

"You mean she's leaving?"

"Heading back to Hollywood, I'm afraid."

"Gee, those California guys don't need her—we do." Laughter spilled out of the jeep.

"Well, we promise we'll be there tonight," one of the soldiers said as they approached the Festspielhaus. The jeep pulled over and parked.

"Thanks for the ride." Betty climbed out.

"Songbird?" the driver called.

Betty turned back to him. "Yes?"

"I was wondering, ma'am, if you could do me a favor. My buddy, you see, is in an awful funk. He's going home soon, but the sweetheart he's been loving all these years isn't going to be waiting. Turns out she shared a kiss with some sailor on V-E Day and went and got married. Not much wonder, I suppose, that he's not looking forward to going home."

"That's a sad story. Whatever can I do?" The wind blew harder, and Betty stepped from side to side, feeling the wind slice through her trousers, chilling her legs.

"Just grin at him. Give him something to think about. Make faces if you have to."

Betty laughed. "I'm not sure our stage manager would be too keen on me making faces, but I'm sure I can manage a wave and a smile from stage. The only thing is, how will I see him? How will I know who it is? The lights are bright and there's a sea of faces."

"Oh, I'll make sure you won't miss him. We'll get there early, and I'll see we get in one of the front rows. He has black hair, a long neck, and big ears. You'll see me—and I'll be right by him."

"Swell. I'll look for him—look for you both." She gave the guys one more quick wave and then hurried around toward the back of the building.

"Sing pretty, Songbird!" one of the guys called, and Betty couldn't help but smile—in spite of the rain.

CHAPTER THIRTEEN

Betty felt the warmth of their acceptance spread through her as she hurried toward the building, her shoes splashing in the rain that collected into puddles. When she approached the corner of the building, she saw Frank standing there. His furrowed brow and wide eyes displayed a hint of pain and betrayal. Betty's own smile faded, and she paused her steps. The rain fell harder now, and she wiped the rain from her face.

"Betty, I came up looking for you." He was standing under a small porch, and he took her hand and pulled her up next to him so that she was protected under the roof. "You shouldn't be out in the rain like this. You're going to catch cold."

He glanced to the jeep that was leaving with a curious expression on his face.

"Frank, those guys—let me explain." Her heart pounded in her chest, and she reached out to take his hand but he pulled away.

"You don't need to explain. I mean, well, we're just friends, right? I—I simply wanted to talk to you about tonight, that's all."

Betty placed a hand on her hip. "You may not want to hear it, but I want to tell you."

"No really, it's not like we had an—understanding or anything. I mean there are plenty of guys around here. My guess is that they were just nice enough to give you a ride."

Betty stamped her foot, splashing water up her leg. "Will you listen to me? I want to explain. I wanted fresh air, you see, or at least that's what I told Mickey. Really, I walked to town, all the way to town, since you didn't come here."

"I had to work all morning. Had photos to process. And I went by headquarters—and did some other things. Uh, work things."

"I'd hoped you wanted to be around. Maybe to see me—" She looked away, suddenly feeling foolish.

Betty felt the gentlest touch on her chin as Frank turned her face his direction. She lifted her eyes to look at him. As she did, she noticed the curiosity from before was gone—replaced by humor.

"Are you saying that you walked in the rain to try to see me?"

"It wasn't raining when I started."

"I'm flattered." Frank laughed. "Betty, no offense but you look a mess." He glanced at his watch. "And you're supposed to be on stage in an hour."

"I know." She patted her hair. "I'm embarrassed to have you see me this way."

"Are you kidding? I think you're adorable. I like messy—it looks wonderful on you. And it's even more wonderful since you ended up this way for me."

"Thanks, uh, I think." She took a step toward the door. "I can't imagine the kind of trouble I'll be in with Mickey as it is."

"Wait a minute. One more minute, please? I need to ask you something. I don't think I can make it through the night if I don't."

Frank studied her and she wished she could tell what he was thinking. He seemed worried about something.

"Okay, but you better make it quick. I'd hate to bomb my performance. Or look like something the cat dragged in, straggling onto the stage."

"So you weren't really interested in any of those guys in the jeep?" Frank winked, and she knew he was teasing her.

"No, I don't even know them," she said, playing along. "I only asked them for a ride—to get out of the rain. I promise."

"And—you most likely wouldn't have gone looking for me unless you thought I was pretty special, huh?" His expression grew more serious.

"That's true—I suppose."

"And maybe you've guessed that I sorta have warm feelings for you too."

Betty felt heat rising to her cheeks. "Sorta? Well, I'd hoped so. I sort of pictured our time yesterday—as a date."

Frank's eyes grew intense, and he took a step closer. "Betty, I know we haven't known each other long, but if all of this is true, well, I'd love to talk to you about us spending more time together."

Laughter poured from Betty's lips, and the warmth in her cheeks moved through her body. "Yes, that's something I'd like to talk about too." She leaned forward and placed the softest kiss on his cheek. "After the concert, I promise!" And then, without looking back, she hurried to the door.

Inside, she ran down the hall as fast as she could, her shoes slipping on the wooden floor.

Dolly was the first one to spot her. "Oh dear, look what came in out of the rain."

Irene's back was to Betty when she approached. "Is that Betty? What took you so long? I told you we need time to do your hair—" She turned, and her jaw dropped. "I knew that was going to happen." She placed a fist on her hip. "I knew you'd get caught in the rain."

Betty nodded. Irene didn't know the half of it, and she wasn't about to spill the whole thing. She wanted to tell them about Frank, yet she mostly wanted to keep it to herself for a while. He wasn't asking her to be his girl, but spending time together was a good start.

Get your mind on the songs, Betty. Think about what you're here to do. You're here to entertain all the guys—despite the fact that a special one has captured your heart. Her mind spun at how fast it had happened, but she couldn't deny it. Before meeting Frank, she didn't believe in love at first sight. But now—now, she wasn't so sure. Frank had certainly demonstrated in the short time she'd known him how wonderful and different he was.

Irene pointed to the chair, and Betty sat like an obedient child.

"I think the rain took all the curl out of it. We're going to have to give you the sleek look tonight—we don't have a choice." With a quick hand, Irene brushed all of Betty's hair back from her face and twisted it in a knot near the nape of her neck, pinning it up.

"Okay." Irene stepped back. "Put on your makeup while I get dressed, and then I'll help you with your gown."

Betty sat at the dressing table, where Kat usually sat, and looked at the variety of small jars in front of her. She opened them one at a time and then picked a few colors that she hoped would work.

"Do you need help?" Dolly sat down beside her.

"Yes, can you tell? I really don't wear much of this—"

"Like my home-ec teacher told me, 'A beautiful face is not made by assembly-line or carbon-copy techniques. It is woven of hand-picked threads into a highly individual pattern.'"

"I thought we were talking about my cosmetics, not my clothes," Betty snickered.

"We are, but what I'm trying to say—what my teacher taught me—is that each person's features are unique. Just highlight your best features. And for you—you really don't need many cosmetics. We simply need to let your natural beauty come through. A little powder. A little blush. Some color for your eyes." Dolly dabbed a cosmetic brush into one jar and then another, brushing it across Betty's face.

A few minutes later, Betty looked in the mirror at her reflection, pleased with the results. "Thank you, Dolly."

"You're welcome. Now get into that gown."

Betty jumped to her feet and hurriedly dressed in Kat's polka-dotted dress.

"Has anyone seen Kat? It's not like her to be late," Shirlee said, slipping on her pumps. "Well, at least never this late."

"I didn't want to think the worst, but I saw a captain heading into the house when I walked out," Dolly said to the mirror as she pinned up her hair.

"Are you saying Kat's having—an affair?" Pearl gasped.

"Kat wouldn't do that. She's in love with her husband." Betty smoothed her dress.

"Well, there's only one other reason for a visit from an officer."

"Edward," Betty murmured the name, and everyone's eyes widened.

"Do you think something happened to him?" Irene placed a hand over her heart. "It makes no sense though—there's no fighting, no battles going on. I mean, there were a lot of telegrams delivered during the war but—now. Now we're at peace, right?"

They didn't have to wait and wonder long. A minute later Kat entered. Her eyes were red and puffy, and her hair disheveled. A captain walked with her, holding her arm.

The chatter of voices grew silent as they entered. The captain spotted Mickey, who had just emerged from his own dressing room in a light blue suit.

The officer approached him. "Sir, can I speak to you for a moment?" He led Mickey to a side room.

Kat didn't look at any of them—didn't say a word. Betty looked to Irene and then to Dolly. All of them glanced at each other, but no one made the move to speak first.

Kat neared the dressing table, and Betty stood, allowing her to have the seat. An eerie silence filled the room, and Betty thought for sure she would burst from the tension.

Then, with slow, tentative steps, Mickey approached, his heeled shoes clicking on the wooden floor. "Kat, honey, you don't need to be here. Not tonight of all nights."

She looked up toward the stage manager, her face a mural of despair. "Listen, Mick, I've never missed a show. Never."

"But honey, you need time to process. Time to mourn."

"Don't you understand, Mick? This is what Edward would have wanted. He loves—loved"—her voice caught in her throat—"he loved my singing more than anything. I want to do this. To honor him."

Mickey studied her for a moment, his face conflicted. "I don't think it's a good idea, but—you know yourself better than anyone."

"This is my last show. I never want to say that I didn't finish what I started."

"Okay." He drew out the word in a way that made it clear he didn't agree. "At least drop the last number? The strain might be too much."

Kat lowered her eyes and pressed her hands to her forehead. She was silent for a moment, and Betty thought for sure she would change her mind—that she would agree with Mick. Agree that canceling was the best thing.

Finally, Kat blew out a slow breath. "No. I want to sing that song too—it'll be my way of sending him off."

"Okay, dollface, if you think it's best."

"Yes, I do." Then Kat scanned the room. "And as for the rest of you, no sad faces. Those GIs deserve just as good a show tonight as they got last night." Kat grabbed her gown and moved toward the private dressing room, then paused.

"Whatever you do, Mick, I don't want word to get out until after I get to the States. Promise me. Nothing is worse than scanning a crowd and knowing they know. I want to sing tonight without seeing pity on their faces. And I don't want to deal with it while I'm traveling back—I'll have reporters at every stop from here to California hounding me."

Mickey nodded. "I promise, Kat. We all promise."

When Kat left to get dressed, the girls hurried to Mickey, circling him in a huddle.

"How'd it happen, Mick? How'd Edward go?" Dolly asked.

"Car accident, somewhere in England."

"Of all things," Irene muttered. "The guy survived sixty bomber missions, at least, and he dies from something like that."

"Just another casualty—my gut hurts for her," Mickey said.

Betty cleared her throat, trying not to show emotion.

"Do you think Kat's doing the right thing? I mean she's working so hard to be strong." Dolly pinched the bridge of her nose as if trying to hold back tears.

"I don't think I could do it," Shirlee answered. "I mean if I loved someone like that."

Betty thought of Frank. She'd only known him a few days, and they were just getting to know each other. Yet, even the thought of not seeing him again caused her lower lip to quiver. How could Kat be so strong losing someone she loved? Had married? And expected a child with.

The baby— Pain pierced Betty's heart, and she placed a hand on her chest. "Oh my gosh, poor thing. How's she going to handle it alone? The little—"

"What? What is it Bet—?" Irene turned to her.

"Oh, did I say that aloud? I'm sorry. I didn't mean it. It's, uh, nothing."

Irene took her hand. "It is something. I can see it on your face. You can't hide the truth very well. Not from us. The little what?"

"I'm just feeling bad—for Kat, that's all."

Mickey turned and drilled Betty with his gaze. "The girls are right. Your face reads like a book. Are you sure there isn't something you want to tell us?"

"I'm sorry, loose lips sink ships. I—I promised I wouldn't. You'll know—all of you will when the time is right. A promise is a promise."

CHAPTER FOURTEEN

Everyone looked like a million bucks as they stood backstage, waiting for the show to start. The gowns sparkled, catching and reflecting every bit of the backstage light. Hair was pinned up, perfectly in place, and even their makeup was flawless. Yet as Betty glanced around, she saw women who appeared as if they were headed to a funeral instead of waiting on the sidelines for a fun, energetic, and exciting show. Heads were lowered, eyes were misty, and lips were turned down as each one grieved for Kat. And as each one thought a little more of her own loved ones.

On stage, the band started, playing for the GIs who were taking their seats. The men's voices were loud, boisterous. Betty dared to glance out into the audience, thinking how the guys appeared so young, so innocent. How did they get through war and keep their boyish smiles? She couldn't imagine their losses, their pained memories that were only one thought away. Realizing that made her want to sing her heart out, despite the circumstances. Maybe this was how Kat felt too.

"The show must go on. Everyone knows that," Betty mumbled through the side of her mouth. "But somehow it doesn't seem right, does it, Irene?"

"I know, but we can't think about Edward right now. Or even about Kat. We have almost two thousand guys out there that want to be home—and we're going to help them forget that longing for a couple of hours. We're going to bring home to them."

The Johnson Sisters were to kick off the show, but instead of only dancing tonight, Mickey had worked with them to add some comedy to their routine.

Mickey introduced them and the girls hustled out. They started by introducing themselves, and then they turned to each other.

"You know, Pearl. I hear the Germans started the war because they wanted the world for their living room," Shirlee said.

"Oh, like a new sofa?" Pearl smirked.

Laughter filled the auditorium.

"No, not like that. More room to live. To spread out. To build their houses." Shirlee nodded.

"Really?" Pearl scratched her head. "Did they get what they wanted?"

"I think so," Esther, the third sister butted in. "Why, the other day I was cruising around town, and I saw there's a lot of room now—where the buildings used to be!"

More laughter sounded, even louder than before, and the back curtain rose to show a living room painted on one of the sets. Betty turned her view offstage, looking for Oskar in the back, wondering how he felt about one of Wagner's irreplaceable sets being painted over for a thirty-second joke. But Oskar wasn't anywhere in sight.

The sisters danced for a while, spinning, twirling, and doing complicated footwork in unison, and then Pearl paused and pointed to the audience. "Hey soldier, bet you can't do this!" After that, the cartwheels started, and with each spin, the guys cheered, perhaps because of the way they cartwheeled in unison, or maybe because their bloomers showed as they flipped upside down.

The band did a few numbers and then it was time for Betty, Irene, and Dolly to do their Andrews Sisters song.

"You've got to accentuate the positive, eliminate the negative," they sang. And although Betty smiled and swayed just as she was supposed to, nothing seemed positive about this situation. Betty was so focused on just getting the words out that she forgot to look for Frank. As the song's last measure began, she frantically scanned the crowd. She finally spotted Frank and smiled. Then she glanced one row forward to where a man—the man from the jeep—was waving his hands and pointing to his tall, dark-haired buddy. Betty offered the soldier a friendly wave as she held the last note. The man's face brightened, and Betty felt lighter. The smile she now offered was real. It was amazing how that one small gesture could brighten someone's day—even her *own* day.

They exited the stage. Betty was about to sit down in one of the stage chairs when Dolly approached. "Mickey said to find you. He said be prepared to sing if Kat can't make the last song. He says you've seen her practice and that you'll know what to do."

Betty's eyes widened as she thought through the words to "America the Beautiful." She didn't have too much time to think, though, because Kat's "Bugle Boy" number was coming up next, and Betty wanted to be standing on the side, cheering her on.

Kat paced the side stage, dabbing her eyes, her jaw set with determination. Then, as the curtain went up, she hustled out with a huge smile. If it wasn't for the obvious puffiness around Kat's eyes, Betty was sure that no one would have noticed anything was wrong.

Kat paused in the center of the stage and then gave a half-salute. At the same time, Mickey entered from the other side and addressed the crowd.

"Listen guys, we want you to know that tonight is Kat's last night in Bayreuth. She's flying home tomorrow."

"Hey, Kat, take us with you!" one young soldier called out.

"Yeah, Kat, I'm short enough to fit in your suitcase," another called.

Laughter filled the room.

"Don't worry, boys, even though I'm flying home, I'll always carry you right here." She pointed to her heart, just as she'd rehearsed.

Then, on cue, the music started and Kat began to sing. She sang loud and clear, and Betty prayed a silent prayer that she'd remain strong. The soldiers got into the music. Many jumped to their feet, boogying with the music, and then more joined them. Soon everyone was standing, dancing, and clapping along.

Kat had made it halfway through the song when Betty saw her exterior start to crumble. First, her eyes widened, as if the reality of the news hit her. Then her feet stopped moving. Her chin trembled as large tears filled her eyes.

"He's the boogie-woogie bugle boy of—Company B. And when he played—" Kat's words caught in her throat, and she placed her hand over her mouth. The bandleader instructed the band to replay the lead-in again, but Kat shook her head. The music stopped, and then the clapping. Silence filled the auditorium. Betty wondered if she should go to Kat, help her off the stage. While everyone watched, it looked like no one knew what to do.

"I can't do this. I don't want to live like this—" Kat turned and left the stage, pushing through the huddle of performers who'd assembled in the wings to watch. Billy, the drummer, jumped from his stool and was right on her heels. As he passed, Mickey grabbed his arm.

"Let her go."

"But she's so upset." Billy looked down at the drumsticks still in his hands. "Everyone can't just stand here and watch her leave."

"Yes, they can. Kat needs time. Give her a few minutes to get some fresh air." Mickey combed his fingers through his hair, and then he set his chin in determination.

"All of you," Mickey called out so loudly Betty was sure the audience heard. "No one goes anywhere." Then he lowered his voice. "The show's going on. There's nothing we can do for Kat now. Nothing anyone can do."

With slumped shoulders, Billy trudged to his drums. The band waited, and the soldiers started to murmur, as if they were trying to figure out what had just happened.

"Who's up next?" Mickey asked.

"It's us, Mick," Irene said. "Our second number."

Betty felt Irene grab her arm. "Okay, get out there and smile wide. We're not going to let this change the show."

Mickey pinched the bridge of his nose, and they knew everything had already changed.

Betty rushed out onto the stage and took her place with Dolly on one side and Irene on the other. Her hands started to shake and she placed them behind her. *Poor Kat. How is she ever going to deal with this? First Edward and now the show.* She knew Kat. Knew how she liked to do everything well. Word would get out about this performance. *Another thing to burden her as she returns home.*

Five seconds later, the music restarted, interrupting Betty's thoughts, and she opened her mouth and let the words flow out.

Their song was a slower melody that seemed to fit the crowd's mood. No doubt everyone wondered what was wrong with Kat. Maybe they thought she was just emotional about leaving. Betty hoped that was the case.

This time when she sang, she made better eye contact with Frank. She saw him snap a few shots, and then he lowered the camera and smiled at her. It felt good, knowing he was there—knowing he was cheering for her, supporting her, maybe even loving her just a bit.

It wasn't until the second-to-the-last song of the night when Betty remembered what she'd been told earlier. "If anything happens to Kat, you need to take over her solo." She looked down and realized she was still wearing the same dress, and she hadn't even thought through all the lyrics in her mind, but as the last note ended on the jazzy number, she knew she was up.

Betty placed her hands over her stomach and took a deep breath. The lights went out and as quietly as she could, she walked onto the stage. She paced herself, guessing where the center was, and hoping the spotlight could find her. Finally, reaching what she thought was the middle, she turned toward the crowd. They were silent, almost as if they weren't even there. Betty drew in another deep breath and then started with one single note.

"O—." She held the note, feeling it fill the room, sweeping over the heads of the audience, reflecting off the wood-paneled walls, and returning to her once again.

In an instant, the spotlight hit her. It was slightly to her right, but the technician quickly adjusted. Two seconds later the band picked up the same note. Then Betty let the first syllable, the first note, develop into the beautiful, heart-felt song.

"O beautiful for spacious skies, for amber waves of grain." She scanned the crowd but this time she didn't look at Frank. She could only think that this was Kat's song—a song Edward would have loved to hear. "For purple mountain majesties, above the fruited plain—."

Betty sang, and thankfully, the words came. Before she knew it, the song ended, and the soldiers were on their feet once more. She smiled and waved, and was walking off the stage when she noticed something out of the corner of her eye. It was Oskar. He was standing on the opposite side of the stage from everyone else. And he was weeping—his hands covered his face and his shoulders shook. Betty didn't know if it was because of the music or because of Kat's news. She imagined both played a part.

* * * *

Frank took his time exiting the auditorium with the other guys, each one engaged in conversation with friends. All of them wondering what was wrong with Kat.

He was about to exit through the lobby when he noticed someone he recognized. It was the woman—that singer—from the cafe the other night. *What did Art say her name was again? Magdalena—that's right.*

Frank approached and he saw the woman's face was pale—even more so than the first night he'd seen her.

"Magdalena, it's good to see you." Frank extended his hand. She looked at it, and the look on her face said that shaking it was almost too much work, but then—forcing a smile—she extended her hand.

"Hello. I am sorry. I do not remember your name. So many men I have met, but I know you are Art's friend."

"Frank. My name is Frank. I'm a photographer, like Art—in fact that's what I was doing here tonight." He wiggled the camera back and forth in his grip.

The woman nodded, but she seemed lost in her own thoughts.

"So—" Frank tried to fill in the conversation. "Did you see the performance tonight?"

The woman lifted her head as if realizing he was still talking to her. "No. I mean, yes. Just last song. That woman at end—she has very beautiful voice."

"I think so too." Frank smiled. "Her name is Betty, she's a friend. Would you like to meet her? I can take you backstage."

The woman took a step back. "No. Not tonight." She looked down at her blouse and skirt. "I am not dressed for it. Another night perhaps." Then she took two more steps back. "I will see you another time. I must go."

"Sure, see you later." Frank ran a hand down his cheek, wondering what that was all about. The night was filled with mystery, but tonight of all nights, nothing could hinder his excitement.

Tonight I'm going to get Betty to agree that we should spend more time together.

Frank's mind told him he was doing it for work—to ensure he was invited to the performers' inner circle. Only then would he be able to keep an eye on what was happening at the Festspielhaus.

But his heart—well, his heart told him something completely different.

CHAPTER FIFTEEN

The mood was sober as they wrapped things up after the show. Betty hung up her gown, put her USO uniform back on, and approached the others circled by the back door.

"So what's the plan?" she asked, scanning the others' faces.

"We're trying to decide if we should head over to the canteen or back to the house to check on Kat. We assume that's where she went since she's not around here."

"I know what my vote is," Betty said, slipping on her jacket. "I think we should go check on Kat. Maybe she needs some company— a shoulder to cry on. Besides, it's her last night. We should be around to tell her our good-byes."

"Do you really think so, Betty?" Dolly took her elbow and held it. "It's Kat we're talking about. She likes time alone. She'd probably think we're invading her privacy."

"Yeah—if you think she'll want us to cry with her, you don't know Kat very well, kid," Irene added. "She only lets people get so close. She's a real star, and she knows it."

"I don't know. She was very kind to me my first night here. Very open. We lay on our beds and talked about a lot of things."

"And last night?" Irene asked.

"Last night she was really different," Betty admitted. "You're also probably right about her not needing us there—or wanting us there—but it doesn't seem right, our going to the canteen and her being home alone. Maybe we can cut out early."

"Okay, agreed." Irene wrapped an arm around Betty's shoulders. "We'll try not to stay out too long."

Betty nodded and followed everyone outside. It wasn't until she spotted Frank, standing at the bottom of the stairs, with a wide smile and bright eyes, that Betty remembered—seeing him in the rain, their brief talk, their promise to talk further. She forced a smile. "Hey, Frank." The others continued on, but Irene remained at her side.

"Hi, Betty, that was a great show tonight. I really liked your songs."

"Thanks. That last one was supposed to be Kat's song—her last solo."

"What's wrong with Kat? Is she okay?"

Betty felt Irene touch her elbow.

"Um, Kat—she was upset about leaving. Overwhelmed with emotion—she really doesn't want to head back and do that next movie." Even as she said the words, Betty felt a heaviness pressing upon her chest. More than anything, she wanted to tell Frank the truth, but she also knew what Mickey had said.

Frank's eyes reflected concern. "That's too bad. I'm sorry. Is she going to be okay?"

"Yes, I think so."

Frank looked to Irene, obviously confused that she was hanging around. "So are we still going to talk tonight?"

"Betty said she's coming to the canteen with us." Irene wrapped her arm around Betty's. "Right, Betty?"

"Just for a little while," Betty said. "Do you want to come with us?"

Frank's eyes studied hers for a moment, and then he offered a soft smile. "Yeah, sure, okay. Do you want to ride with me, Betty? I have my own MP—a nice guy named Howard—and jeep tonight." He winked.

"Every soldier needs his own MP," Betty quipped.

Twenty minutes later, Frank and Betty were seated at a round table in the soldiers' canteen with the other USO singers and dancers, some of the band members, and a few soldiers. A phonograph played Benny Goodman, and around the room, more soldiers sat in small clusters while a few German women served drinks.

Betty looked around the table. From the look on everyone's faces it was clear that even though they were pretending that everything was the same as yesterday, nothing was the same. For Kat, nothing would ever be the same again without Edward.

"Would you like something to drink?" Frank touched her hand.

"A cup of coffee, please."

"Sure." He stood and walked across the room to the small counter to place the order.

"So, I was walking back from town today, and I got caught in the rain," Betty said, trying to help the mood around the table. "You should have seen me by the time I got back to the Festspielhaus. I was a mess. Tell them, Irene, what my hair looked like."

"It was a mess all right. Slicking it all back was the only thing I could do with it."

"Your hair looks good like that." Billy nodded. "You're brave, Betty, for going down there."

"Brave?" She palmed her hair, making sure every strand was still in place.

"I don't like hanging out around town too often." Billy flashed a knowing look around the table. "There are too many sad people. They come, they go. Every day there's a new group. I don't like seeing them without homes, without hopes. If anyone needs a concert to help get their minds off things, it's them. And seeing all those bombed-out buildings really puts me in a sober mood."

"Are you saying you don't like what had to be done?" Frank approached. He placed a mug of black, steaming coffee in front of Betty. "I know a lot of guys who risked their lives, and some who died, on those missions."

"I'm not sorry that we had to do that. We were out to win a war, right?" Billy shook his head. "But I can't be glad, either. I'm human. Sad stuff makes me sad. I just hope we can all forgive and forget."

"I don't know how I could forget. I was on those front lines," one soldier commented. "I can tell you that I cheered for every one of our planes flying overhead. I knew that the harder they hit, the easier things would be for me—although in the end things weren't easy."

"Tell these folks about what you saw in Berlin," the soldier's buddy commented.

"Berlin?" Frank leaned forward, resting his arms on the table. "When was that?"

It pleased Betty to see Frank's interest in her friends, in the conversation. *He really cares.* She scooted closer to him.

"Just last month," the soldier continued, "my friend and I wanted to check out the Russian zone, and, boy, were we in for a surprise. While I was there I gave my watch to an English-speaking Russian commander, and he gave me a tour of Hitler's personal air-raid shelter."

"You did what?" Dolly gasped. She patted her chest as if trying to still her racing heart. "You went where?"

"You're joking, right?" Irene piped in.

Betty glanced at Frank, waiting for him to crack a smile. She was sure this guy was joking, and she was waiting for someone to make him admit it. *Surely you can't be serious, buddy.*

"So what did you see?" Frank asked.

"Well, first of all, I couldn't believe it was right there, in the middle of town. It was just a few hundred yards from the Chancellery in a garden. My friend and I followed the Russian down a hundred steps—or so it seemed. And when we got inside it was like stepping into a mansion or something. There were kitchens—more than one—a huge library, servant quarters, and a room for Hitler's girlfriend."

"Did you go into the room where Hitler—you know—" Irene ran a finger across her throat.

"No. The Russian didn't show me that, and I didn't ask. I did learn something there, though, something that's tied to this place. Did you know that when Hitler killed himself, one of the Wagner operas—an original—was in his possession?"

"Really?" Betty's brow furrowed. "Which one?"

"*Rienzi.*"

Betty felt chills travel up and down her arms. "Well, I suppose that makes sense."

"Do you know that opera, Betty?"

"I don't know it, but I've heard of it before. I heard about how Hitler first got his ideas for 'German freedom,' if that's what you want to call it, after listening to that opera. I heard about how he used the music from it for his rallies and such."

Betty didn't tell them that she'd heard all this from a driver. She didn't tell them that before coming over here she didn't know a place called Bayreuth existed, or that Wagner's music was such a big deal to Hitler.

"Did you sing in the opera, Betty? Have you sung professionally before?" Billy asked.

"I sang at the Douglas factory—at the Santa Monica canteen, actually."

Eyebrows lifted as the other singers glanced at each other. She could read on their faces that being a canteen singer did not impress them. She thought about asking where they'd all sung before their stint in the USO, but she was almost afraid to know. She hadn't thought much about her musical experience—or lack of it. From the looks on their faces, it mattered more to them than she realized.

"Sounds swell," Dolly said.

"Sounds easy to me." Billy rested his chin on his hand. "Sounds easier than traipsing all over Europe in the middle of a war, like us."

"Well, I did other work in the canteen too. It wasn't just about the singing. I helped wherever I was needed. It wasn't that easy—we'd get an express telegraph saying three hundred men were on their way. After that, you should have seen the blur of cotton aprons as we fixed up sandwiches and orange squeezers—the guys always appreciated those on a hot day."

Laughter burst out at her table and the sound carried around the room. Other soldiers quieted and looked their direction. They all eyed

Betty as if they wondered what was so funny. Betty sat back in her seat, feeling heat rise to her cheeks and wondering if she'd already turned three shades of pink. Her throat felt tight and she felt like a little girl sitting at a table with professionals. She glanced over at Frank. His jaw was tight and anger flashed in his eyes. Yet he didn't speak. She could tell he was holding back his words, which she appreciated. After all, she had to work with these people.

"Sweetheart." Irene reached across the table and patted Betty's hand. "There were times we dodged bombs and sang in hospital wards where injured men were contemplating how to write their girls back home and tell them they'd be returning minus a limb or an eye. I don't think you can understand how hard it really was unless you were here."

"Yes, but I don't think you understand what things were like back in the States either." Betty jutted her chin. "It's not like everyone back home wasn't sacrificing and working their hardest for the war effort—everyone back there made this win possible too. Do you know that some women—like my mom—worked twelve hours every night and then took care of their homes, their families, and tended their Victory gardens during the day?" Betty paused, seeing that not only the eyes of everyone at the table were on her, but also others from around the room. "I'm sorry, I don't mean to be disrespectful, but—things were hard there too."

"She's right." Frank spoke up from beside her. His voice trembled slightly, as he controlled his tone. "Everyone did their part. We all worked together to win this war."

"If anyone should know how hard things were here, Frank, it's you," Billy said. "You have the pictures to prove it. I knew I recognized your name when Mickey introduced you yesterday. I went over to headquarters and checked out some old copies of *Stars and Stripes* and saw your photos. It was sad to hear what happened to the Klassy Lassy."

Betty glanced at him, wondering what Billy was talking about. She'd have to ask Frank later. They had *many* things to talk about.

"It was painful, I'll admit that. But just because one person's experience was hard doesn't make another's situation any less difficult." Then Frank smiled and turned to her. "Betty, you look a little tired. I'd be happy to give you a ride back to your quarters when you're finished here."

"Yes, I'd like that." She wiped her face and took another sip from her coffee.

Frank stood.

"But…" She glanced at him. "I need to talk to Irene about something first. It will only take a minute."

"No hurries. I'll be waiting outside. It's a little stuffy in here." He ran his finger under his shirt collar. Then, without a word to anyone else at the table, he turned and strode away.

"Gee, talk about Mr. Unsocial. Did it seem to you like he was trying to cut our party short?" Dolly asked.

"Maybe he has a lot on his mind—you know, stuff that happened in the war." Billy warmed to his subject like a reporter delivering the news. "I read a little about him in the *Stars and Stripes*. There was a short bio to go with his photos. The article said he lost a sister back in the States. She was one of those WASPs and crashed her plane. Then—well, I don't want to be one who spreads rumors."

"What? What happened?" Dolly prodded, scooting her chair closer to Billy's.

Betty felt her stomach tightening, as if someone were twisting it into knots. She didn't like this. Didn't like how they were talking about Frank now that he was out of earshot, but she had to admit she wanted to know.

Maybe I'm rushing into things too quickly. Frank wanted to talk about us spending more time together, but I didn't even know he had a sister—or that he lost her. I know nothing, in fact. Nothing except that I think he's handsome and kind. Surely a relationship had to be based on more than that.

"Well, the article was about the loss of a whole B-17 crew," Billy said. "Although, as a photographer, Frank wasn't assigned to a crew, this was the crew he flew with most of the time."

"The Klassy Lassy," Betty said. "Was he with them? Was he the only one who made it out?"

"No, nothing like that. It was his plain luck, really. The article said Frank had leave coming or something like that. He was supposed to go up that day with the bombing crew—to photograph their run. The pilot—his good friend—told him to sit this one out. If he didn't take the leave, he'd lose it. The paper said the crew never made it back. Their B-17 crash-landed. No one saw any chutes. Ten men gone, just like that. Frank missed the right flight."

"How sad. No wonder he seems reserved and withdrawn," Irene pouted.

Betty pressed her fingers to her temples and a sharp pain shot across her forehead. "He's not always like that," she spouted. "And even if he was, do you blame him?"

"No, I don't blame him, especially since he's lost all credibility as a photographer," Billy added.

"What do you mean?" Another shooting pain hit Betty's forehead.

"I mean just three months ago he was taking photos of battles and concentration camps, and now it's of showgirls and jazz bands. Got to be a gut punch to one's ego."

"It's nothing I'd be crying about," the soldier sitting next to Irene said. "It might mess up his career, but he's gotta be looking forward to going to work every day."

Betty stood, not wanting to hear anymore. First Kat's news, then her friends' offhand dismissal of her work on the home front. And now this news about Frank. It was too much to take. "Irene, can I talk to you—for a second?"

"Sure, kid."

Irene stood and Betty took her hand, leading her to the far corner of the room where the music wasn't quite as loud. Betty felt tears rimming her eyes.

"Listen, you didn't take that joking to heart, did you?" Irene's eyes searched hers. "I understand how hard things were for you all back home. And I think that singing in a canteen is perfectly adorable."

Betty placed her fingers to her lips, hoping to hold her emotions inside. Then she fanned her face. "No. It's not that. None—none of those things matter now. I'm just thinking about Kat—and the fact that I lied to Frank about what's wrong. I hate not mentioning Edward's death. Frank knows something's wrong. I can tell."

Betty looked away. She looked to the door, realizing that she was going to have to walk out there and smile and act like everything was fine—that she didn't feel sad for her friend or that she didn't know about everything Frank faced, including the fact the he most likely wished he could be taking photos anywhere else. And then, when she made it through all that and got back to the estate, she'd have to face Kat. She'd have to see Kat's luggage packed and maybe even listen to Kat cry into her pillow through the night. Her stomach ached just thinking about it.

"I feel so bad about Frank—but more than that, what am I going to say to Kat when I get back to Wahnfried? I just don't know what to do."

"Oh, honey." Irene pulled her into a hug. "I don't think you're going to have to talk to Kat about anything. I think it's going to mean a lot to her just that you're there." Irene stepped back and held Betty at arm's length. "And don't worry. We'll be leaving here soon. I just want to grab a quick snack. I always get hungry after a show."

Betty nodded and started to turn, but then she paused as Irene's hand touched her shoulder. "Wait, there's one more thing."

"What?"

"Whatever you do, you can't tell Frank about Edward, no matter how bad you feel. No matter how hard it is."

"I know, that's what Mickey said." Betty bit her lip.

"No—I mean you *really* can't tell him, Betty. You can't even tell him and then ask him to keep it a secret. Frank is a photographer.

He works with the papers and stuff. He no doubt has photos of Kat rushing off the stage. This is big news. Big. If he knows and the word gets out, everyone will want those photos."

"You think Frank would—would tell?"

"Well, think about it. Like Billy said, he's most likely not too happy about taking photos of singers. But this could be his big break. If he's the first one to report the story about Edward, then his photos of Kat would be in big demand."

"I don't think he'd do that." Her throat felt raw and thick. "But I won't tell. For Kat—for her peace. I won't tell until Mickey gives the okay."

Betty sighed then hurried outside. Frank was standing by the jeep, chatting with an MP. The wind was cold, but the crisp breeze against her face wasn't as sharp as the pain she carried inside. Betty wiped her eyes and forced herself to smile. She'd lied to Frank enough today, and she didn't want him asking why she was crying.

She walked up to him. "Thanks for waiting." Then, so she didn't have to look him in the eyes, she turned to the MP. "I wish you could have come inside, Howard." She rubbed her arms, trying to warm them. "It's cold out here."

"Oh, I have strict orders not to leave my jeep, unless I have another MP watching it. We've been having problems with people siphoning off our fuel. More than one jeep has run dry far earlier than it ought."

"I bet that's not the only thing that's being stolen around here," Frank commented. Then he helped Betty climb inside. "Sometimes it's hard to figure out who to trust."

Betty felt the sting of those words. More than anything, she wished she could tell the truth, to earn Frank's trust.

CHAPTER SIXTEEN

Frank took the seat next to Betty and glanced at her. She was quiet. Disheartened. Something had happened, and he had a feeling it was more than Kat getting emotional. He just didn't know what. She was a different person than the one who'd entered the Festspielhaus all smiles only hours earlier.

Betty's probably worried about Kat—about her breaking down on stage and leaving.

That made the most sense, but another thought trailed close behind.

Or maybe Betty's changed her mind. Maybe she's had time to think about wanting to spend time with me. Frank knew if Betty decided that, keeping an eye on things around the Festspielhaus would be harder.

"Listen, Betty, I really need to apologize."

She glanced over at him. "Frank, no…"

"Earlier—you know, when you got to the Festspielhaus. I shouldn't have teased you about getting a ride with those guys, and I shouldn't have forced my feelings on you like that."

"Frank, wait."

"No, let me say it. We promised to talk, but maybe it's happening too fast. I want to treat you right. I don't want to mess things up—with us."

Betty nodded. "Okay, I understand."

The MP glanced at them over his shoulder, as if listening, and Frank wondered if this was how things used to be in the olden days when all dates were chaperoned. Frank wanted to say more, but he thought it would be better to talk to Betty when she didn't have so much on her mind. He needed to be around the Festspielhaus as much as possible, and Betty was his ticket to doing that.

They drove through the quiet, dark town, and Frank noticed MPs in rain slickers policing the streets—more patrols than he remembered, most likely because of the gas being siphoned off. The whole place seemed darker than usual. Clouds had blown in, blocking out the moon. He wished it were brighter, wished he could get a better look at Betty's face. The evening hadn't turned out as he'd hoped—not even close.

Wahnfried was dark when they arrived. A breeze had picked up, blowing dry leaves off the trees that lined the drive. The leaves carried on the wind across the dead lawn and potholed driveway.

"That's strange. Kat didn't turn any lights on." Betty's voice was heavy with concern.

"I should go in with you—to check on things." The jeep stopped, and Frank jumped out. Something felt wrong. He pulled his small flashlight out of his jacket pocket and turned it on. The yellow beam stretched to the front door, and he too wondered why Kat wouldn't have turned a light on.

"You can come in, but you know what Kat said." Betty's lips smiled, but her eyes looked just as worried. "You can't go any farther than the foyer."

"Sure, that's fine. I'll wait there, and when I see that Kat's here and everything's okay, then I'll head out and let you get some rest." He attempted to make his tone light. "I'm a modern man, but there's no way I'm going to let a beautiful girl enter a haunted house alone—in the month of October."

Another smile—a real one this time—curled on Betty's lips. "Yes, it *is* the month of October."

They walked to the front door and found it locked.

"I'm not surprised. If I was a woman home alone I'd do the same." Frank knocked.

"I wonder if Kat walked home alone. I feel bad if she did."

"Surely she wouldn't do that. This isn't Kansas." Frank knocked again.

"She says she walks back and forth all the time. Remember when we got here that first night and she was already back? Well, the next morning she told us something had really scared her on that walk. She said there were some kids trying to spook her. She said there were footsteps or something following her, but she never saw who it was."

Frank stepped back and eyed the house, looking for movement in the windows, but didn't see anything.

"I don't think Kat's here, Betty," he finally said. "And if she was here, she's not anymore. Maybe she got a ride and went for a midnight drive—to get one last look at the place. Or maybe she decided

SONGBIRD UNDER A GERMAN MOON

to meet up with your friends over at the canteen after all. Do you have a key?"

"No. I didn't even think to ask for one." She shook her head. "Back home our house doesn't even have a lock."

"Yeah, my parents' house doesn't either. Or at least if it has a lock I've never used it. Do you know where they'd keep a key if they were going to hide one around here?"

"Well, if it was my guess…" Betty glanced around. Then she moved down the steps toward the shrubbery. Frank followed her with the flashlight beam. She squatted and lifted up a palm-sized rock. Nothing was there so she did it again, lifting up the next one. Finally, after the third rock, she smiled, stood, and held up a key.

Frank felt tension in his gut. He wished he'd known about Kat walking alone. He would have made sure she had an escort. He wished he would have known about her getting scared on the trail. Maybe whoever had spooked Kat was sending a warning. Maybe since the letters hadn't done their trick, more drastic measures were being taken. *Please let Kat be okay.*

"Great job." Frank glanced back at Howard, signaling the MP to join them as Betty unlocked the door. Stepping inside, Betty turned, seemingly surprised to see Howard walking up the steps.

"What's going on?" she asked.

"Well, Kat's not here, and if we're going to wait until your friends get home, then I don't think it would be polite to let our friend sit out in the jeep."

"I'm just here for backup, miss," Howard said. "To—chaperone." He winked.

"That would be understandable if Frank were staying, but there's no need. I'm a big girl. I traveled halfway around the world alone. You really don't need to stick around." She found the light switch and flipped it on, flooding the foyer with light.

"Well *that's* a surprise," Howard said. "It's amazing the lights still work, especially when half the building is gone. Someone must have worked on it. If I knew who, I'd like to talk to him. We're still without electricity at our place in town, along with most of our block."

"I don't know who it was, but I'm thankful," Betty said as she hurried down the hall.

"Kat," she called. "Kat!"

Frank stepped forward, following her. His footsteps echoed on the floor.

Betty paused and shook a finger at him, stopping him cold. "I don't think so. Not a step farther. I'm not going to get on Mickey's bad side, remember?"

"Kat!" she called again.

Frank stood at the entrance to the hall and watched Betty disappear into a door at the end.

It took thirty seconds for Betty to reemerge. Her white face was the picture of puzzlement, and as she approached, Frank noticed her hands were shaking.

"Betty, are you okay?"

Instead of answering Frank, she turned to Howard. "Can you do me a favor, please?"

"Sure, miss."

"Can you go back to the canteen and get Irene and Dolly and tell them Kat isn't here? Or, better yet, can you ask them to bring Mickey too?" She turned to Frank in defeat. "I—I can't believe that I'm so ill-prepared. I don't even know where Mickey lives. I don't know—" She turned to Howard. "I don't even know how to find someone like you. I mean, if I'm in trouble or someone is in trouble—in the future. I wouldn't even know where to look for help."

"Wait." Frank held up his hand, stopping the MP. "There has to be a good reason why Kat isn't here. Don't you think you're going a little overboard sending for Mickey?"

Betty crossed her arms over her chest and stared at her shoes. "It's really not good. I knew I should have followed her," she mumbled.

"Betty?"

She lifted her head and looked at him.

"Is there something in the room? Is there something troubling you?"

"Yes—I mean there's nothing different about the room, and that's what's troubling. Kat's supposed to fly home tomorrow. I can't imagine her not having everything packed, or at least working on it. I can't imagine why she'd want to be out, driving around or whatever..."

Frank reached out for her arms, gently touching them, hoping to stop their trembling. "Yes, but just because you don't know where Kat is doesn't mean there's trouble. Is there a reason why you think Mickey needs to be here? Is there something you're not telling me?"

"No. Maybe. I don't know. Kat's not home, and I can only assume she would have walked home—after she ran off stage, I mean. Where could she be? By the time we finished the concert, got out of our dresses, went to the canteen—it's been nearly three hours."

"I really don't know her, Betty. I can't say where she'd go."

Betty pulled back from his grasp and turned her back to him. "I just can't think of a good explanation."

"I can head to town and spread the word to keep an eye out for Kat," Howard suggested again. "From what I hear she didn't seem herself tonight—and as we all know, it's better to be safe than sorry."

"Maybe we should talk this through first, Howard." Frank stepped around Betty so he could face her again. "Listen, Betty. I imagine Kat was embarrassed for letting her emotions get out of control. She might have wanted to apologize to Mickey. Maybe she's over there now, talking to him. Maybe we missed her on the road— passed the jeep she was riding in."

"Okay, maybe all that is true, but what if it's not?" She persisted with Howard. "Can you *please* go get my friends at the canteen and ask them to bring Mickey?"

Howard looked to Frank, who nodded. He felt bad getting Howard wrapped up in this, but it wouldn't hurt anything and would ease Betty's conscience. Betty was hiding something—something that made her more worried about Kat than he had reason to think she should be. Maybe she'd share the burden with him once Howard was gone. He needed to know these things. He was the one with secrets to keep, not the other way around.

Howard left, and a few seconds later, they heard the jeep driving away.

Betty paced for a minute, and then she sighed and plopped down on the stairs that led to the second story. Her face was contorted with worry.

Frank approached and squatted down in front of her. "There's something you're not telling me."

"I don't know why you're saying that." Her lips were pressed into a thin line, her eyes wide, but she refused to look at him.

"I can see it all over your face."

"Maybe when Mickey comes…" Her voice trailed off, and she looked to her lap.

Frank paced while they waited. He made a large loop, walking from the front door to the walled-up area that used to lead to the main part of the house, to the back door, which was also boarded up, and then he passed the stairs and the hallway, which led to the annex with the rooms, finding himself back at the front door.

He walked the same route fifty times at least, not knowing what else to do. Not knowing what else to say. He wanted to press Betty to tell him the truth. He needed to know what was happening. Then again, if he pressed too much, he might push her away. Frank couldn't let that happen, so he stayed quiet.

Betty yawned, and then leaned back against the stair behind her. Her eyes were closed, and at first Frank thought she'd fallen asleep, but then he saw her lips moving. Frank paused his pacing and approached Betty, sitting down beside her. And as he sat, a strange sensation came over him. He realized that he wanted to be here for *her*. Not only for his job.

"Betty," he whispered.

Softly her eyelashes lifted, and she glanced up at him.

"Are you praying?"

Betty nodded.

"Can I pray with you?"

Betty nodded again.

Frank took her hands in his. Earlier today, such a gesture would have made his heart pound with her closeness. But now—now he just wanted to protect her. To give her peace. To ease the worries that mounted in her heart.

"Dear God, I know Betty is worried about Kat," he started.

The sound of a jeep motor revved up the driveway. Betty must have heard it too because she stirred. Frank quickly wrapped up his prayer, and as soon as they both whispered "Amen," they rose and hurried to the door. Betty opened it, and Frank saw Mickey mounting the steps, followed by several of the singers and Howard.

"Betty!" He opened his arms to her, and she hurried into his embrace, like a little girl turning to her father for comfort.

"Mickey, do you know where Kat is? She's not here."

"You checked the room?" Irene rushed down the hall.

"Did you look upstairs?" Dolly hurried up the stairs.

"Did anyone check the trail?" Shirlee asked. "We've told her more than once that she didn't need to be walking alone."

"Checking the trail is a good idea," Mickey said. "There's no reason Kat shouldn't be here. No reason at all."

Irene came out of Kat's room with a yellow piece of paper in her hands. Frank recognized it as a telegram, and he wondered what was on it.

The dark-haired singer moved to Mickey. "This is here, and her things are just as she left them. She hasn't even packed for her flight tomorrow. She'd never take off like this and not tell anybody. I mean, even if she wanted to be alone she'd do it here—she'd just kick us all out of her room, that's all. She's done it before."

Dolly came back down the stairs. "She's not upstairs, either. Where could she be?"

Everyone quietly exchanged glances. Frank couldn't help but notice how each one glanced at him, as if uncomfortable with his presence. *They know more than they're letting on. There's something in that telegram they don't want to tell me about.* Again, a war erupted inside Frank. He could stay and pester them for the truth, or he could go. He decided that the latter would be the wisest thing to do. He didn't want to get on their bad side after only one day. He needed these performers to trust him. To allow him into their lives. Who knew what was at stake if they didn't?

Frank cleared his throat. "I'm sorry Kat's missing, but I'm not sure if I can be of any more help." He stepped to the door.

"Howard, are you coming?"

"Actually," Mickey said, "I think we'd like Howard to stay here. But thank you, Frank, for all your help." Mickey walked forward and shook Frank's hand.

They want Howard to stay but not me?

Frank nodded good-bye, and then he glanced back at Betty. Her eyes met his. She offered him a sad smile, and then she turned her attention back to her friends.

It wasn't until Frank was outside and down the front steps that he realized he no longer had a ride. He buttoned his jacket, flipped the collar up, and then stared down the tree-lined lane. It shouldn't take more than twenty minutes to walk up the hill, past the Festspielhaus, and then down the other side. *I'll keep an eye out for Kat. although it can't be good if she's on the trail after all this time. Maybe she twisted her ankle. That would explain things.* Frank didn't let his mind wander to what else could have happened to a beautiful girl in a dark, secluded place.

He grabbed his camera equipment from the jeep and patted his side where his pistol was, just for reassurance. Finally, fixing his flashlight beam down the driveway, he headed out.

It was cold, but it wasn't the walk that bothered him. It didn't even bother him that he and Betty didn't get a chance to talk. What bothered him most was the look in Betty's eyes. The look that said she was hiding something.

The look that said she didn't trust him with the truth.

* * * *

Betty lifted her head, listening as the wind blew outside. She hated sending Frank away without an explanation, but she didn't have a choice. Kat had clearly stated her wishes, and Betty had to stick by that. Even though she trusted Frank, she knew the others didn't. She wished they would have let him stay though. Even with all the questions that hung over them, Frank's presence calmed her.

"Do you need a description of Kat?" Irene asked Howard. "They always ask for a description in the movies."

The MP chuckled. "No offense, miss, but I don't think we'll need that. This is Katherine Wiseman we're talking about. We've seen her in the pictures. We've seen the shows. Why, I wouldn't be surprised if half the guys here have her picture pinned up near their beds, right next to Betty Grable. But do any of you know where Kat went after leaving the Festspielhaus?"

"Dolly, Betty, and I didn't see her leave." Irene twirled her finger in the air. "The three of us went on stage right after she left."

"How about you, Mick? Did you see her leave?" Esther asked.

"No, I had to scramble to figure out what to do with the rest of the show."

"Did she take any of her things? She'd laid out that large pile. Did anyone check?" Irene asked.

Betty noticed that the worry lines on the others' faces deepened.

Mickey ran his fingers through his hair. "Why didn't I follow her? What was I thinking?" He pointed to the window and the dark night. "There are so many crazies out there."

Irene patted Mickey's shoulder. "It's not your fault, Mick. Kat's a big girl. She's the one that left. I'm sure someone saw where she went."

"Yes, and there were MPs in the parking area by the jeeps." Betty felt a small ray of hope. "They've had problems with people siphoning gas, you see, so they're posting guards. Surely someone saw her leave. We just have to trust that Kat is just doing what Kat does— pushing everyone away so she can work through some things on her own."

Mickey sighed. "Yeah, kid, I'm sure there's a good explanation. Let's hope that she comes waltzing in that door soon. I'll even take her tears right now. I'll even cry with her if that helps."

* * * *

Frank walked up the hill with slow steps, his flashlight sweeping back and forth as he scanned the path. He supposed at one time, years ago, the trail had been well maintained. He could almost picture Wagner walking from his home to the opera house. He imagined fine, well-dressed women strolling in the park with parasols poised over their shoulders. He saw Wagner's children, innocent of how their father's music would impact the world, laughing and playing as they scurried around these woods.

His feet plodded through mud from the recent rainfall. His eyes searched for anything that looked out of the ordinary. His ears focused on the night sounds, the wind whispering through the trees. As he neared the pond area, Frank slowed and took an even closer look. By now, the moon had peeked out from the clouds, casting more light and reflecting off the surface of the pond. The breeze had died. The water was still. The forest quiet.

"Dear God," he whispered, "I know You know where Kat is. Please take care of her. Please watch over her. I'm not sure—" A faint sound interrupted his prayer. His heart seemed to leap into his throat, and he turned his flashlight in the direction of the brush lining the pond. A small rabbit scurried into the dry branches. Nervous laughter spilled from his throat, and he could almost hear his sister's voice in his ear—her twelve-year-old voice, that is.

"Scaredy cat," she'd told him more than once. "You'd be afraid of your own shadow, Frankie, if I wasn't around to protect you."

Lily had always been the brave one, climbing to the top of the tree, running through the cemetery near their home at night, taking flying lessons and getting her pilot's license when most people believed girls needed to keep their feet firmly planted on the ground or—more accurately—firmly planted in the kitchen, where they could cook and clean and take care of their families.

"God, I know You're watching over Kat." Frank continued his prayer. "There's been enough pain in this world lately, don't You think? Can You help us out with this one?"

Then he turned and continued up the hill. The night was dark, the trail was empty, and Frank's pistol remained in its holster where it belonged. Frank supposed he should be glad for that.

CHAPTER SEVENTEEN

Betty didn't realize she'd fallen asleep until she felt her head jerk, and she opened her eyes, noticing rays of morning light filtering into the room. She sat up with a start and saw the silhouette of a body on Kat's bed.

"Kat." She jumped to her feet and hurried over, almost tripping over Irene, who slept on the floor. Then confusion filled her when she saw the red, curly hair splayed on the pillow.

"Kat?"

"Is she here?" Irene mumbled behind her.

"Did someone say Kat's here?" the red hair mumbled, and then the silhouette sat up. Dolly ran her hand down the side of her face. "I didn't mean to fall asleep. Kat's going to kill me if I shed red hair on her pillow."

"That'd be okay—I'd like to see Kat wring your neck." Irene sat up and leaned her back against Betty's bed. "Then at least we'd know she's okay."

Betty moved to the window. She was surprised to see a line of jeeps in the driveway. "Ladies, look. This is getting serious." She pointed out the window at the jeeps. Dolly and Irene hurried to her side.

"Look over there too," Irene said. "There are guys walking down the road and up the hill. They must be searching for her."

Betty's stomach rumbled and nausea overtook her. *This can't be happening. This can't be happening.* She covered her mouth with her hand and returned to her bed, perching on the edge.

Last night Howard had come back with more MPs. They'd asked questions, but even then, Mickey hadn't revealed the news about Edward's death. Some of the guys offered to hang around and watch the house. A few more offered to walk the trail.

She and the other USO ladies had waited up, hanging around the foyer, alternating between sitting on the steps and pacing, until finally—after two hours had passed—all the guys returned and said their search had come up empty.

Only then did they head to their rooms. Dolly and Irene had joined Betty in her room, vowing to stay up until Kat returned. But she never did.

"I think we should head out there." Dolly ran her fingers through her wild hair and snagged one of Kat's scarves to hold it back. "Or better yet, maybe we should go to the opera house and check out things there."

In her mind's eye, Betty pictured Kat where Kat was at her best—at the Festspielhaus. She imagined her singing and smiling. She thought of her running around, dressing, practicing, getting lost in the halls....

"Oh my goodness!" Betty turned to Irene. "That's it. Oh, what if that's it?" Betty squeezed Irene's arms tighter and did a little hop. "What if that's it?"

"Betty? What are you talking about?" Irene tried to pull her arms away. "Ouch, you're hurting me."

Betty released her grasp. "Remember the other day during rehearsal, and Kat was trying to figure out the best way to get on stage for her last number?"

Irene nodded.

"Yes, I remember that too," Dolly piped in.

"Well, when Kat ran off, what if she went down the wrong hall? I mean, that doesn't sound too crazy, does it? What if she got turned around. You know what a bad sense of direction she had, and then there was the fact that she was upset."

"So you're saying that it could be possible that she went down the wrong hall and ended up in some back room. If that was the case, she'd never find her way out."

"Oh, that makes me feel so much better!" Irene embraced Betty.

"What? The idea of Kat being lost in the Festspielhaus makes you feel better?" Dolly shook her head.

"Well, it's better than all the other things I've been thinking," Irene said.

"I suppose it *would* be horrible, I mean getting lost and stuck there overnight, especially when she'd just received that news about Edward." Betty pulled on her USO jacket and trousers. It didn't matter what her makeup looked like after sleeping in it. It didn't matter what her hair looked like. All she wanted to do was to get up to the opera house and find her friend.

They headed down the hall and found Mickey still there. He was sitting on the stairs, staring at the front door. Betty followed his gaze and noticed two MPs leaving. They refused to look at her and instead stepped out, shutting the door behind themselves.

"Mickey, we have an idea where Kat is," Betty said. "We're going to the opera house. You know Kat, she always got lost…"

"Yes," Irene added, "we think that she must have gotten lost down one of the halls. It must have been so sad and lonely last night, and she—"

"Girls." Mickey stood, and for the first time Betty noticed tears on his face.

"And she's going to have to take another airplane flight to get home," Dolly picked up where Irene stopped.

"Listen…" Mickey's voice was hoarse. He coughed into his hand and then lowered his head, his shoulders shaking.

"What is it, Mickey?" Irene asked.

"They found her." He said it without looking up.

"Oh, that's great news. Is she okay? Was she at the opera house?" Dolly asked.

Mickey shook his head. "She was—in the pond."

"I don't understand." Betty's eyebrows furrowed.

"They found her this morning floating in the water. There wasn't a mark on her from what they can see, and it didn't look like there was any type of struggle. They—they say she committed suicide. And after I told them about Edward—well, we don't have any reason to think otherwise."

"Suicide." Betty looked around wildly. "Dead? Kat's dead?" She felt her knees tremble. Then her legs gave out and she reached for the banister for support, sinking onto the bottom step.

Irene gasped. "No, that's impossible. Kat would never do that—she's not dead. How dare they say she's dead?"

Mickey didn't answer. He just sat on the stairs, appearing older than he had last time Betty had seen him. His face was a map of wrinkles and his eyelids looked heavy, as if they were going to close under his grief.

"She doesn't like the water." Betty's voice sounded hollow, even to her own ears.

"Yes, that's right. She doesn't like the water. Kat would never go into the water." Irene placed her hand over her mouth.

Mickey rose. "They're waiting for me. They're going to take me to the scene. I—I need to identify the body, although everyone knows it's her. She's even still wearing her white dress."

Betty rose. "She wouldn't have done that. Kat wouldn't have killed herself. Something else must have happened." She rushed toward Mickey. "I know she lost Edward. I know Kat—well, she ran off the stage, but there was something else. Something to live for."

Betty knew that she'd promised Kat not to say anything about the baby, but things were different now. Betty wanted them to know, wanted them to understand that Kat wouldn't have done this to herself.

She turned back to Irene and Dolly. "She was pregnant."

"What?" Irene strode to her.

"Are you sure? How do you know?" Dolly gasped.

"She told me. That first night—actually she didn't tell me, I guessed by the things she was saying."

"You can't tell anyone that." Mickey grabbed her arm. "That does not leave this room—do you understand?" Mickey's eyes were wide, wild. "First of all, who do you think you are to say such a thing? Kat wasn't like the other girls. She never, never would have cheated on her husband. Do you want to slander her name in order to take her place? Is that it?" He squeezed harder. "You will never take her place. Never."

Where is this coming from? Why is he acting this way? Pain shot up Betty's arm, and she struggled to pull away.

"No, never." Tears sprang to her eyes. "You're hurting me, Mickey, you're hurting me. I'd never do that."

Dolly and Irene both rushed toward her.

"Let go!" Irene cried. "You can't do this again, Mickey. Let go!"

Mickey's eyes widened, and he released his grasp. Betty turned toward Dolly, as if hiding behind her could provide some protection. Her steps paused when she saw the angry look on Dolly's face.

"Mickey's right, Betty. It's not possible." Dolly's voice was hard, sharp.

"Kat said when she was in Paris, Edward came and they had one night together."

"We were in Paris with her, Betty. Edward wasn't there. If this gets out—it's even worse than her being dead." Dolly stepped away, walking to Mickey, as if lining up on his side.

Betty's chest ached, and she sucked in a shuddering breath. "Irene?" She turned to her friend. "You believe me, don't you? I wouldn't make that up. Why would I make that up?"

"I don't know what to think, Betty, but they're right. It's sad enough with everything that's happened, and this will only make things worse."

"So do you really believe that she committed suicide?" Betty directed her panicked expression around the group. "That she walked to that pond, went in, and let herself drown?"

Irene shrugged. "I don't know what to believe, but I do remember what Kat said when she exited the stage. We all heard it. She said she didn't want to live like this. Maybe she came to the point where she didn't want to live at all. You weren't around her as much as we were. You hardly knew her—not like us. She'd lost her joy lately. She didn't want to be performing, and she didn't want to be doing that movie. She pushed us away—isolated herself from us. Edward was all that she had. He was the most important thing to her. Maybe she did kill herself, who knows?"

Betty felt the energy drain from her arms, and they dropped limp to her sides. She watched as Dolly walked Mickey outside to the MPs and the waiting jeep. After the door closed, Irene patted her shoulder and then climbed the stairs, heading up to her room.

Betty sat down hard on the stairs, not knowing what to think, not knowing what to do. She didn't want to go to her room—all Kat's stuff was there. She was too afraid to go for a walk. She didn't have anyone to talk to.

Her arm still stung where Mickey had grabbed it, and Betty rubbed the sore spot.

I can't believe it. I can't believe Kat did that. Someone must have done that to her—but who? Nothing made sense.

Frank. She wished Frank were here. She could talk to him. He would believe her.

Footsteps sounded from above her, and even though Betty knew it was Irene walking around—most likely waking up the others to tell them what had happened—a wave of fear washed over her.

"Kat knew something was wrong. She told me things weren't right. She told me she had a bad feeling," Betty mumbled to herself.

Maybe none of us should be here—or in the opera house. Evil had dwelt in this place. Madness had walked these halls.

Maybe I should leave, go home. Betty stood and hurried to the window. *I don't belong here. We aren't wanted.*

Someone had made that perfectly clear.

CHAPTER EIGHTEEN

A pounding on the door of their house had awakened Frank before 5 a.m., when it was still dark out. Had Art had forgotten his key and wanted in? He leapt out of bed, ran to the door, and opened it to find Howard there instead of Art.

"Frank, we need you up at the gardens near the Festspielhaus—they've found Kat."

"Yeah, sure." He rubbed his eyes, wondering why they needed him.

"Is she okay? Does Betty know?"

"No to both those questions." Only then did Frank notice Howard's red eyes, his weary face. "They found her body in the pond. We need you to take some stills—for evidence." Howard lowered his head. "I knew something was wrong. She didn't seem herself, and everyone knew she was unhappy about returning to Hollywood. And after what she said on stage, they're all guessing it's suicide."

Suicide? The thought hadn't crossed Frank's mind, yet he had information the others didn't. He had the letters. Of course they'd think it was suicide. *Everyone around here thinks things are safe.* Yet he'd have to check things out before he gave his opinion on the matter.

It took two hours for the sun to cast enough light on the scene for Frank to get good shots. He swallowed hard and tried to control his trembling hands as he photographed Kat, floating near the bushes at the far end. Another hour passed, while he took more photos of the area around the pond, and they waited for someone to get Mickey. A low fog hung in the valley, hiding the town below and chilling Frank to the bone. But even worse were his pained thoughts.

It's happening just as the letters said. Why didn't I do more? I should have stuck closer to those singers. Someone's after them, all right. How come I let Kat go—running off without following her? It's my fault. I could have stopped this…

Frank lifted his eyes and spotted Mickey walking up the trail, with his head hanging low. The older man was distraught when he arrived, and he hung back—not getting too close to the pond—staring in disbelief.

Every face mirrored Mickey's. The five MPs on the scene had seen Kat at the show the night before. They'd discussed her words and the way she ran off the stage. They talked about the reasons why she'd want to take her own life. And their assumptions about suicide were confirmed in their own minds when Mickey told them about Edward's death. Frank listened with interest, but he still wasn't convinced. *Marv has me here for a reason…*

As soon as Frank heard about Edward's death, he knew that's what had bothered Betty yesterday. Frank didn't know Betty's reasons for not telling him, but he had two ideas. First, it was just the type of story the news would jump on, giving Kat no peace. And second, Kat needed time to process it herself. Frank only wished he'd known last night—it would have made more sense about why everything had happened as it had with Betty. More than that, he might have taken Kat's disappearance more seriously. He might have acted sooner when Kat wasn't at the estate.

There was also the matter of trust. A twinge of regret circled his heart, and he wished the innocent, sweet Betty could have trusted him.

If Betty had told me about Kat, and she told me not to tell, I would have kept it to myself. And maybe I could have proven myself to her.

Of course, while he knew keeping his word was something he took seriously, Betty didn't know that. As much as they were attracted to each other, they hadn't yet built any level of trust.

And he couldn't be too hard on her when he also hid so much. His excuse was that he couldn't tell her—just like he hadn't been able to share any of the information the OSS had given him. Before now that hadn't bothered him. Now it did. Frank wished he could talk to Betty about the letters. To warn her. Obviously there was some truth behind them. His only answer was that they all pack up and leave before anyone else got hurt. Maybe he didn't need to figure it out. Maybe just getting everyone to leave would be good enough. But what would happen then? Would he ever see Betty again?

Frank looked toward the valley and the fog below, kicking at a stick on the ground.

We need answers. We need truth. He hoped time was on his side, and that no one else would lose their life while he tried to figure out what was going on.

They waited until Mickey had left, and then the MPs pulled the body from the water. Frank took more shots. He also waited around to talk to the officer from the special investigative division of the military police, who had driven up from Nuremberg. Frank assumed that once the MPs heard whose body was found, they'd decided to send in their bigwig.

"Hey, Frank."

Hearing his voice, Frank turned and saw Howard approaching with an older MP. The man wore the familiar black armband with white letters. He was tall, with reddish blond hair. His jaw was tight, his eyes sharp.

"This is Officer Gordon Frey. I told him you got shots of the scene, and he wondered if he could get copies today."

"Sure. I can develop them after I finish up here." Frank looked to where a few of the other MPs loaded Kat in a large, canvas bag. "I told the other guys to try to disrupt as little as possible around the pond—said you'd want to get a look at it."

Officer Frey waved a hand in the air. "I told them not to worry too much about that. From what I hear there were some sixteen hundred witnesses who heard Miss Wiseman say she no longer wanted to live." Officer Frey turned, staring at the pond. "Sad, isn't it. Someone with so much beauty, so much potential, not feeling like going on."

"Can I talk to you about that?" Frank rubbed his brow, trying to figure out which concerns he wanted to talk about first. "I know the other MPs think it was suicide. Is that what you think too?"

"Well, I still need to look at the body before I can give an official ruling, but that's where we're leaning—off the record, of course," Officer Frey said.

"Off the record—yes. I'm an Army Corps combat photographer, not a news hound. Writing the news isn't my job." Frank cleared his throat. "Would you consider other possibilities, sir, such as murder? I'm friends with Kat's roommate, Betty Lake. I was with Betty when we first got to Wahnfried last night and discovered Kat wasn't there. After Howard stayed around to assist Mickey, I hiked home, from the estate to town, and I passed this pond."

"This pond?" The MP's eyes sparked new interest.

"Yes. I was here—around midnight I think—and there wasn't a body. The woods were still, and I didn't see any footprints close to the bank."

"You looked that hard? You actually stopped and looked around on your way home?" The investigator's brow furrowed, and he pulled a small notebook from his jacket pocket, jotting down some notes. "Can you tell me more?"

"I took it slow and swept my flashlight over the whole path along the way. I'd been with Betty for a few hours by that time, you see, and we were worried because Kat hadn't arrived home. Betty told me how Kat walked that trail home after the concerts, and how she'd been spooked a few nights ago—Kat thought someone was following her."

"You know all this, and you didn't come to the MPs?"

"The MP was there. Howard was there as we talked it through."

"Yes," Howard quickly jumped in, "but nothing told us there was a problem, sir. All we knew for sure was that Kat hadn't arrived home. She could have been out with friends, or—"

The investigator eyed them again. Then his lips curled in a half smile. "I'm sure you couldn't have known. No one could." Then he turned his gaze and focused on Frank. "But I'd like to talk to you more—when you drop those photos off, maybe? You can be a big help." Officer Frey's smile widened, but the look in his eye was focused, intense.

Frank's stomach flipped, and for some reason the request didn't seem as simple as it sounded.

"Yes, sir, of course."

* * * *

Betty looked up at the trees, spreading like an umbrella above her. It was strange how this town was still under German control when the leaves first budded. Now, they were changing colors and falling to the ground. It made her wonder what her life would be like here by the time the leaves budded again.

She glanced at the fountain on the back patio of Wahnfried, imagining how beautiful it would have been when water actually bubbled and flowed. Then she turned her attention back to her friends, sitting around the patio with her, as they talked about their next concert. The idea of a memorial concert came up before it really sank into everyone's mind and heart that Kat was gone.

"We should do it big—just like Kat would. We should sing all her favorite songs," Irene said.

Betty listened and nodded, but it was the house—not her friend's words—that drew her attention. She stared at the back of the large structure and realized that the bombing was more evident from this side. The back wall was crumbled, revealing interior rooms that had been looted. Even though she knew their part of the house had been walled off and declared perfectly safe, it still made Betty feel vulnerable to see everything exposed like that. She was thankful two MPs had been posted by the front door and two more at the end of the long driveway, but wondered if that was enough.

"I wonder what Mickey will think of our idea?" Dolly said, picking up a yellow leaf from the lawn and twirling the stem in her fingers. "He looked pretty crushed this morning when he told us the news. I wonder if he'll stay around? Or if this will be too much for him."

"Of course he'll stay. He really doesn't have much to go back to." Shirlee shrugged. "Whether he likes it or not, we're it."

"I wonder if the band knows?" Pearl asked. "Do you think Mickey told them?"

"I'm sure he did—or found some way to let them know." Irene lowered her head. "I just feel so bad. I mean if any one of us would have followed her—talked to her. She might have made a different choice."

"But what if it wasn't her choice?" The words were out before Betty had time to weigh whether she should say them.

"What do you mean?" Esther glanced over at her, eyes narrowed.

Betty shrugged, and then she pulled her crossed legs closer to her chest. "I don't know. I just keep thinking about what Kat said the other morning—remember when we were at breakfast? She didn't want to walk the trail up to the Festspielhaus alone anymore. She said that she heard footsteps following her."

"Don't talk like that." Shirlee rose to her feet. "It's bad enough being sad about Kat. You don't need to get us all scared about living here too."

"I'm sorry." Betty shook her head. "I can't believe Kat did this—to herself."

"I can." Pearl's lower lip trembled. "She didn't want to return to Hollywood—and now she didn't have her husband. She had nothing to live for."

Out of the corner of her eye, Betty saw Dolly and Irene's gazes on her, and she knew what they were thinking. Mickey had demanded she not tell anyone about Kat's condition, in order to save her reputation, but Betty wondered if it wasn't to save *his*. Something had happened with Mickey back in Hollywood, and no doubt Kat's death would add another stain to his reputation. Maybe the idea that Mickey couldn't control his girls—that they were sneaking around with who-knows-who, doing who-knows-what—would be something he couldn't rise from. That—and the fact that Betty was the only one Kat had confessed her pregnancy to. And who was she, a canteen girl who'd only been in Bayreuth for a few days. What did she know?

"I'm sorry I made you upset, Shirlee." Betty stood. "I'm going to change and head into town. I need to stretch my legs—do something. Anyone want to come?"

No one commented. Instead, they averted their gazes as she looked around the circle. "Okay, well, let me know if you need anything at the PX. I'll be happy to get it for you."

Betty tried to keep her steps light as she walked past the boarded-up back door, around to the front of the house.

The MPs watched as she neared. One of them opened the door as she approached. "Doing okay, miss?"

Betty nodded. "As well as can be expected, I suppose."

She entered the house and walked down the hall, preparing herself for what she knew she had to do. She'd be walking into her room for the first time after hearing of Kat's death.

"I just won't look at her things. I'll only get what I need and leave," she told herself.

As Betty approached her room, she saw that the door was open, and she paused. Her heart pounded in her chest and she was thinking about turning around and getting one of the MPs when she heard the voices of two men—one of which she recognized.

Betty walked to the doorway and peered in. Her gaze first fell on Howard, the MP who'd helped them so much last night—although he looked more official today in his full military uniform, including his helmet. Betty also noticed his pistol on his hip. She was sure it had been there last night, but now it took on a whole new meaning. Howard was talking to an MP officer, and both scanned the room, talking in low tones.

"Can I help you?" she asked.

"Sir, this is Betty Lake, Kat's roommate—the one I told you about."

The officer strode over, taking her hand in his. "Hello, Betty, it's nice to meet you. I'm sorry we startled you, being in your room like this. We were just looking over Kat's things." He patted her hand then released it.

"I understand." Even as she said the words, her brow furrowed. "Is there anything I can help you with?"

"Yes, in fact there is. First of all, we were looking for the telegram— the one that told her of Edward's death. It's a very important piece of evidence. Have you seen it?"

"Yes, I saw it yesterday. My friend Irene had it. She's out back. Would you like me to go get her?"

"In a minute, dear." He spoke to her as if she was a child, and looked at her in the same way. The man cleared his throat. "Before you go to find your friend, I have another question—did you happen to see anything? A letter or note that Kat might have left? Something that would have stated her intentions?"

"A suicide note?"

The man cocked an eyebrow. "Well, I wasn't going to state it so bluntly, but yes, that is what we're looking for."

Betty glanced around, remembering how she and the other girls had hung out in here and how Dolly had fallen asleep on Kat's bed, but as far as she could remember, they hadn't seen a note of any sort. They hadn't moved anything like that—and they would have known what it was if they'd found it.

"No, sir. When I came back here last night, I assumed everything was as Kat left it when she went to the opera house—and I didn't see a note." Betty moved over to her bed and sat. "I don't think Kat committed suicide. And if I'm right, there won't be a note."

The man approached, standing in front of her. He had reddish blond hair and a ruddy complexion. He reminded Betty of the young soldier sitting next to her on the plane ride into Nuremberg, but this man was older and much more serious. He pulled out a small notebook. "And can you tell me why you don't think that, Miss Lake?"

Betty brushed her hair from her cheek and tried not to let the war inside her become evident on her face. More than anything she wanted to tell the man about Kat's pregnancy, but that was impossible.

If she told, Mickey would be mad at her for sure. She'd most likely get fired—sent home.

"Well—" she finally said. "Even though everyone thinks Kat didn't have anything to live for, I have a feeling she did." She blew out a slow breath. "And then, the other night, Kat told us that someone had been following her on the trail. She tried to shrug it off and said it was only kids, but I think it really spooked her."

"The mysterious footsteps on the trail. That photographer—what was his name?" The man flipped back in his notebook. "Yes, here it is. Frank Witt told me the same thing. While that's interesting, it's not enough for me to change my mind."

"You spoke to Frank?"

"Yes, this morning. He was the one who took photos for us—of the body."

Betty was glad she was sitting, because with his words, tears filled her eyes, and her chest felt as if someone had set a piano on it. She found it hard to breathe.

"Bet— Miss? Are you okay?" Howard asked, kneeling in front of her.

She nodded that she was, and sucked in a breath, forcing it down. In her mind's eye, she tried to picture Kat in the water. But she quickly pushed that thought away. *Don't go there. Don't think of that. Remember how she was yesterday, before the telegram. Remember how she was during rehearsal, singing and dancing. Don't think—don't think of the pond.*

"Howard, can you do me a favor?" She wiped her eyes with the back of her hand. "Can you see if someone would be interested in giving me a ride to town? I'd like to talk to Frank. I just need his support right now."

Howard looked to the officer, and the man nodded his approval.

"Sure, Betty. Just tell me when you're ready, and I'll see what I can do."

"Thank you." She watched the man scribbling down more notes. She wondered what he wrote—wondered if she'd said something she shouldn't have. Something that would upset Mickey.

Dear Lord, I don't know what to do here. I know this feeling I have in my gut, but I don't know what to do with it.

It was a fleeting prayer. There and then gone. She wished she could get an answer from God—wished He could just stand before her and tell her what to do, what to say. But since that wasn't possible, she hoped to get help from the next best place.

I need to talk to Frank.

CHAPTER NINETEEN

Frank couldn't begin to estimate the number of photos he'd taken during the war. Of troops, of bomber squads, of mid-air fire fights, of bombings and even of bombers—filled with guys he knew—crashing to the ground. He'd also taken photos of Nazi spies, of citizens caught in the bombing, and of former prisoners of the camps, but nothing was as painful as developing the photographs of Kat. Maybe it was because the war was supposed to be over. Or maybe because she looked like an angel.

She lay on her back, her arm entwined in a branch. Her eyes were closed, and her face was deathly pale. Her hair fanned out around her face, one strand crossing her forehead. Even as he was taking the photo, Frank had the urge to reach down and brush it back from her face.

She wore the white dress she'd worn for the last performance, and in mid-range shots, she looked like a large white flower floating on the top of the pond—her dress splayed out as it would if she were twirling during a dance number.

Anger bubbled up inside him. Someone had done this. Just like the letters had promised. But who? Why?

He hung the photos to dry and then paused. From the way the investigator sounded, this was a suicide—open and closed. Yet as

Frank looked at the developing photos, his thoughts ping-ponged back and forth in his mind.

Why was Kat a target?

Was the person who wrote the letters the one who killed her?

What was he trying to say? Trying to prove?

Were Betty and the other girls in danger? Should he advise Mickey to send everyone home?

He also thought about Kat's body showing up like it had. It didn't make sense.

Maybe Kat's body was under the water. Maybe that's why I didn't see her. Or maybe she did it after I left. Maybe it was suicide after all, and there was no connection with the letters.

I need time—more time to look over these photos. More time to think this through.

Frank looked to the film. As always, he would turn the film over when he turned over the prints. In the normal military, his job was to take the prints and the army's job was to put them to use, to copy them or distribute them. But for his work in the OSS, he could make prints for himself as needed—just as long as he destroyed them when he was done.

With an extra set of photos, I'll have more time to try to figure this out.

And if not...

Frank pushed that last thought out of his mind. That wasn't an option. If he didn't figure it out, someone else could be next. The thing was, he couldn't let anyone else know about the extra prints. Making them and having them was enough for him to be discharged in his "normal" line of military work, and he'd hate to have to dance around the questions of why he was the exception to the rule.

Frank kept his gloves on and returned to the film. Of course, then there were those times he made copies for himself that had nothing to do with his undercover work. From the last set of photos, he'd made a few copies for himself—of Betty. One of her on stage and two behind the scenes.

Frank had finished hanging the second set of prints when a knock sounded on the door of the darkroom. His shoulders tightened, he took in a breath and approached the door.

"Yeah?" he asked, leaning close to it.

"Hey, it's me." Art's voice filtered through the door.

"Do you need to use the darkroom? I'm almost done," Frank asked.

"No, uh, that's not it. There's actually someone here to see you."

"Okay, let me clean up. I'll be out in a jiffy."

Frank's heart pounded in his chest, and he wondered if it was the MP Officer, Frey, coming for the prints. Frank had told Frey that he'd bring the prints to headquarters, but what if he'd changed his mind?

Frank cleaned up the solutions, but there was nothing he could do about the prints. If he took them down he'd ruin them for sure. He'd have to leave them there and hope for the best with Art.

Taking another deep breath, he exited the darkroom and made his way down to the living area of the house, which had mostly been unused by him or Art. Rounding the corner of the hall, he saw Howard sitting there, and next to him, Betty.

Frank released the breath he didn't know he'd held, and then his heart seemed to split in two when he saw how sad she looked—how frightened. Her hair was held back by a scarf and she wore her USO trousers and jacket. She looked more like a factory worker than a USO singer—so young, innocent, and completely overwhelmed. *I have to protect her. I have to figure this out.*

"Hey there." Frank entered and sat on the sofa next to her. "How are you doing?"

Betty shrugged. "Fine—I suppose. I—I don't know what to think. I just feel bad. Poor Kat."

"I know." Frank patted her hand, resting it there. Then he looked to Howard. "Thanks for giving Betty a ride. I assume you're checking out things at the estate?"

Howard shrugged. "Not too much. Especially not anything that rules out suicide." He rose. "Maybe your photos will make us see something in a new light, but I doubt it."

Frank felt Betty's hand ball into a fist under his hand, and he could tell she didn't agree with Howard. He didn't either.

"Can I ask you?" Frank rose. "Is there a reason why the MPs are content with simply calling it a suicide? Are they afraid anything else will stir trouble in the local population?" Frank ran a hand down his chin. "Or maybe there's just so much happening in Nuremberg, with the war trials and all, that hunting down a possible murder suspect is the last thing the investigator wants to think about?"

Howard's eyes narrowed. "Are you saying our offices are negligent in handling this case?"

Frank shrugged. "I'm not saying any such thing. I'm just surprised your superior didn't take my statement more seriously, that's all."

"Just because you didn't see Kat in the pond last night, doesn't mean she wasn't there—or at least that's what Frey said." Howard cocked his chin upward.

Frank could see Betty studying his face from the corner of his eye, but he refused to look at her. *Foolishness!* Didn't these guys know how to investigate? More than that, didn't Howard know how to keep his mouth shut?

"Also, it's because of what we've learned," Howard spouted before Frank had a chance to respond. "No matter what happens there will be one hundred different people who will see the same thing one hundred different ways. We're here to enforce the laws handed down to us, and as far as I'm concerned, we've handled this case fairly."

"Sure." Frank nodded, trying to hold in his frustration. He led the man to the door, realizing he'd probably pushed his questions as far as he could without making an enemy. "Forgive me for my bluntness. This is so close to home, you know? I mean, I think all of us feel that Kat's death was preventable. I guess I'm used to being removed from the human drama. After being up in the air during most of the war, maybe I don't know how to handle this stuff on the ground." He softened his face with a smile. "I trust your judgment."

Howard nodded his acknowledgment and then tipped his helmet to Betty. "Hope things are better soon, miss."

"Yes, me too. It's a shock. I'm sure we'll adjust, after we have time to grieve." She offered a sad smile. "We're already discussing a memorial concert."

"That will be good," Howard said, striding out the door. "I think a little music to lift our spirits would do us good."

After the door shut, Frank turned back to Betty.

"I'm so sorry, Betty. I didn't listen to you last night. Maybe if we'd acted sooner…"

Betty looked to her hands folded on her lap. "I don't think it would have mattered. I'm assuming that by the time we realized she wasn't at the Wahnfried she was already—gone." She then stood and walked to the front window, looking out at the houses and the park across the street. "I'm thankful you're at least challenging the officials to not just accept that it was suicide without looking into it."

Frank nodded and approached her. "You know what I think. You heard me tell Howard my thoughts. What about you, Betty?" Frank wanted to know her heart. He also wanted to know if she'd heard anything from anyone else. Quiet lips, he was learning, was not standard procedure around here.

"Well." She sighed. "I'm the only one at the estate who thinks Kat didn't kill herself."

"Is it because of Edward? Do they all think Kat did this because of his death?"

Betty's eyes widened in surprise. "You know?"

"Yes, Mickey told the MPs this morning—and I was there."

"Yes, taking photos. I heard. It must have been awful."

"It was…" He let his voice trail off, thinking of the photos hanging in the darkroom.

Art's footsteps echoed upstairs, in their shared bedroom, and Frank knew it would be better if he and Betty continued their talk elsewhere. He'd most likely have a better chance of Betty opening up if she wasn't worried about someone else overhearing.

"You know, Betty, I think we both want to talk about what happened, but I—I was wondering if you'd like to walk and talk? It's a bit chilly, but I'd feel more free, talking as we walk."

"Yes, of course." She stood and buttoned the top button of her jacket. "Fresh air will do me good."

They walked to the edge of town, past the current shopping district—the area that used to be military barracks but was now flattened by bombing—to the road leading out of town.

When they got to a small street with simple houses, Frank took Betty's hand.

"I'm sorry I couldn't tell you about Edward's death," she said. "Kat, well, she asked us not to tell."

"I understand, Betty. It's hard keeping secrets, isn't it?"

Even as Frank said the words, he thought of so many things he couldn't tell her about, including the extra set of photos hanging in the darkroom. Frank had locked the door, and he was pretty sure Art wouldn't try to go in there, but just knowing that two sets hung there made him worry. He was usually more careful than this.

"I have a question, though." Betty's brow furrowed. "Howard mentioned you didn't see a body in the pond. When was that? What was he talking about?"

"Last night when I walked home from Wahnfried..."

Betty paused to face him. "You did have to walk home, didn't you? Howard was with us. I'm so sorry. I didn't even think about that."

"Don't worry." He continued forward, and she picked up her pace, keeping in step with him.

"Betty, I walked by the pond, and I didn't see Kat. Either her body was under the water or it happened after—and that was around midnight."

Betty was silent, and for a moment, Frank wondered if she'd heard him.

"Betty?" he asked.

"I heard you. I'm trying to think about it. Trying to make sense of it, but I can't get it straight in my mind."

Frank eyed the heaps of rubble and broken fragments of walls standing like monoliths, stark against the gray sky. "Yeah, I can't make sense of it either."

His soul ached from the sights around him and from the fact that things weren't getting better.

"This whole place is broken, isn't it?" Frank said, noticing the sadness etched on Betty's face. "You'd think we'd get used to pain and loss, but I don't think we can."

"No, especially when it doesn't make sense. Pain in war is understandable, but—not this." She sighed. "Things are supposed to be better, right? We won the war. Where is that happily-ever-after ending we looked forward to?"

"It's not on this earth." Frank kicked at a piece of crumbled brick. "Sometimes I doubt if we'll ever find it."

"We still search for it."

"Yes, I know." He shook his head. "We try to bring normality into hard places, don't we? The other day I was surprised to find gift shops, tailor shops, and a portrait studio that had already popped up amidst the rubble to serve the Americans. I hear a movie theater and soda fountain are coming next."

"And let's not forget the candy and tobacco in the pocket of every GI." She sighed. "It's as if we think if we focus on those things we'll forget the brokenness around us."

They walked for a little while longer and crested a hill. When they reached the top, Betty tugged on his arm. "Frank, look."

He followed her gaze and his eyes narrowed. It was a long, wretched column of men, women, and children.

"Where are they coming from? What's going on?" she asked.

"I've heard the guys talking about this," he answered. "They are Sudeten Germans pouring over the border every day from Czechoslovakia. Hitler took that part of Czechoslovakia first, and many Germans took up residence there. Now they are no longer welcome."

"Is that a nice way of saying they're being driven out?"

"Yes."

Frank eyed the sad-looking group for a while. Everyone looked so weak and scared. Seeing them made his heart ache. Frank placed his hand on the small of Betty's back. "Maybe we should turn back." *We've had enough heartache for one day,* he wanted to add.

They turned away from the spectacle, and then they walked in silence, lost in their thoughts. As they drew closer to Frank's house, he looked over at her. "I can find a ride for you—back to Wahnfried if you'd like. I wish I could go with you myself, but I have to deliver some photos."

Betty looked over at him, and her expression said she knew exactly what photos they were. "A ride would be great. Thank you."

"Betty, I also want you to promise me you won't go anywhere alone. That you will keep the house locked—"

She cut him short. "They've posted MPs at the house. Mickey's not going to let anything happen to us. I'm pretty sure that even if they officially say it was suicide, we're going to have security watching over us for a while."

"That's good. That makes me feel better."

He said the words but he didn't mean them. Only discovering the truth would make him feel better, Frank knew.

They turned back onto his street. Frank paused, and then he softly took Betty's shoulders and turned her toward him. "I—I've also been thinking about us, Betty. I want you to know me. Trust me. Trust my heart. And I want to get to know you better too."

"I appreciate that." Betty nodded as she said the words, but Frank could see something else in her eyes—confusion.

"I'd still like to spend more time with you. Maybe it's my way to make sure you're safe." That wasn't a lie.

"You better get going." She patted his lapel, and he appreciated how she tried to smile despite her sadness. "I see Howard up there. I'll go ask for a ride."

Sure enough, Frank turned and spotted Howard. He was sitting in his jeep, clearly watching them. He didn't avert his gaze when Frank met his eyes. He just continued to stare, to watch.

An icy cold wave of panic washed over Frank, and he wondered if Howard had returned after they'd left. If Art had let him in. If so, they could have found the second set of prints—

"Uh, sure, Betty. Go ahead and ask Howard for a ride." Frank smiled, hoping she couldn't see the worry in his gaze. "And you're right. I need to get back to work. I can guess that right now the press is being notified about Kat's death—Edward's death too. And maybe my photos will help them know what to officially report." He shrugged. "Or at least they'll have one more clue leading to the truth."

CHAPTER TWENTY

Frank tried not to act surprised when he walked into Denzel Bailey's office and saw Officer Gordon Frey sitting there with a scowl on his face. Something was wrong. Very wrong.

When Frank had first returned to his house, he'd been relieved to find Art gone and their house locked. The darkroom had remained locked too. Looking around the darkroom, Frank's guess had been that no one had touched his things. He packed up one set of prints and hid the second in his room, satisfied his secret was safe.

But now, from the look on Officer Frey's face, Frank wondered if Howard had gotten in, seen the second set of prints after all, and told Officer Frey about them. If so, he had a lot of dancing around the subject to do.

"Frank, would you have a seat?" Denzel motioned to a high-backed wooden chair.

Frank sat.

"Oh, can you close the door, please," Denzel said, and Frank's shoulders tightened at his friend's forced smile.

"Yeah, sure." Frank rose, closed the door, and his brow furrowed. He sat in the chair again, his posture erect and his stomach tight with tension. He looked from Denzel, to Officer Frey, then back to

Denzel again. Frank held the large folder of photos he'd developed, along with the film.

Frey had mentioned earlier that he might ask Frank more questions about what he saw—or rather, didn't see—last night on the trail, but from the tension in the room, something more was going on.

Why is Denzel acting so strange? Why is Officer Frey looking at me like that?

"So"—Denzel leaned forward, resting his arms on his desk—"Mr. Witt, I hear you have a problem with Officer Frey's investigative skills."

Frank's eyes widened. Mr. Witt? "Oh, no, sir." Back in England, he and Denzel had hung out at least once every week, maybe more. They'd trained together and taken leave together, but he'd never seen this side of his friend.

"Really? Is that true, Mr. Witt? You are *not* having a problem with my investigation?" Officer Frey crossed his arms over his chest. "One of the MPs, Howard Lenard, said you had a few questions for him today. He said that you questioned whether we'd investigated as we ought. According to him, you accused us—me—of falling short because I'm so focused on the war trials coming up in Nuremberg."

"No, sir, that's not what I meant. That sounds worse than I intended. I just know what I saw last night when I walked by that pond. I didn't see any sign of Kat in the water."

"That *is* a problem, you not seeing her in the pond. Especially when you claim to have been there after the time we assume she waded into the water. In fact, your statement is the one thing that keeps me from making a firm declaration. Everything else stacks up to suicide." Officer Frey rose and moved to the window, peering out. He stood there for a moment, watching whatever was happening in the street below him. Frank wondered if he should say something. Then he decided it was probably better that he kept quiet.

Frank looked to Denzel, but his friend quickly looked away, staring instead at the ticking clock on the wall as if timing the silence.

Finally, Officer Frey turned and leaned back, sitting on the wide windowsill. "We examined Katherine Wiseman's body and there indeed is no sign of injury. Her body was unmarked except for one small bruise on her arm that could have come from just about anything." Officer Frey turned and studied Frank's face.

"What about an autopsy, sir? Surely that would be the one thing that would tell us if she died by drowning—or by some other way."

"Where do you think we are? Do you think the Los Angeles County General Hospital is right next door? This was a war zone just a few months ago. We have thousands of bodies in the morgue— shouldn't all of them get the same treatment? Katherine Wiseman had a motive. She had the time to walk down there without anyone bothering her. There was no suicide note, but she spoke her intentions to an entire audience."

Frank nodded, wondering why Officer Frey would take the time to explain all this to him.

"There's only one thing that has me bothered, you see— it's your statement." Officer Frey's gaze bore into Frank. "Because of what you said, I've taken more time to think about who could possibly want Kat dead and what his, or her, motive would be. It was not a robbery. She was still wearing her wedding band. She was not physically assaulted. She was loved and adored by many. Then…"

"Then?" Frank asked.

"Then, I started thinking about who would benefit from her death, and there were only two people that came to mind—you, and your friend Betty."

Frank jumped to his feet. "Are you crazy?"

"Go ahead and sit, Frank. No one's saying you did it." Denzel rose, walked around the desk, and placed a hand on Frank's shoulder.

Frank felt his chest tighten, and he placed a hand over his heart. It had never beat so wildly—not even when he was in a bomber that was being shot at by ground artillery. Reluctantly, he sat.

Denzel released Frank's shoulder and returned to his chair behind his desk. "You're not saying that you think either of them did it, right, Officer Frey?"

Officer Frey folded his hands on his lap. "No. I don't think you killed her, *but* if someone did, the two of you would have the best motives."

"How's that?" Frank forced his voice to hold steady. "I don't know how you could say that."

"First of all, Songbird had the most direct access to Kat. She was no doubt trusted too. And now—" Officer Frey sighed. "Now, she'll always be known as the girl who stepped up to save the day, by singing Kat's last number. More than that, now she's gonna be the star."

"Betty was either singing or with me. Besides, there's no way she could have killed Kat. She's as gentle as a kitten. If you knew her, you'd know it's impossible."

"That's also the conclusion I came to. That's why I turned my attention to you." Officer Frey said this in such an even tone Frank wasn't sure he heard him correctly.

Frank placed the envelope on his lap and pressed his hands into his forehead, feeling an ache come on. Then he turned his gaze to his friend. "Oh, come on, Denzel, we've known each other for years. How can you possibly sit there and listen to this?"

Instead of answering, Denzel looked away.

Officer Frey stretched out his hand to the package Frank held. "Are those the photos?"

"Yes, sir." Frank handed him the envelope.

Officer Frey opened the envelope and slid the photos out onto the desk. On the top of the pile were photos of Kat on stage the night before. There were a dozen decent shots. There were also a few of her running off the stage.

"I'm sure the newsmen will ask for these." Officer Frey turned to Denzel. "You know how those newsmen are, don't you? They're always on the lookout for that one shot that will epitomize what they can't say in a thousand words. We've seen it before. There are photos of D-Day and Iwo Jima that have made their way into the hearts and minds of every American. There wasn't a paper in America that didn't print those shots. I have a feeling, these last ones of Katherine Wiseman will get the same attention."

Officer Frey sat at the desk, took one of the photos from the stack, and placed it in front of Frank. It was one of Kat on stage. Frank had captured her just as she first stumbled over the words to the song. Her blond hair was perfectly coiled. Her white dress flowed around her like an angel's gown. The tops of soldiers' heads were barely seen at the bottom of the photo, but Kat was not looking toward them. Instead, her face was lifted. She looked up into the sky with sad, mournful eyes. Her mouth circled in a sweet O, and tears rimmed her eyes. Her hands were partially lifted as if she wanted to lift off the stage and escape. It was a beautiful shot if Frank said so himself.

"This is a great photo, Frank. If Kat were to head home and start her movie, it might have made it to the back page of the Society Section. But now…"

Frank felt his hands begin to shake, and he was unsure if he was hearing correctly. He knew where Officer Frey was leading the conversation, but he didn't know what to say—how to stop his words.

"Now that Katherine Wiseman is dead, this photo is going to make the front page of a thousand papers. No, make that ten thousand papers. Everyone is going to know this photo, Frank. And how lucky for you. You got the worst assignment known for a combat photographer, taking photos of showgirls—and now it's the best luck you've had. I saw you signed up for high school classes too—need to finish, do you, so you can get a better job? That's not going to be needed now. Not with this photo of Katherine Wiseman."

Frank felt sick, and he wondered if he'd lose his lunch. Pain tightened around his gut and moved to his chest. He looked to Denzel, waiting for his friend to comment, disagree, anything. Denzel met his gaze, but his face remained expressionless.

Denzel's not falling for this, is he?

"Do you—you really think—" Frank swallowed hard, forcing down the mix of anger and pain that tried to force its way up his throat. "Do you think that I would do this? I can't believe you're saying that." Frank scooted to the edge of his seat, reaching a hand to Denzel as if reaching for a lifeline. "You know me. We've worked together for years. I'm a good man—a Christian man—I would never do such a thing."

Denzel cleared his throat. "You put yourself there, on the crime scene, Frank. You told us you walked up that trail alone…"

"If there were any chance I was guilty, do you think I would have admitted to you that I was on that trail?" Frank ran his fingers through his hair and then lowered his gaze. He wished Marv were here. Marv would stick up for him—wouldn't he?

Dear God, please. I know I haven't been talkin' to You much lately, but I need Your wisdom. You've got to help me out here.

"Frank," Officer Frey said softer, gentler than the harsh tone he'd used earlier.

Frank lifted his face, wiping the sweat beading across his brow. He met the man's gaze, and then Officer Frey laid out the other photos on the desk. The photos of Kat in the water. The ones of her floating, eyes closed, pale, dead.

"Did you do this, Frank?"

"No, sir. I didn't."

"If you didn't, do you know anyone else who would have a motive to kill such a beautiful woman?"

Frank shook his head. "No, I'm sorry. I don't know that either. I mean if she wasn't robbed or—hurt." Frank thought of the letters. He couldn't discuss them, even if they'd save him from these accusations. Not that they held any answers, only more questions.

"I can't think of any other motive either—not a good one. Not one that's worth pouring time and resources into. Besides, there's the fragility of our situation to consider. If I even mention the word *murder,* it's going to stir up a lot of old fears that have been boiling under the surface. Right now, everyone's getting along as well as can be expected. Jews are living among the Germans again. American GIs are welcomed around German tables for dinner. Displaced persons are finding jobs, homes. Fear leads to many unpleasant things. Old pains could be resurrected. A lot more people could lose their lives if they turn on each other. All the good we've done could vanish overnight."

Frank nodded, understanding what the man was saying. There would be fear. There could even be further problems between the numerous nationalities living within the borders of the town.

Maybe they should be afraid. More things, worse things could happen if the killer isn't caught—if there is, in fact, a killer.

Frank thought about it for a moment. To say Kat was murdered opened the door to looking for a murderer. Someone who set out to hurt her. Someone who would have a reason to do such a thing.

Maybe the letters had no connection. Maybe the letters were just a way for someone to try to get the Americans to leave.

Maybe Officer Frey's right—maybe it was suicide.

"And then there are the other USO women we have to think about," Officer Frey continued. "I can't imagine them wanting to stay if they think they could be next."

"Yes, I could imagine that happening," Denzel commented, finally saying something.

Betty could leave. I'd never get to know her.

But maybe she should leave—maybe it's dangerous. Maybe she should go where it's safe.

The two thoughts battled each other.

Frank wanted her safe, but he also wanted her here. Near him.

"I understand all this, sir."

"I don't think you do, Frank." Officer Frey leaned forward in his seat. "I honestly don't. But if I were to investigate, you know now the direction I'd head first."

"Yes, sir, I understand."

"I don't want to investigate. I'd like to stick to my initial conclusion that Katherine Wiseman lost her life at her own hand."

"Thank you, sir." Frank let his arms drop to his sides, letting tension slide off his shoulders.

Officer Frey nodded, and then he turned his attention to Denzel. "Denzel, from what I hear, there will be newspapermen arriving soon. I've prepared a statement discussing Katherine Wiseman's unfortunate suicide."

Officer Frey lifted a satchel from the floor, took out a slip of paper, and placed it in front of Denzel. "I'd like this release to go out to each reporter, and"—He took the angelic photo of Kat and also placed it in front of the man—"and this photo. The statement talks about the death of Katherine's husband, and her gracious attempt to perform one more time for the servicemen she loved, before being overcome by grief. It's a touching story, if I say so myself. It's a nice final tribute to a beautiful woman."

Officer Frey rose, returned the rest of the photos to the envelope, tucked them into his satchel, and then walked to the door. "I'll walk you out, Frank. You can attend the press conference with me."

"If it's okay with you, sir, I'll sit this one out." Frank stood, willing his legs to support him.

"The newspapermen might be interested in speaking with you—in hearing the thoughts of the man who took this last, beautiful shot of Katherine Wiseman."

"No offense, sir. I'd rather stay out of this. I'm sorry she's gone, and I don't need any honors."

Officer Frey nodded. "I understand, Frank. I think you're making a wise decision. Let's let Katherine's memory remain, with all the wonderful things she accomplished in her lifetime. She's responsible for her life—and her death. Let's not muddle that up with opinions."

CHAPTER TWENTY-ONE

Frank walked aimlessly down the cobblestoned street, unsure of what had just transpired in Denzel's office.

"What was that about? How could Frey think I had anything to do with this?"

He stopped short when he realized he was mumbling to himself. He turned and stared at a small church, replaying the events of the last twenty minutes over and over in his head. Trying to make some sense of the situation. Finally, he realized what he was staring at.

Unbelievable. Frank hadn't noticed the small church before, even though he'd walked from his house to headquarters and back numerous times. It was a small, brick building, tucked between two taller, partially destroyed structures, as if forgotten. Its size and location had probably protected it from the bombs. While the commercial buildings around it had crumbled, the small church stood.

He stepped to the side as other soldiers and citizens walked by.

As Frank gazed at the church, awed that even the stained glass windows were still in place, he thought about a scripture passage his mother had taught him as a child, "And the rain descended, and the floods came, and the winds blew, and beat upon that house; and it fell not: for it was founded upon a rock."

A rain of bombs fell, and this church still stands. If God protected it—He can protect me.

The thought filled Frank's mind even before he had time to process it. What amazed him, really, was that during his whole time in the war he'd never felt as attacked as he did now. When he flew bomber missions, an unseen enemy shot at their plane, but it wasn't him—personally—they were shooting at. It was the larger threat the plane represented.

There'd even been times during his undercover missions when he'd thought his cover had been blown, yet the tension he felt then was nothing compared to the ache inside of him now.

When Officer Frey—someone on *his side*—hurled those words, those accusations, it hurt. What rained upon him, pelted him hard, wasn't a physical attack, but fear. Fear that his effort to learn the truth about Kat would lead to unthinkable accusations. That by trying to find her and help her, he would be considered a potential suspect should her death be ruled a murder.

The thought of hurting another human being like that sickened him. And then, the realization that others would believe it. An accusation like that would hit every paper, just as Kat's death was about do. Marv might be able to come to the rescue, but not before Frank's name was slandered. That would be something no one would forget.

Poor Mom. Even though Frank knew she'd never believe it, he also knew her life would never be the same. *She'd never recover.* Lily's death had already shattered her heart. He wasn't sure she could handle more.

Lord, please don't let that happen—please.

Frank walked down the cracked sidewalk toward the church, feeling the pull of fellowship with God that he hadn't felt in many months—not since the battles had ended. It had been easy to pray, to read God's Word, and to think about eternity when he knew tomorrow he'd fly over enemy territory or head into dark alleyways. Sometimes he and the other guys would even pray together and encourage each other before the flight. Maybe that was because if the danger was close, they wanted—they needed—God closer.

Frank touched the door handle of the church, expecting it to be locked. Instead, the latch turned, and the door opened.

"Hello?" He stepped inside and let his eyes adjust to the light.

The room was small, dim. There was a narrow aisle and no more than ten worn, wooden pews on either side. Candles flickered at the altar. One woman—he assumed from her slumped position that she was older—sat in the front right corner, head lowered and covered with a shawl that hid most of her face.

He took in a deep breath, almost expecting to breathe in the same scent of flowers and women's cologne as he would at his church back home. Instead, odors of old wood, dust, and mildew met his nose. But that didn't matter. Peace overwhelmed him as he continued forward. Frank moved to the back pew, and his legs seemed to give out as if unwilling to carry his weight any farther.

In front of the wooden pew was a kneeling bench—dirty, torn, inviting—and he sank onto his knees. A million thoughts swirled around his head as Officer's Frey's words played in his mind.

You walked up that trail alone…

Everyone is going to know this photo…

How lucky for you...

He folded his hands and rested them on the back of the pew in front of him. Then he rested his forehead on his hands and realized they were shaking. Frank opened his mouth to pray, but the words didn't come. It was as if all the worries had built a wall between him and God. Even now, even here, he couldn't escape them.

"I want to give everything to You, God. Help me," he finally whispered. "I'm sorry I didn't come to You sooner, more often. Forgive me for forgetting You when things were going so well. How did I ever think I could handle life without Your daily help?"

The prayers continued, one at a time, as he had the strength to pray them.

"Protect"—he blew out a soft breath—"protect those that remain."

That was his greatest fear—that whoever killed Kat would strike again.

"You are the Protector," he prayed. "You watch over them even when I'm not there."

He still had a nagging in his heart that told him there was more going on with Kat's death than what was seen on the surface.

Should I trust this feeling, Lord? Should I continue to seek answers—even if I might be the one accused? He yearned for God's answer, right now, out loud. Even a letter, a telegram would be nice.

Am I putting the lives of the other USO women at risk because I'm afraid of hurting my own reputation? Or because I'm afraid of losing Betty?

"Lord, I don't know what to do. I've never felt so helpless as I did in that room. And my friend—even my friend didn't stand up for me."

As he prayed, Frank felt God lift some of the weight he carried. God was there. God was with him. God would always be with him.

Lifting his head, Frank noticed the woman who'd been praying near the front had disappeared. Then his gaze landed on the mural on the wall at the altar. In the painting, Jesus stood in the Garden of Gethsemane. Jesus' arm was outstretched to a man who carried silver coins in his hand. Behind the man, an army of Roman shoulders stood with swords ready to arrest the Son of God.

Jesus, You were accused. Your friends abandoned You...

"Dear Jesus," he whispered, the truth of that hitting him more than it ever had before. And it was at that moment that the ache of his heart transformed. The pain he felt wasn't simply the pain of his accusation and betrayal, it was that of Christ, who endured so much more. Tears rolled down his cheeks.

"Thank You, Jesus. Thank You for taking that on—for me."

He continued to sit there, thinking of all the times God had helped him and protected him since he left home and joined the army. Thinking back, there were too many to count. He should've died in the fighting. Many of his friends had, yet he still lived. God must have a reason. Maybe God had brought him to where he was for a purpose. Maybe it wasn't just Marv trying to set him up with a pretty girl. Maybe God did need a combat photographer shooting stills of pretty girls for a reason only God knew. And from the peace Frank felt deep inside, it wasn't to walk away.

Frank took in the mural again. "I understand, even if it means I lose everything, I need to stand firm," he whispered. "If something inside me tells me Kat did not do this to herself, I need to keep looking."

The scripture verse that had popped into his memory returned. Frank whispered it into the quiet of the sanctuary, "And the rain descended, and the floods came, and the winds blew, and beat upon that house; and it fell not: for it was founded upon a rock."

He didn't know what it meant, except that God would help him stand—or better yet, only with God as his foundation could he stand at all.

Help me to stand strong. Help me to be faithful. I won't give up. I'll continue searching for the truth, pursuing the truth.

Peace came over him, sweeter than anything he'd experienced, and then he rose, turning to leave. As he did, something on the pew—a slip of paper, torn from a book it seemed—fluttered to the floor.

Bending to retrieve it, Frank saw that someone had written a phrase in German, *Angst verleiht Flügel*. He scratched his head, almost certain that the paper hadn't been there before. Did the old woman leave it for him?

If so, what does it mean?

Then he looked at it again, closer.

I know this handwriting. It's the same as on the letters!

* * * *

Frank wondered if he should knock as he approached the back door of the Festspielhaus. He did, twice, and then waited. Maybe Oskar wasn't even here today, especially since there wouldn't be any practice—at least for a few days.

He stepped from side to side, rubbing his arms, hoping to keep warm. A chill numbed him as he'd climbed the hill. He wondered if he should test the doorknob, to see if it was open, but he changed his mind. Even if Oskar were here, working in one of the deep recesses, he didn't want to try to hunt him down. Or scare him by tromping up and down the halls.

Frank was just turning to walk away when the door opened.

"Yes?" It was Oskar's voice.

Frank turned.

"Oh!" Oskar's face brightened. "Mr. Witt—it is you."

"Please, call me Frank."

"Habits learned in one's youth are hard to break. I am older, yes, but you are an important man." Oskar ruffled his hair with one of his hands. In his other hand, he held some type of clamp.

"Yes, well, I don't know about that." The wind picked up, felt like an icy gale. Frank blew in his hands. "Can I come in for a moment?"

"Please do, it is cold out, but I am afraid there will not be rehearsal toda—" Oskar scowled. "Did you hear the horrible news?" He stepped back and let Frank hurry in, shutting the door behind him.

"Yes, Oskar. It is horrible. I feel so bad for Kat. But the truth is, I didn't come because of a rehearsal. I came to speak with you." His words echoed down the hall, and the silence overwhelmed Frank. Every other time he'd been to the Festspielhaus there had been singing, dancing, voices. Not today.

"Me? You came for me?" Oskar cocked an eyebrow curiously.

"Yes." Frank pulled the piece of paper from his pocket. "I found this note written in German, and I don't understand it."

He handed the paper to Oskar. Oskar's eyes widened for the briefest moment, and then his face returned to the same pleasant smile again.

"Did someone give you this note?" he asked.

"I—I don't think so. I found it on a church pew, and I suppose someone left it there. I'm curious, that's all. I don't know German."

"Yes, well, it is just a simple poem. Or rather proverb—I think that is how you say it. *Angst verleiht Flügel.* It would translate, 'Fear lends wings.'"

"Fear lends wings?" Frank rubbed his chin. "I have no idea what it means."

"It means, Mr. Witt, fear would make you do things you think impossible in any other situation."

"So you've heard this before? Is it common?"

"It is not common—not as common as other proverbs. But I have heard it before." Oskar's eyes narrowed, and for a moment, Frank wondered if Oskar remembered he was there. "I had someone I loved who told me this once. She is gone now."

Frank turned the words over in his mind. "I suppose it's true. Maybe fear does get us to do things we thought were impossible before. Mostly if our fear draws us to the places where we should have been in the first place." Frank thought about his moments in the church. Fear had driven him to the arms of God. Even though he wished he'd gone to God as easily during the good times as the hard ones, at least he'd gone.

Oskar nodded. A tear pooled in his eye, and Frank wondered if it were due to thoughts about his lost love.

"Yes, Mr. Witt. Sometimes the situations we are given change everything—even who we are deep inside," he said with a heavy sigh.

* * * *

Dierk viewed the opera's set, wondering where he'd gone wrong. He had never expected anyone would find this place—his secret room. But she had. How?

When Dierk had first seen the beautiful singer inside, he considered walking her home. Any gentleman would do such a thing. He'd walked her home many times, out of sight, just to make sure she arrived. There were many bad men in the forests.

Then, after they talked awhile, he saw that she had noticed things she shouldn't. The crates, the plans. He had no choice. No choice.

Dierk wished she could have sung one last song, but the plunge of the needle had caused a scream instead.

She was an angel. A beautiful messenger. And he had dressed her as such.

CHAPTER TWENTY-TWO

Betty glanced around the rehearsal room at the forced smiles, and it amazed her how everyone could sing, dance, and play when the only thing on all their minds was the fact that Kat's body was being shipped home tomorrow. It had been two days since Mickey had told them about her death. It still didn't seem real.

"Betty, did you hear?" Irene said during their first break. "They found another body. A lieutenant. It got me thinking about what you said."

Mickey strode out of the costume room. "No need to fret, Irene, no one's out to do harm. The guy's buddies heard the shot and said the lieutenant was the only one in his room. He was just depressed, you see, over so many of his men killed during the campaign. Took his own life."

Irene shook her head. "That makes no sense. His poor family. He fought to stay alive the whole war and now this."

Betty took Irene's hand. "Seems to me that it's another victory for the Germans. I wish he would have seen it that way. I wish someone would have known, would have talked to him."

Betty wondered if what Mickey said was the truth. She hoped so. *I wish I could talk to Frank about it.* It had also been two days since she'd seen him.

How come he isn't coming around?

The last time they'd talked was on their walk to the outskirts of Bayreuth, and since then he hadn't even stopped in to say hello.

"Okay, girls, take a ten-minute break while I talk to Oskar here about a backdrop idea I have for your next number," Mickey said with a wave of his hand.

"Sure, Mickey." Irene pulled up a chair, turned it around, and straddled it. "It's not like we haven't been sitting around enough. Practice makes perfect."

"I think I've forgotten how to sing," Dolly complained. "Or maybe my heart's not in it. I don't care if Mickey gives us an hour break. It just doesn't seem right—us being here."

Newspapermen had descended on the town of Bayreuth—or so they heard—telling the world the horrible news. They'd seen jeep after jeep of reporters coming down the main road, seeking to interview them on the death of their friend, but as ordered, the MPs on duty sent them away. They had no desire to talk about Kat's death—they were having a hard enough time coming to terms with it themselves. The hardest moment, perhaps, was when they saw the first headline. It became even more real at that moment.

Hollywood Starlet Katherine Wiseman Lost Husband and Will to Live. Wiseman's Death Ruled Suicide.

Mickey had brought a copy of the *Stars and Stripes* to Wahnfried. He'd also worked it out that their meals would be delivered too—at least for a couple of days. MPs had guarded the house day and night, to ease Mickey's mind. Even then, Betty had a hard time sleeping. Even after she and the other girls had packed up all of Kat's things and given them to Mickey to be sent back to the States, Betty couldn't help but think that Kat should be there—sleeping in the bed next to her with her silk eye mask on. Sometimes at night, she'd have to turn on her flashlight and check—she'd been so certain she'd heard Kat's breathing.

Ten minutes later, as promised, Mickey returned. He tried to run the rehearsal like everything was normal, but everyone could tell he was having a hard time of it. His hair wasn't combed as neatly as Betty was used to seeing. His smile wasn't nearly as bright. Even his complaints, his orders, his anger wasn't as sharp as usual. Betty found it strange that she actually missed those barks.

"Okay, I'm thinking through the line-up. I have the band playing four numbers, the Johnson Sisters doing three of their cha-cha acts. We also have the triplets singing two numbers. Good enough?" He looked up, peering out from under his bushy eyebrows, as if waiting for comments.

"What about solos?" Irene tapped her foot on the ground. "I mean we always have a few solos in the show."

"What would you like to sing? Give me some suggestions. What are some of Kat's favorites—something that could be a tribute to her?" Mickey asked.

"Oh, I wasn't thinking about me. I was thinking about Betty," Irene said. "The guys will be expecting the songbird to chirp." Even though Irene smiled as she said those words, Betty felt an underlying tension—possibly even resentment. Ever since her big blow-up with Mickey, things hadn't been quite right. All the women treated her with courtesy, but after she mentioned the possibility that maybe Kat didn't commit suicide—that someone could have taken her life—they remained distant. As if considering the thought would put them in danger too.

Mickey glanced over at Betty, and she could tell from his gaze he didn't want to use her, but Betty wasn't going to let him get off that easily. She bit her lip, wondering what she could do to get in his good graces again.

Maybe if I take back what I said about Kat's pregnancy and my concerns that someone did this?

Betty knew it would help, but she wondered if she could actually do it. *Do I lie? Do I shove down what I know and believe to be true in order to get them to like me?*

"Yeah, Mickey, give Betty a shot to show you what she has up her sleeve," Dolly said.

"Okay, Betty. The girls want you to sing." It was the first time Mickey had used her name, but it wasn't the sweet sound she'd expected.

She smiled as she remembered who she was and what she was here to do. *I've come to sing. It doesn't matter if Mickey thinks I'm trying to slander Kat. It doesn't matter if the other girls have a shield of protection around them—the guys will accept me. And they deserve a good show.*

"Okay, I have an idea. I remember hearing Kat on the radio once. She was singing 'Ain't Misbehavin' and she did it really jazzy like." Betty turned to the band, who awaited their instructions from Mickey.

She focused on Wally. "Why don't I start with a tap of my foot, and then you pick it up?"

Mickey eyed her and then stepped back. "So Betty thinks she's running the show now." He gave a harsh chuckle.

"Sorry, Mick, I don't mean to be stepping on your toes, but can we try?"

"Sure, Betty. Go for it."

Even though the look on his face was stern, Betty hoped by the time she finished singing, Mickey would warm up to her.

She turned to the band members. "Okay, I know you guys know the song—let's just try it and see what we come up with."

"Sure, Betty." Billy cast her a smile. "C'mon boys, let's jazz it up."

Betty started by tapping her foot in a lively rhythm, and on the tenth beat, Billy joined her, followed by the horns and then the wind instruments. Finally, the complete band played. On cue, Betty started to sing, "No one to talk to, all by myself...."

She smiled at the band, who indeed added their own jazz to the mix. Betty launched into the next line and decided to add her own flair with her feet. She sashayed up to the front of the practice stage just as Kat had modeled.

Seeing her, Irene whistled, and Dolly jumped to her feet and joined in. Not wanting to be left out, the Johnson sisters mimicked the steps until they had their own little production happening.

When the song was over, laughter spilled from Betty's lips, and cheers erupted around the room.

"See, I knew you had it in you," Dolly said, clapping.

Betty turned toward Mickey, her eyes wide, anticipating his excitement. Instead, he looked at her through half-lidded eyes. He didn't smile, didn't even nod.

"I think we'll wait on that one. It seems too cheerful, too soon. Besides, it needs work. The timing wasn't right. Betty's voice sounded weak."

Betty didn't know how to respond. For as long as she could remember, she'd never had a reaction like that when she sang.

"But Mickey, it was one of Kat's favorite songs. She would have loved it," Irene dared to say.

"Does anyone ever listen to me?" Mickey threw his hands up in the air. "We're not going to do that song. Maybe we're never going to do it." Then looking around, he lowered his voice. "We're all going to work together. Like a team. There aren't going to be any stars. Everyone's gonna be the same. These are the numbers that stand." He slammed his clipboard with the schedule on the floor. "This is the program. Everyone satisfied?"

"Yes, Mickey," Dolly started.

"Yes, Mickey," everyone else chimed in.

"I understand." Betty did her best to hold back her tears. She was a professional now. This wasn't the church choir. This wasn't some canteen. Mickey knew what he was doing, even though it didn't feel good.

"Fine. Why don't you take the rest of the day off. And maybe do some warm-ups or something. Your voices really stunk today." Mickey stalked out of the building, and they all stood quietly for a moment.

Betty stared at her feet, feeling foolish. Maybe her voice did sound as bad as Mickey said. She heard someone crying and looked up, and saw that Irene had her face in her hands.

"Hey, are you okay?" Betty asked.

Irene shook her head. "No."

"It's okay. Maybe our voices did sound bad, but we can practice tonight back at Wahnfried." Betty approached Irene and placed a hand on her shoulder.

"It's not that. I miss Kat being here. She would have stood up to Mickey. She would have given him a piece of her mind."

Dolly nodded. "Yeah, she would have. And she would have told Mickey that if he thought he could sing better to put on a dress and try it."

"I just can't believe she's really gone," Tony the saxophonist jumped in. "Even though I keep telling myself it's true, I keep expecting her to stomp out of that dressing room like she owns the place."

"I can believe it. I happened to be up here at the Festspielhaus when they were carrying the body bag off the trail," Billy said. "More than anything else, I'm mad at her. How could she do that? It was so selfish. Didn't she think how we'd feel? How all her fans would feel?"

"Enough of this moaning and weeping." Dolly stood. "We really should get our outfits ready for tomorrow. Should be easy enough, though, since we've got no solos. We just have to find some dresses that match and that look half-decent."

They went through the dresses on the racks quietly, yet Betty noticed that none of them tried on any of Kat's dresses. They stayed far from her rack. Betty had a feeling that trying one on would bring tears to her eyes. She couldn't imagine actually performing on stage in one. She'd be a mess for sure.

Things were better when they returned to Wahnfried that afternoon. Everyone spoke about ordinary things—and Betty found herself more comfortable around the other women again.

Even though she still hadn't given up on the idea that Kat's death wasn't by suicide, she was content leaving the conversation for another time—when the pain of her death wasn't so fresh on their hearts.

Three handsome soldiers delivered their meal to the estate. As always, they requested a few songs.

Betty and the others sang some Andrews Sisters favorites and then sat down to the now-cold ham and biscuits.

"You know," Irene mumbled, "after all this boogie-woogie, I'd give anything to hear some Bach. Sometimes I find my foot tapping along to this jazzy beat—even as I sleep."

"Are you serious? I have a collection," one of the soldiers said as he was gathering their tins to take back. "My mother sent me a small crate from home, and it had some recorded cantatas in it."

"Really? Do you think you can bring them over? We have a record player in the foyer. It looks as if it works."

"Sure. It'll be worth a try."

"As long as you stay in the foyer!" Irene insisted, pushing a finger into the chest of one of the men. "It's Mickey's rule."

"Mickey?" he asked.

"Our boss. And believe me, you don't want to get on his bad side," Irene added.

"Unless you want a broken nose and busted eardrum," Pearl added.

"Seriously?" Betty's eyes were wide. "Mickey did that to someone?"

Dolly leaned over and softly pushed Pearl's arm. "Way to go— don't you think before you speak?"

"Sorry. It's not like these guys are going to make a big deal out of it. They don't know anyone in the business. Besides, Mickey's been real good since he's been here." She scanned the room, seeing the amused looks on everyone's faces. "Or rather, mostly good."

The guys left, and thirty minutes later, they were indeed back with the records.

With eager anticipation, everyone circled up in the foyer with the record player in the middle. Expertly, Irene set up the player and placed the first record on it. A few seconds later, Bach flowed out.

"I can't believe this thing didn't get messed up in the bombing," Dolly said. "In fact"—she scanned the room—"someone must have taken a lot of time to get everything ready for us. I've seen the buildings downtown. There are buildings that were in shambles from a bomb falling two blocks away."

"If I ever learn who got the place in order for us, I'll have to thank them," Irene said, sitting back in her chair. "It's as if I've found a little culture again, listening to this."

Betty listened to the music that filtered through the quiet of the room. "To tell you the truth, I didn't get much culture growing up. We didn't have our own radio. In fact, my only singing experience had been in church. Then in high school, a friend of mine had a radio and we'd sing along. I hadn't even heard about Wagner until I got here. It's a shame, isn't it."

"Not really. I'm the same. When we first got here Oskar gave us a tour," Shirlee said. "He seems to know everything there is to know about Wagner. When an opera was first performed, who the singers were, what costumes they used. Sometimes we get a little anxious because Mickey pushes us so hard, but it sounds like those Wagner people really took things seriously. Before the war, people made pilgrimages here every year to attend the performances. Also, singers from all over the world would come and perform nearly for free—just for the honor of singing for Wagner on this stage."

Hearing Shirlee talk reminded Betty of the first MP she'd met when she arrived, and the stories he told of his mother—the opera singer—who used to sing in Wagner's operas—until she discovered the connection with Hitler.

"You know, I'll have to ask Oskar for the official tour sometime. It doesn't seem fair that I don't get it just because I came in late," she pouted.

"Make sure you ask on a day when there are no concerts, no rehearsals. It takes awhile," Shirlee said.

"And wear comfortable shoes." Pearl giggled. "I knew the building was huge, but walking it made me realize how many halls and rooms and closets there are."

Betty twirled a strand of hair around her finger, wondering why she'd never connected what Mac, their MP driver, had said with Kat's death. She vaguely remembered him talking about being warned by his mother to stay away from the Festspielhaus in the month of October. *What could he have meant?*

"Pearl, do you remember Oskar saying anything specific—or important about the month of October at the Festspielhaus?" Betty dared to ask.

"October? Like this month?" Pearl wrinkled her nose as she frowned. "Not that I can remember, but you can ask. If anyone knows, Oskar does."

CHAPTER TWENTY-THREE

Betty sat up in bed. Were others walking in the halls? Had she over-slept? She opened her eyes, her confusion deepening when she saw that it was still dark. What were the others doing walking around in the middle of the night? She listened, wondering if the noise had only been in her dreams.

She heard it again. Shuffling—not in the halls. Not upstairs, but under her. Betty was afraid to move. She almost felt frozen in place.

"Irene? Dolly?" she called softly, hoping one of them wandered the halls. No one answered.

Then she remembered... There were MPs stationed outside. As quietly as she could, she stood and tiptoed to the window. Looking out onto the front lawn and driveway, she saw the MPs' jeeps still parked out front, which meant the guys were still there. She considered asking them to check—in the basement? She wondered if there was one.

Or maybe they could patrol inside the house—just in case. No, that would wake everyone.

She could head out there and ask the MPs to walk the perimeter of the building and find—what? A person? The person who'd hurt Kat? No, that didn't make sense. If someone wanted to hurt any of them, he most likely wouldn't do it when they were guarded.

It's probably an animal. One that's found its way under the house. There were plenty of displaced animals, just as there were people.

You can't let your fears take over, Betty. There is going to be a time when the MPs aren't here. You can't spend your whole life obsessing about every little noise.

She returned to bed, but the unsettled feeling wouldn't leave her. For the last few days, she'd told herself the uneasiness deep inside had to do with Kat's death. It was only right to feel sad and worried. Add to that the way Mickey had treated her at the rehearsal, and it only made sense why the anxiety wouldn't leave.

Mickey's rejection couldn't compare with the sorrow—and even fear—she felt after Kat's death, but the pain was almost as acute— just in a different way. It seemed to stab the tender place in her heart where she'd tucked away her dreams.

Her dreams were something she'd held inside for as long as she could remember, and in the last year when she'd entertained at the canteen, it all seemed to be building to something greater—a wider audience for her songs.

Betty thought she'd achieved the pinnacle of her dreams when she came here, and although she had a lot to learn, she'd never expected Mickey to reject her as he had today. The sharpness of his words and disdain in his eyes made her question if she had any value. She thought she'd done well, but maybe the applause was more because she'd shown up.

Added to all that, she wondered why Frank hadn't been around. *Does he still care? Has he given up on me? Has he found someone else?*

Maybe I've fooled myself. Maybe it's time I face reality. Fame isn't achieved overnight. True love isn't birthed within the span of a plane ride, jeep ride, six songs, and one date.

Realizing she'd let naïve, romantic ideals run away in her mind and heart made her feel empty and aimless. Or rather, it intensified the emptiness that lingered in the shadows of her soul. Feelings she'd tried to ignore.

Betty got back into bed and curled onto her side, pulling her blankets up under her chin. Thankfully, the shuffling underneath the floor had stopped. She took in a deep breath and then blew it out slowly, trying to think back to when she started feeling this way. The more she thought about it, the more she realized the aimlessness most likely started when she'd set her mind on singing for the USO. That made no sense. The USO meant she was doing what God had created her to do, right? From the time she was a child, everyone had told her that her voice was given to her by God. Not a Christmas pageant was held without her singing an angelic song. She'd sung in every school play. She sang because it sounded good and brought smiles to other people's faces.

When she was moved from the factory to the canteen, she gladly used her gift for a greater good. And when she heard about the auditions with the USO, it seemed right in line with what had been happening. She could bring smiles to more soldiers—those who longed for home. But it was only here, now, that she realized she'd never really prayed about it. She'd never sought to see if this was what God had planned for her life. If this was where He wanted her to go.

The fear that had been there moments before transformed into remorse. She rose and moved to the light switch, turning it on. Then she hurried to her dresser and pulled out her Bible, taking it back to bed with her.

Did I miss Your path completely, God? Am I completely off track?

She opened her Bible and turned to the bookmark she'd put there the last Sunday service before she left home. She looked again to the verse she had underlined, Psalm 37:7. "'Rest in the Lord, and wait patiently for him,'" she whispered.

"Wait patiently? Is that what I was supposed to do, God? Did I run ahead?" She thought about that for a few minutes—trying to still her mind enough to think about God and how He saw the situation. She pictured her Heavenly Father looking down on her. Watching her smile as she sang. It seemed as if it would make Him happy to see her using her gift to bring smiles to others.

She also considered if she'd intentionally forced her will—pushing even though she felt God telling her to stop. She didn't think so. Even when her family questioned her decisions, she never felt as if she disobeyed God by pursuing the USO.

Of course, there was the way she handled it. Perhaps she could have figured out a different way to plan for the trip. A way that wouldn't have made her parents worry. She could have figured out a better way to treat her friend too. It wasn't very kind the way she made her take a bus to come get her car.

Lord, I'm sorry. Forgive me for not treating people as kindly as I could in my haste.

She had been selfish in the small things, but Betty felt her heart had been in the right place when it came to singing. She truly wanted to bring joy to others, rather than build up her own name and find fame. She hadn't acted immorally to get this job—as many young women did in Hollywood. Yet, maybe in all her attempts to sing and serve she'd forgotten what it meant to care for others in small ways. More than that, she'd forgotten what faith was all about. She'd taken too little time to build a relationship with someone special—a loving God.

Meet Me. Come to Me. She felt the words whisper in her soul.

"Lord, maybe being part of the USO *is* what You had planned. But maybe there is more than that. Are You asking me to quiet down and be prayerful before You?" She thought about how much she enjoyed seeing Frank and spending time with him—and that was only someone she'd known for a week. How much more should she enjoy spending time with God, praying to Him, thinking about His love, imagining His smiling face?

As she sat there, her back leaned against the wall, Betty considered the times over the past week when she'd said quick prayers to God, seeking His help. She'd prayed for safety on the plane. She'd prayed for comfort after Kat's death. She'd even prayed for answers about what really happened. But thinking back now, those were reactions more than communication. Sure, God wanted her to turn to Him, but maybe He wanted more. Maybe He wanted her to see Him there too—with her. Maybe instead of giving her an answer, He wanted to *be* the answer, the protection, the peace.

Is that what You want, God? Is that what You're trying to tell me? Betty tried to remember what Pastor Lambert had preached on her last Sunday at home. It was something to do with trusting God—or at least she thought that's what it had been about. She remembered she'd worn her favorite red dress and the choir had sung her mother's favorite hymn. They'd gone to her aunt's house for lunch and… Betty let her mind wander through the weeks prior, trying to remember any sermon she'd really listened to. Trying to remember any moment when she really felt connected with God. Maybe she'd been keeping God at arm's length longer than she thought.

The thing was, she'd been able to get by with that then. Or maybe the emptiness had been more manageable, since her life had been filled with so many other good things.

But now?

Now she didn't know how she'd make it through the day if she continued to keep God at arm's length. She wasn't in a safe, protected place anymore. She wasn't surrounded by people who loved her singing whether she did a good job or not. She didn't know what waited for her outside the front door. She needed God as she'd never needed Him before.

She placed her Bible on the dresser, hurried over and turned off the light, and then jumped back into bed, snuggling under the covers again. And as she closed her eyes, Betty realized how needy she was. Yet now she saw her need differently. In all those places she felt scared, empty, and incomplete, she knew God would come in and fill them with Himself. Even as she lay there thinking of Him, she felt His sweet, gentle presence seeping in—filling her to overflowing, as He'd promised.

And even though nothing had changed on the outside, knowing God was with her flooded her with more of His special, supernatural peace than she'd felt in a very long time. Even though Kat's bed was empty and the world outside could be harsh, God gave her an assurance that He was there. And that if she looked to Him, all would be well—if not always outwardly, then deep in her heart.

CHAPTER TWENTY-FOUR

Frank spread the photos on his bed, looking at them in the mid-morning light. Art had been up and out of the house early, shooting photos of buildings at various stages of cleanup and construction.

When Frank wasn't watching the Festspielhaus from afar, he'd looked at the photos a dozen times over the last few days. Some thing wasn't right, but he couldn't put his finger on what. *Kat looks too peaceful.* For some reason he thought she shouldn't look that peaceful. But the thing that bothered Frank the most was the fact that there seemed to be no trauma on her body. There was just that one small bruise. No cuts. Nothing.

Maybe I'm wrong. Maybe she did walk into the pond and drown herself. If someone had done this to her, Kat would have put up a fight.

Yet even as he thought that, something inside told Frank to keep looking for the truth. To not give up. He'd prayed about it a lot—trying to decide what to do. In fact, the only time he wasn't thinking about what had happened to Kat was when he was in class. He and two hundred other guys had hopes of getting their high school diplomas before shipping home. Sometimes he felt like a dope for being there, trying to learn algebra again. Still, he'd stick with it. He knew where he wanted to be, what he wanted to offer, before he got more serious with Betty.

A knock sounded on his door, and Frank jumped.

"Hey, why is the door locked? You got a girl in there or something?" Art called.

"No—just trying to nap. Don't want to have any bad Germans getting me while I'm snoozing." Frank gathered up the photos and slipped them under his blankets. Then he strode to the door, unlocked it, and stepped back.

Art had a sly look on his face, and he quickly glanced inside the room as if expecting to see a girl there. He walked in with a disappointed look.

"I don't know why you're so concerned—why you think you need to lock the door." Art chuckled. "You'd just be *another* body in their books—in their morgue. It's not like they haven't seen enough around here already."

"What do you mean 'another' body? They haven't found another body, have they?"

"I'm not talking about the suicide. I'm talking about the fact they're still pulling bodies out of the rubble. One guy I was talking to, working with the clean-up crews, said they unearthed three hundred German soldiers caught in their barracks by American bombers. Been there since April. What a mess."

"I wonder if I was on that bombing run. I seem to remember flying over this area."

"I wondered the same thing."

"Actually, I don't understand why we don't have more murders—problems," Frank said. "Maybe whatever happened to Kat was because she was at the wrong place at the wrong time. The Festspielhaus is surrounded by forests. Who knows who's lurking out there?"

"So you really think it was something more than suicide?" Art asked. "I talked to Denzel, and he said your thinking that way is a bad idea. He told me what went on down in his office."

Frank crossed his arms over his chest and turned to the window. "Did he tell you how he just sat there and didn't stick up for me? Didn't say a word?" Frank tried to keep his voice calm. He'd already talked to God about his feelings of betrayal a number of times, and didn't want to stir up those angry feelings again.

Art sat on his cot and removed his boots. "If I were to go with my gut feeling, I'd side with you. There's a lot more going on in those woods than anyone realizes." He leaned back on his bed and put his feet up. "I was talking to a guy today who supervises whole work crews of former German soldiers. Just him, his gun, and one hundred prisoners of war."

"So how's it going? Does he have many *Volkstrom*, soldiers, running away?"

"There were some, he guessed. But for every one he loses, he gains three more."

"I don't understand. How is that possible?" Frank sat on his bed, being careful not to disturb the photos.

"Well, every day the prisoners get a hearty breakfast, they work all day, and then we feed them a good meal at night too. That's more food than the average German citizen gets—and it's far more than those former German soldiers have, hidden in the woods. That soldier said they head out with one hundred and then he counts them when they come back—99, 100, 101, 102…"

"I wonder how many more are out there?" Frank shook his head. "All it takes is one guy with a big grudge to do something like what happened with Kat." Frank rose and tucked his .45 Colt into the wooden holster. "There's not a person in town who admits they were a Nazi, but I have a feeling it's the quiet before the storm. Hatred doesn't disappear just because somebody signed a peace treaty."

"So, where you headin'?" Art yawned.

"First mess, then class, and then the Festspielhaus tonight."

"Oh yeah, I heard about that show to honor Kat. I think I'll try to make it. I might try to sneak in Magdalena. She told me she was interested in seeing a show."

"I'll look for you there." Frank opened the door, glancing to where the photos were hidden. Art had never messed with his things before, and he hoped that would still be the case.

"Oh, wait."

Art's words halted Frank's steps. "Speaking of Magdalena, she wants to talk to you."

"To me?" He glanced back inside the doorway.

"Yeah, she said she sang for the Festspielhaus for many years, and she has something she wants to tell you."

"About what?"

"She didn't say. Maybe we should meet up after the show tonight? We could meet over at that German club where she sings."

Frank shrugged. "Sure, that sounds good, but I need to talk to Betty first."

"You're still interested in her? I thought that had cooled."

"I'm still interested. I just want to do things right. I don't want to pull her down. She deserves someone who has his act together."

"Okay, we'll be at the club if you can make it. Magdalena made it sound really important, whatever it was."

* * * *

Betty glanced around the mess hall at the soldiers' faces and forced herself to smile. It was Pearl's birthday, she discovered, and Pearl's sister Shirlee had talked to the mess sergeant last week about making a cake—which ended up being the size of a small plate with four little candles. Even though no one was in the mood to celebrate, Irene thought they all should try their hardest to have some fun.

Betty broadened her smile and rapped her spoon against a tin tray. "Is it anybody's birthday?"

"It's mine, ma'am." One soldier raised his hand.

"It's mine too," called another fellow.

"It's my wife's," another soldier called with a wistful look on his face.

"I'm sorry there's not enough cake to go around for everyone in the room," Shirlee said, "but if the birthday guys would like to come forward, you can all make a wish and blow."

The men came forward, and in unison with Pearl, they blew out the candles. When the cake was divided, they each had a small slice.

"So what did you wish for?" Betty asked a tall blond soldier.

"I wished you'd have a lunch date with me." He pointed to the table where he'd been sitting. "Do you care to join me, miss? My name is Abe."

"I can join you for lunch, Abe." She smiled. "Just let me get a tray."

Two minutes later, she was sitting across from the blond soldier, wishing it were Frank. Still she tried to be polite. It was the guy's birthday, after all.

"So have you been to any of our shows?" she asked.

"Yes, two in fact."

"What did you think?" Betty took a bite of her sandwich.

"Well, I saw Bob Hope right before the Battle of the Bulge, so it's not a fair comparison."

"Really?" Betty bit her lip, and her mind immediately returned to Mickey's criticism of her voice.

"Yeah, I mean, how could he compare with the likes of you?" He winked.

"So tell me about the Battle of the Bulge," she said, attempting to change the subject. The guy's eyes brightened, and he launched into a story of a battle near Chenogne even before she had a chance to take a breath.

Twenty minutes later, he was still talking. Betty ate her lunch in silence as he talked about people and places and battles she'd read about in the newspaper back home. His take was different from what she'd read and seen on the newsreels, that was for sure.

"So when we got to the town—we were in Germany by this time— there were white sheets hanging in the windows." The soldier's face was narrow, and with his blond hair sticking up, he reminded her of the scarecrow in *Wizard of Oz*. "We thought that meant they were surrendering the town, but as soon as the first tanks rolled in, snipers from the windows opened fire. I wasn't going to let that happen. I let them have it…"

He continued talking, and she looked around. It was interesting, she supposed, hearing about the fighting from this guy's point of view. The thing was, the way he talked, you'd think he'd won the war by himself. After another ten minutes had passed and she'd still not supplied a word, Betty was looking for a way to excuse herself.

Then she saw her excuse as Frank entered the side door and got in the chow line.

She interrupted the blond soldier as he was in the middle of telling about the Germans he'd rounded up. "Excuse me, Aaron, was it?"

"Abe. Abe Gentry, ma'am."

"Yes, Abe, I'm so sorry but I just saw someone—a friend—that I need to talk to. It's about the death—the other night."

"Saddest thing. To think someone so beautiful, so talented, would end her own life like that."

Betty nodded. She still didn't think it was suicide, but that was something she'd keep to herself, unless she was with someone she trusted, like Frank. Besides, she didn't want Abe to have to try to defend his opinion.

"Katherine Wiseman was a beautiful singer, and she did a great job in movies too," he continued. "I think Hollywood is really shaken up and—"

"Yes, I know," Kat said. "I completely agree with you, but I need to talk to my friend, you see."

Without another word, she stood, dropped off her dirty tray, picked up a clean one, and then hurried to slip in line right behind Frank. She knew the soldier was still watching her, most likely stunned by her rudeness, but she didn't care. If she could talk to anyone concerning her suspicions about Kat's death, she knew she could talk to Frank. She still thought he was handsome and kind, and even if he'd changed his mind about the possibility of them having a future relationship, she hoped she could consider him a friend.

"Hey there, mind if I join you for lunch?"

Frank looked back over his shoulder and his face brightened. "I don't mind, Songbird, but what are you doing here? Don't you have a show to prep for?"

Betty's chest tightened, and she pushed back the grief she'd tried to forget all morning.

"Mickey is gone for most of the day. Irene said that last night, at the last minute, he flew to England. There's been a change of plans, and Kat's going to be buried next to Edward. I'm sure that's what Kat would have wanted. Mickey's supposed to be back this afternoon."

"So is the show still on for tonight?" Frank had a pleasant look on his face, as if he was happy to see her.

"Yes, as far as I know. You know how Mickey is—Mr. 'The-Show-Must-Go-On.'"

Betty held up her tray and accepted another sandwich. The soldier behind the counter looked curiously at her, but he didn't say anything. *I'm hungry today, buddy, okay?* she wanted to say.

After their trays were full, she followed Frank to a table, which happened to be only four tables away from Abe. *Poor Abe.* His face appeared more sad than angry to see his lunch date dining with another. Betty wondered now if he regretted wasting a wish.

She and Frank talked about ordinary things—the weather, the Bach record that had made Irene so happy, and Art's story about the Germans who were slipping into the POW line. A work crew had value since it meant warm food and a warm bed.

Betty waited for Frank to get half of his sandwich eaten before she launched into what she really wanted to talk about. "Frank, do you think we could continue what we were talking about the other day, about Kat?"

Frank looked around, and she could tell he was wondering if it was safe to talk there. Betty glanced around too, seeing that the tables nearest them had cleared out, and also noticing that the cackle of soldiers' voices around the room would make it nearly impossible for anyone else to pick up on their conversation.

"Okay." Frank leaned forward. "What do you want to talk about?"

"Well, I know before the show you were backstage the night— well, the night Kat ran out. Did you see anything, you know, that caused you to believe she was suicidal?"

Frank lifted his face and stared into the air above Betty's head, but he didn't speak. After a few minutes, he looked into her eyes. "That's strange you're asking that. I've wondered the same thing. I saw a range of emotions going through Kat that night, but I think the fact that she committed suicide is probably the best evidence of her emotional state."

"Yes, that's what everyone is saying, but that's not fair. Kat was my roommate. If anyone should have picked up on her fragile mental state, I should have."

"Betty, do you really think anyone's going to believe that argument? You were her roommate for three nights—and none of those nights happened after she heard the news about Edward's death. News like that is enough to push someone over the edge, right? At least that's what everyone says. Most people think she didn't have anything to live for. She loved performing for the soldiers and that was ending. She was flying back to work for a studio she no longer respected to act in a movie she didn't like. Then, with Edward—maybe she just decided she didn't want to live like that."

"Is that what you think, Frank?" Betty leaned forward, studying his face—his strong jaw, chiseled features, and dark eyes that didn't do very well hiding what he truly felt.

Frank didn't answer her.

"Frank…" Betty bit her lower lip. "What if I told you she had something to live for?"

Frank's eyes widened in surprise, and she leaned forward so that Frank's nose was only six inches from hers. "Kat had a condition," she whispered. "Mickey told me not to tell anyone, but I just have to. I trust you."

"A condition?" Frank furrowed his brow.

"Yes, a *condition*. Kat was pregnant. Only a few months along. She met up with her husband in Paris and…"

Frank cocked an eyebrow. "She told you that? She told you she was going to have a baby?"

"Not directly, but in a beat-around-the-bush type of way."

"Maybe you misunderstood her." Even as Frank said the words he knew Betty could be right. A distant conversation filtered through his thoughts, and he remembered being in Paris and hearing some of the other guys talking about seeing a famous movie star with her husband. The more he thought about their conversation, the more he realized it had been Kat. He hadn't made the connection before until Betty mentioned Paris.

"I'm young, but not foolish. Kat said she was expecting as clear as she could without speaking those exact words. I know what someone means when they say the things she said."

"If that's true, which I don't know if it is, then it could have been another reason she decided to take her own life." Frank glanced away, expecting the words to come, then he looked at her again, angry at himself for the way he was treating her. *I have to do it.*

"*If* that's true? You don't believe me?" Betty's eyes widened in anger. "Do you think I'm lying to you, Frank?"

"No. I think you believe it, but maybe you misunderstood." He rubbed his jaw. "But *if* that was true then that could be another reason why she took her life."

"What do you mean?" Betty folded her arms over her chest and her anger was still evident.

"Think about it, Betty. How would it look if she returned to Hollywood with everyone knowing her husband had been stationed away from her—and then he died. They would all wonder about her pregnancy. There she'd be, fighting to protect her good name."

"But I always thought of it as a reason she'd want to live. It was a child, Edward's child."

"Yes, but when someone's scared, sometimes they don't think straight. Sometimes their actions are rash and they do things they later regret. Only with Kat, her rash decision wasn't something she could take back."

"You don't believe that." Betty reached across the table and took his hand. "Deep down I know you don't."

"Maybe I need to. Maybe it'd be easier if I did."

"It wouldn't be easier for me. I need you." She sighed. "If, in the end, we talk things through and we both decide Kat did this, then I'll be happy to walk away. But something inside me isn't letting go. Maybe it's God encouraging me to keep asking questions. I'd like to think so."

"But what if asking questions, talking about this, brings problems for us?"

"You mean we'd be in danger from the person who hurt Kat?" A chill moved up Betty's spine. "I hadn't thought about that. I suppose if someone did this, they'd do whatever it took to make sure they aren't found out."

"What if our own reputations are at stake?"

"I'm not sure why that would be the case, but right now I just want to be the advocate for Kat that I know she would have been for me."

Frank chuckled. "Are you serious? The Kat I witnessed, those few times, didn't seem like someone who'd stick out her neck for someone else."

"Well, maybe I saw another side of her. People aren't always as they appear…" She glanced around the room and sighed. "There's more going on inside people than we think."

"Do you believe that, Betty?" Frank's gaze was intent on hers.

"Yes. I suppose I believe that more than I used to." She leaned forward, the edge of the table pressing against her ribs. "Frank, why are you saying this?"

"I'm saying it because I have something to tell you."

Betty studied his gaze, and she could tell she wasn't going to like what he was about to say.

"I used you, Betty. I used you to get to Kat. To get to the others in the Festspielhaus."

Betty felt her chin drop, but her heart dropped further. She stared into Frank's eyes and knew it was the truth.

Betty swallowed hard. "Why are you telling me this?"

Frank reached for her hand and then changed his mind and pulled it back. "I think you should leave. There's nothing for you here. You'll never be anything but a back-up singer. And"—he lowered his gaze, but not before she saw sadness there—"I don't want you staying around for me."

Betty hid her trembling hands under the table. "Yes, well, thank you for telling me the truth." *It was just like Kat had said.* She looked away, hoping the tears wouldn't come. Then she stood. "I need to go now. I have work to do. And…" Her voice rose. "And even if I'm never anything more than a back-up singer, it will be enough. In—in time, God's plan will…" She covered her mouth with her hand and hurried away.

It will work out. God's plans will work out, she thought as she hurried outside. But even as she thought that, pain filled her.

This is not how it's supposed to be.

Lord, I can't handle any more.

Who do I have now? Who do I have besides You?

* * * *

Frank strode home, not looking to the right or the left. He'd sat in class that morning, but he hadn't learned a thing. His thoughts had been on Betty. Finally, just before lunch, he'd decided the most logical thing to do would be to let every romantic thought of her go. No—more than that, he needed to force her away. It had seemed like a good plan at the time. No family needed to go through the pain of losing a daughter, a sister, like his family had gone through with Lily. Now he wasn't so sure about his decision.

She needs to leave. Needs to go where it's safe. He couldn't live with himself if anything happened to her.

Yet, if that was the right choice, why had he felt so bad about what he'd said? The pain showing in Betty's eyes had obviously cut to her heart, and seeing that made him wonder if he'd done the right thing.

Frank approached his house, pulled the key from his pocket, and unlocked the door. Then he strode up to his room to get his camera. He was halfway across the room when he noticed something on his bed. A white envelope.

Did Art get into my things? Did he pull out the letters and read them?

Frank hurried over and opened the envelope. He recognized the script, but the words were new.

> *The singer may be just first. A warning of what is to come. Her death is sad mystery. The new Songbird holds the knowledge of the answers, if she looks upon the photographs. She will see truth.*

How did this get here? Frank's heart pounded in his chest and his hand reached for his gun. Was the mysterious messenger still around?

He was right about one thing—Kat's murder was perhaps just the first. He knew something else too. *Songbird*—was this note saying that Betty might have the answer? Was it possible that Betty would see something he missed by looking at the photos? Frank had never shared top secret information before, but this seemed like a shot worth taking.

I need Betty. She's a key to this somehow. If this is correct, I need her to look at the photos.

CHAPTER TWENTY-FIVE

Betty watched Oskar as he set up the stage for the evening's events. He seemed lost in his own world as he hoisted the large wooden backdrop and set it in place. As Betty watched, she wondered what she was doing here. She wondered why God would do this to her—make her go through all this pain. She had already faced so much, and now she had to face Frank's rejection. *He didn't care about me. He just cared about using me to get to the others.*

"Do you think we should run through the numbers?"

Betty turned at Dolly's voice.

"The band's getting all set up," Dolly continued. "And from what I hear, Mickey's landed in Nuremberg and is on his way."

Betty nodded, remembering that drive. Had it only been a week since she headed here with stars in her eyes? That didn't seem possible.

"I'm game for practicing. I want to do as good a job as I possibly can." *While I'm still here*—she wanted to add. Maybe Frank was right. Maybe she didn't have anything to stick around for.

Betty looked around. She saw the band, dressed in white suits and blue shirts, but she didn't see the third wheel of their trio. "Where's Irene?"

"Probably hiding in the orchestra pit, smooching with Billy."

"Billy? Are you kidding? I didn't know they were sweet on each other."

"Oh, I think he's liked her for a while, but it's only recently that she started liking him back. I think Kat's death, and her feelings for Edward, have made all of us want to have someone special in our lives."

"I can agree with that." Shirlee piped in from where she had been practicing her dance steps on stage. "I've been with the USO for two years, and even though I'm used to the word *obey*, I hope sometime when I use it in the near future it'll have a 'love, honor, and' in front of it."

Betty chuckled, surprising herself, and then she stepped forward to the edge of the stage and looked down into the orchestra pit. It made her stomach quiver to see the big cavern. It was as if a cave existed under the first row—and it was dark beyond that.

"I'm not sure I see anyone," Betty said.

"Not there, underneath," Dolly pointed. "The pit goes way back, under the stage. I heard from Oskar that the *Ring* orchestra needed over one hundred and fifty musicians."

Then, remembering Oskar was on stage, Dolly turned to him. "Is that right, Oskar—one hundred and fifty?"

"What? Oh, yes." Oskar finished setting up the scene, and then moved to them. "It was a sight to behold."

"Don't say *was*—I'm sure it'll happen again. Maybe after we leave, some of the old performers will come back." Dolly placed her hand on her hips. "Things aren't going to be like this forever. Believe it or not, we will go home someday."

Oskar's eyes narrowed. Then he lowered his head. "I wish that were the case, but I do not see this happening. The world has changed." His lips pressed together into a thin line, and Betty could tell he wanted to say more, but held back.

"I bet it was magical," Betty whispered, looking around the auditorium. "The music must have been overwhelming. I can imagine it moved the listeners deep inside their souls."

Oskar nodded. "Wagner alone knew how to use the music and the words to change people. Those who watched, listened—left different. That is why they came—so many came—faithfully over the years."

"I can imagine the singers and musicians enjoyed the experience equally as well." Betty dared to take another step, her toe touching the edge. "How did the musicians get down there?"

"There is no need to go down there." Oskar's voice was firm. "There is no need." With that, he turned and walked away, back behind stage.

"I think Irene is going to get in trouble if she's caught," Betty whispered to Dolly. "I guess that leaves out me asking him for a tour."

"That's strange," Dolly said, her gaze following Oskar. "He's always been eager to show us around before—but you're right. Let's hope Irene doesn't get caught."

* * * *

Betty was pacing backstage in her red velvet dress and black satin pumps when Mickey showed up fifteen minutes before the show was set to start. His hair was disheveled, and his eyes looked puffy, as if he hadn't slept all night.

Seeing his weariness, Betty wanted to work harder—wanted to prove that bringing her on hadn't been a mistake. Made her want to put a smile on his face and maybe help him forget for a few minutes that he'd just buried Kat. It was the least she could do before she flew the coop, which she was beginning to consider more and more.

The rest of the performers must have had the same thing on their minds, because everyone seemed to be in top form. Betty noticed the sweet grin Irene gave Billy as their trio walked on stage. It made her think of Frank, and she searched the crowd looking for him. She found him, sitting up in the box that she'd heard had, at one time, been Hitler's private box. She noticed he was looking at her, watching her, and she quickly looked away. A sadness filled her, joining with a thousand other sad thoughts that she'd been collecting lately.

The first set of songs and dances went off without a hitch, but halfway through the trio's second number the lights went out. The stage lights, the auditorium lights—everything dropped to a black so thick it almost felt alive. The rest of the musicians and singers stopped, and Betty's voice rang out, the note carrying clear and bright as a songbird, through the hall. She stilled and the silence seemed to breathe. Everyone held, waiting, as if wondering what to do.

"The army must not pay its bills either," Betty said, projecting her voice. "What do you think, Dolly? Irene? Should we take up a collection?"

Men's laughter carried around the room.

When the lights still didn't come on a minute later, Betty heard Irene sigh.

"Sorry, I'm afraid we won't be able to go on," Irene said.

"I can help with that." The beam from one soldier's flashlight hit the stage near Betty's feet. It was amazing how one little light could do so much to break the darkness.

"Yeah, I can help too." Another flashlight clicked on, followed by dozens more.

Betty looked to Dolly and Irene, then the band, noticing the large smiles on their faces.

"Okay, boys, I've always been a sucker for spotlights," Betty said. "What do you think, Wally? Can you take this one from the top?"

"Sure can, Songbird." With that, the band started. At that moment, it didn't matter that Betty was singing as part of a trio. Or that Frank didn't care for her as she cared for him. She was singing under the light of flashlight beams and to the applause of nearly two thousand men. She was where she was supposed to be. And she knew things were right, really right, because in her heart—for the first time—she felt as if God were right there—clapping along.

* * * *

After changing into her USO uniform, Betty scanned the faces of the others backstage, wondering if Frank would be there. She felt a cold chill move up her arms when she saw him, standing in the back corner of the practice area talking with Oskar. She tried to look away, but Frank's eyes met hers and he motioned her over.

Betty cocked her head, unsure if she'd just seen that. But then Frank did it again, motioning her over with a wave of his hand.

Betty approached, but instead of acknowledging Frank, she turned to Oskar.

"So I assume you're the hero who got the lights back up and running?" she asked.

Oskar shrugged. "Yes, well, it was only a minor problem—the electrical board is getting tired." He chuckled. "Both of us have been around this place more years than we know."

"I'm glad you got it working, but I have to admit it was sort of fun singing with those spotlights.'"

"Yes?" Oskar nodded. "I can arrange again."

"Well, maybe not." Betty laughed.

"It did look like you had fun." Frank winked. "Maybe I'll have to join you up there one day."

"You sing?" Betty cocked an eyebrow and anger built inside her. How could he tell her what he'd told her earlier and then act as if nothing had happened?

"No, but I could pretend, if it would get me in one of those fancy white suits." He ran his fingers down the lapel of his olive drab uniform. "I clean up well."

"What are you doing?" The words spilled from her mouth. "You told me today that you were using me, that you don't really care about me, and now you want to act like nothing is wrong? Do you expect me to forgive you? To be your friend and pretend that nothing's wrong? To let you use me some more?"

From the corner of her eye, Betty realized Oskar still stood there, watching the scene. A pained look colored his face. Had he ever been married or fallen in love? Maybe he'd lost his love too.

Maybe the war tore him apart from the woman he loved, as so many others had experienced...

"Betty, can I talk to you for a minute?" Frank lowered his voice and led her toward the back door. "I know you usually go to the canteen, but I need to talk to you. I need your help."

"Now you need me, huh? You want to use me again?"

"It's not like that. I said what I said because I was hoping you would leave."

"Is that supposed to make me feel better? That you were hoping I'd leave?"

Frank continued, unfazed. "I lied about my feelings so that you'd go home where it was safe."

"Where it's safe?" She focused on him, considering his words. "Are you serious? Because it sure sounded like you were telling the truth."

"Please, Betty, there's too much to explain now. All I can say is that I was lying. About everything. I need you. I need your help in figuring out what happened to Kat. I can't do it without you." He looked around at the other performers who pushed their way past them. Then he leaned forward. "I have the photos of Kat's body," he said barely above a whisper. "I need you to look at them. And I'm actually passing up another invitation because I need your help."

"You really need my help?" She studied his face, hoping to see that he was telling the truth. And she could see that either he deeply cared for her or he was a better actor than Humphrey Bogart. "Okay, I trust you—I think." She placed a hand on her hip and cocked her chin up at him. "So what was the other invitation?"

"My roommate invited me to this German club. He has a friend—a girlfriend who used to sing opera here. She said she wanted to talk to me about something."

"That sounds interesting—curious too. I'd like to be there—hear what she has to say."

"Sure, okay. I want to meet with her soon. I'll let you know when. But first…"

"The photos." She whispered. "I'll try."

Betty's stomach ached just thinking about it, but she could tell from Frank's tone that he really did need her.

"But there's one more thing I need to know. Are you sure you said all those things because you were worried about me—and wanted me to go home where it's safe?"

He leaned down, his face close to hers. "Yes, Betty, that's the truth." His face was gentle, yet protective also. As if he did care—really care for her.

They strode outside, and Betty was pleased to see it was warmer than she had expected. She wrapped her arm in his. "You might have your personal MP again, but do you think we could walk? I've been shuttled around and cooped up for three days." Even as she spoke, Betty wondered if deep inside she was stalling what was to come. She couldn't imagine having to look at Kat—that way.

"Sure. I haven't seen Howard since he drove you home the other day anyway."

The night was dark, the moon half-hidden behind large, gray clouds. The parking lot around them was full of GIs. Others, like them, walked down the road to town.

"Sometimes I find it hard to believe I'm really in Germany. It's like a little America here," she said, trying to act like everything was normal. "I shop at the PX and eat at the mess. I'm not sure if I've even had a conversation—or tried—with a German citizen since I've been here, other than Oskar."

"I think we get too comfortable. We forget. I have to remind myself of the buddies I lost. I have to remember the photos of the concentration camps. Remember there was one here in town. I have to remember the fear of being a target."

"Tell me what it was like, the war. We've talked about many things, but not that."

"I was an aerial photographer attached to headquarters of the Ninth Air Force."

"So you shot photographs from the planes? Like you did during our flight?" She reached for him. He slipped his hand around hers and smiled, pulling her closer to his side as they walked.

"I took photos—among other things."

"What do you mean?"

"The B-17 crews loved it when we photographers were on board. And there were times, when we were in a sticky situation, when I manned the waist guns."

"That sounds dangerous."

He shrugged. "It was our job, what can I say?"

"Did you get to fire those guns?"

"Only a few times. We were also often escorted by American or British fighters—so they kept the bad guys at bay." He chuckled. "It wasn't always exciting. We'd also take photos of the ground crews with their individual aircraft. And we were always on the flight line when a mission took off and returned. The worst feeling was when a plane landed and it shot a red flare as they taxied down the landing strip. Then we knew wounded were on board.

"Once when that happened, we found out the waist gunner had been hit. He died a few hours later. After that, I talked the captain into getting permission for me to fly with the crew as a temporary waist gunner. The crew that I flew with ended up being my favorite— I wasn't assigned to them, but I flew with them as often as I could. I think I went out with them thirty times—maybe forty."

Betty looked up to the night sky and tried to imagine what it would have been like to live there at that time—hearing the roar of the planes and knowing what was to come. "Is it strange, being here now?"

"It is." He chuckled. "And, if I'm honest, the hardest thing I've faced since being in Europe is this assignment. I used to shoot the war, and it was a big boost to my ego. I've chatted with God about it, and He's assured me I'm exactly where I need to be. Still, it's not really something that's going down in history."

"What about the photos you took of Kat? Those made the news."

He sighed. "I'd give that fame back if I could."

They neared the bottom of the hill and moved into town. MPs and soldiers patrolled the streets. Except for small clusters of people who slept in the shells of bombed buildings, and the various baroque structures that still stood, one would think they walked on a military base.

Betty noticed many of the soldiers had girls on their arms, and she was thankful she had her USO uniform on. Glad no one would think she was a German girl, trying to bum her next meal.

"So have you ever seen your photos in the papers?" she asked.

"I've seen a few in *Stars and Stripes*. My parents read the papers religiously. They cut out all they can find, and I'm glad. I don't have any of the originals."

"You don't get to keep them?"

"We're not allowed. My photos are the property of the U.S. Army." He chuckled. "Even the ones of you girls—those photos are important to national security, I'm sure."

"So—you haven't made *any* extras? Not even of the USO girls? I mean if you have to take a shot, you might as well enjoy them."

"Well, no, I haven't made any extra prints of the USO *girls*, but I have to admit I did make a few extra copies of someone." He winked at her.

Betty wished she could be excited by his words. Under other circumstances maybe.

Soon they'd reached Frank's house.

A rush of nausea moved to Betty's stomach, as she realized again what was to come.

Frank opened the door. He flipped on the lights, scanned the room, and then entered. She'd never seen Frank act like this before. So intense. So serious, as if danger lurked around the corner.

He closed the door behind them. "Are you going to be okay looking at them? I wouldn't ask, but I need your help."

"Truthfully? I just don't know." She crossed her arms over her chest, and then pulled them tight against her. "I'm afraid of seeing Kat like that."

"If you don't want to…"

"I do. I—" She took in a deep breath. "I will. If it'll help."

He nodded, and they entered the darkroom. Frank walked to a shelf in the corner and pulled down a small stack of photos. His face was serious as he flipped through them, but then he paused, smiled, and singled out a photo.

"Let's start with this one—put the beautiful one before the harder ones."

Frank handed the photo to her, and Betty saw herself. She wore Irene's white dress with the black polka dots. From the way one side of her skirt flipped up, she must have swayed. A soft smile curled on her lips that were open slightly, as if she was preparing to launch into a song. The camera had been focused so none of the GIs were seen, just her on the stage.

"I love this one. It looks like you're having a good time." He stepped closer to look at it.

"I do have a good time. Sometimes when I'm up there, I think I was born for this. It's as if God created me just for that moment."

"I can tell."

"But I have to admit, after today, I was seriously considering leaving. I still might."

Frank nodded. Then studied her face for a moment. Finally, he turned back to the photos in his hands. "Are you ready to look at the other ones—the ones of Kat?"

"Yes." She felt her hands trembling. "I think so."

"Okay, but I think we should go sit down. You should sit for this."

CHAPTER TWENTY-SIX

Betty took a deep breath and then looked down at the first photo Frank held on his lap. He passed it over to her and she looked closer. It was Kat's face. Her eyes were closed, her face white, and she looked as if she were sleeping.

"Oh, my—oh, dear God." She whispered it as a prayer. The tears came, and she turned and pressed her face into Frank's shoulder.

"I'm so sorry, Betty. I shouldn't have asked you to do this."

Collecting herself, Betty looked at the picture again, trying to notice anything that stood out to her. Besides being pale, Kat looked exactly the same.

"I don't see anything wrong. She looks just like she's sleeping, doesn't she? Do you have another photo?"

"I do, Betty, but I don't think you should look at any more."

"But if I could help." She gripped his arm, feeling his support.

Dear God, help me. If I'm supposed to do this, give me the strength.

"Okay, but take your time. Only if you're able."

She waited a few minutes and then sat back. "Okay, but I think I can only handle one more." She tried to force a smile. "I'm afraid I won't be able to sleep tonight as it is, and I'll need sleep. Mickey told us we're repeating the show tomorrow. I suppose a whole passel of guys couldn't get in. He wants to make sure everyone gets to see it."

She sat back, pressing her back against the couch, averting her gaze from the photo.

Frank looked at her, and from the sad look on his face, she knew that if he didn't truly need her help he wouldn't have asked her to do this. "Okay. I'm ready."

Frank placed another photo on her lap, and she looked down at it. It was a photo of Kat, floating in the water. Her white dress flared out in the water—only...

"Wait." Betty sat up straighter. "This isn't right."

"What do you mean?"

"This is not Kat's dress." She lifted the photo and studied it closer. "I've never seen this dress before." Her heart pounded. "Kat's dress didn't have sleeves—and she had a black belt. The style is different. This dress looks old—like a costume or something. But that's impossible. I mean why would she change? When did she change?

"This doesn't make sense at all." Betty shook her head. Then she handed the photo back and stood. "Her dress—the one she wore that night. I wonder what happened to it. Maybe she did change before she left. Maybe it's on the rack." She paced the room.

"Do you think it could be there?"

"It could. We never checked. Mickey told us they found her in her white dress and we never questioned that. We should check in the morning."

"Yes, but let's think about this. Where would she get the costume?"

Betty felt the warmth and concern in Frank's gaze.

"There might be some around the Festspielhaus. I haven't seen all the rooms, but Irene and Dolly told me there are rooms with props. I can imagine there are rooms with costumes too." Betty could almost picture the dress that Kat wore being in some type of production or play.

"Do you think—" She paused and turned to Frank. "Do you think Oskar might have had something to do with this?"

"Oskar? Why would you think that?"

Betty moved to the chair across from the sofa and perched on the edge of the seat. In her mind's eye, she saw Kat, stalking down the wrong hall, heading to—who knew where.

"What if Kat ran away, but she headed down the wrong hall? She had a horrible sense of direction and she could have gotten lost."

"Yes, but that doesn't mean Oskar did anything to her. He's a nice guy. He seems to work alongside Mickey without saying a word."

"Exactly." She looked to Frank, lifting her eyebrows. "He makes us comfortable there—very comfortable."

* * * *

Betty scanned the mess hall and noted Frank sitting across the room. He caught her gaze and lifted his hand, and she saw he had a tray of food already waiting for her—not that she was hungry.

Last night they'd sat in his living room, talking until nearly midnight. Their conversation was interrupted by a loud knock on the door. Frank had quickly hidden the photos, and then he'd opened the door to find Howard saying that Mickey was beside himself with worry and that Betty needed to get back to Wahnfried right away.

"Did you get in trouble?" Frank asked when she sat.

"I got an earful. Felt like I did when I was ten and got caught stealing candy from the general store."

"You did that?" Frank smirked.

"You didn't?" she shot back. Then she grew serious. "But…" She let out a low sigh. "I apologized. It wasn't right, making Mickey and the others worry like that. I should have thought it through before I left with you without telling anyone."

"I should have found a ride back for you sooner."

"We won't have to worry about that anymore. I have a chaperone now too."

"Really?"

"Well, sort of. I'm not allowed to go anywhere without my personal MP." She looked to the doorway where Howard stood and he waved. "Did you think of a plan?"

Frank leaned close and talked only loud enough for her to hear. "Sort of. But I'm not sure. I think first we need to search the Festspielhaus."

"Well, Irene and Billy snuck away to smooch a few days ago. Maybe we should try that excuse and go sneaking down the halls?" She winked.

He gave her a soft smile, but she could tell his mind was still focused on getting information.

"There's something else I've thought of," he said, taking a sip of his coffee.

"What's that?"

"The other day I was talking to—well, someone, about the photos, and he mentioned Kat only had one mark on her—on her arm. I looked at the photos closer and I saw it. Even though her arm was partially submerged in the water, it looked more like a scrape than a bruise. Maybe even a burn from a rug."

"But there are no rugs in the Festspielhaus." She thought through all the rooms—the practice areas, the dressing rooms. "I thought of something too," Betty whispered. "It was Kat's skin. I know when I take a bath my skin gets all wrinkly and bumpy—"

"Which could mean she hadn't been there long, I think. Maybe we need to start somewhere else first," Frank said, leaning in.

"Where's that?"

"Oskar's house." His gaze was intense. "Do you think you can come down with something—get real sick? Maybe stay back at Wahnfried? From what I hear, Oscar lives not far from there. His father used to work at Wahnfried and at the opera house, so he has a house nearby."

"It would work except for my shadow." Betty resisted glancing back at the door where Howard still stood. "It'll be hard to get out. It would be easier to get sick at the opera house and ask to hang out in the dressing room or something. Maybe Howard will get interested in the show?"

"Oh, I'm not talking tonight," Frank said. "Maybe tomorrow—during rehearsal or something. I'd hate for you to miss a show. And, I need more time to think. I need to figure out where to go and what we need to do about Howard."

She shook her head and sighed. "Why do I need a bodyguard? The other girls just have one for all of them."

"And you get Howard"—Frank smiled—"all to yourself."

"Yes, it must mean I'm special. I just don't understand why Mickey is going overboard all of a sudden."

"It doesn't make sense, unless…" Frank ran a hand through his hair. "Unless Mickey knows something he's not telling you."

* * * *

Betty walked into the opera house that afternoon, and one look at Mickey's face told her that Frank was right. Mickey did know something.

"Hey, gang, gather around." Mickey's voice was raspy and his face was blotchy. Betty's guess was that he'd been crying, and it choked her up just to see him like that.

He sighed. "There's something I need to talk to you about."

Betty pulled up a chair and sat next to Irene. She reached over and took Irene's hand—she wasn't sure if it was to give comfort or receive it. Judging from Mickey's intense, narrow gaze, she guessed both.

"It's not official yet, but we no longer believe that Kat committed suicide." Mickey scanned their faces, and then lowered his head.

Betty felt as if her body was being pricked by a thousand needles. Even though she'd always thought that, it didn't seem real. And from the looks on the faces of the others, they seemed to have a hard time believing it too.

"A lot wasn't done right when her body was found—this is not something the military is used to tackling," Mickey said. "One MP moved her body, and the investigator in charge didn't think she needed an autopsy. Everyone's focus is on the trials in Nuremberg, and it was easy just to call it a suicide and be done with it." Tears welled in Mickey's eyes, and he wiped them away with the back of his hand. "The studio, though, got involved. I suppose the idea that Kat ended her life didn't sit well with her fans. They hired a private medical examiner who conducted an autopsy in England. I don't know the details, but they could tell from Kat's lungs that she was dead before she went in the water."

Irene's hand tightened around Betty's. Then Irene looked at her. "You were right…" Tears welled in her eyes. "The baby," Irene mouthed.

Betty nodded, and the room blurred as her own eyes filled with tears. The sadness of that thought wrapped around her like a heavy cloak and her mind filled with fear. *Someone did this. Whoever it is, he's still out there…*

"Oh no, poor Kat." Dolly broke out in sobs, crying into her hands.

"I should have said something last night, but I was still in shock. That's why I've asked the military police to provide protection—at least through this last show."

"Last show?" The words spilled from Betty's mouth.

"I talked the USO into allowing us to perform tonight. Their first inclination was to send everyone to England so that no one else gets hurt. I assured them we'd take utmost care to watch over you—"

A crash sounded behind Mickey, overwhelming his words. Dolly squealed, and Irene almost pulled Betty onto her lap as she jerked her hand back.

"I apologize." Oskar rushed forward, picking up the large wooden frame he'd dropped. Betty eyed him, wondering what he was thinking—wondering if he was involved. She tried to get a look at his face—to see what his response was to Mickey's news, but Oskar quickly looked away before she had a chance.

"But Mickey, I don't want to leave. Maybe we can all work together to solve this." Betty glanced around the room, and she could tell by the anxious faces of the others that they didn't agree with her.

Irene patted her hand. "I know you just got here, kid, but I think this is a sign for the rest of us that the show is over. It's time to hit the road. You agree, don't you, Betty, that it's not worth risking anyone else's life?"

"Yes, of course I agree. I don't want to see anyone else hurt." Betty felt her stomach constricting, and she wished she had a way to get the news to Frank before the show. *It's gonna have to be tonight—we don't have another choice.*

* * * *

The last time Betty had played sick, it was in the fifth grade when she didn't want to go to school because Les Duran had broken her heart by giving Lucy Salisbury the prettiest valentine in class. She started by thinking of the photos that she saw of Kat last night. If anything could make her feel ill, it was that.

She watched Howard and the other MPs as they walked around the backstage area. They were looking at some of the sets that Oskar had worked on recently. They looked excited to be back there. They also looked relaxed. *How lucky for them to be able to see the show from behind the scenes. Hopefully they'll be paying more attention to what's on stage.*

She moved the rack of Kat's gowns, looking through them, hoping to spot the white one, but not really surprised when she didn't. Her friend's gown had to be somewhere. What had happened to it? How did Kat get into that costume? How did she die? Betty pictured her friend—scared and alone, and her knees grew weak.

"Betty, are you okay?" Irene approached as Betty sifted through the gowns.

"Truthfully? I don't feel so good."

"I think you should lie down before you topple over." Irene led her to the lounging couch in the corner of the dressing room. "Go ahead and rest here. I'll go talk to Mickey."

"Irene…" Betty stretched her hand to her friend. "Can I ask you something first?"

"Sure, kid, what is it?"

"Is Mickey going to be okay? I mean he really doesn't look like he's doing well at all."

"Mickey will pull out of it somehow, although it's going to be harder without Kat around."

"What do you mean?"

"I guess you haven't heard the whole story, have you?"

Betty shook her head.

"Well, it was Mickey who discovered Kat—her talent—years ago. She was a background singer in some low-budget film. Mickey talked to his friends at the studio and they signed her and made her a star."

"I had no idea."

"Yeah, well, there's more than that. When Mickey got in trouble with the studio for losing his temper—getting too abusive with his hands and his words—his career was pretty much done. It was Kat who got him this job—by promising to come here and sing. Mickey committed to being on his best behavior and Kat stayed around as long as she could."

"So Mickey's usually worse than this?" Betty cocked an eyebrow.

"Oh, kid, he should get an Academy Award for how well he's acted while he's been over here."

Irene pursed her lips then sighed. "But I imagine he's feeling pretty bad. I mean if it wasn't for him, Kat wouldn't have been here. And hearing about the baby. I'm sure that's just another knife to Mickey's heart. I think that's another reason why he doesn't want it to get out—the guilt is already too much as it is."

Betty nodded, and Irene stood.

"Wait." Betty reached out and grabbed Irene's arm.

"Yeah?" Irene turned.

Betty scrunched her brow. "Where does Mickey live?"

"In an apartment in town. I've been there a few times with the other girls. It's a nice place."

"This is a strange question, but does it have any rugs or carpet?"

Irene thought for a few seconds. "Yeah, I suppose it does. Why?"

Betty shrugged. "Just wondering."

"Wow, kid, you really are sick, you're getting delusional. I'll go get Mick—tell him you're not looking so hot."

Mickey approached a few minutes later. "How are you doing,

Songbird?" His voice was gentle and he patted her hand. "Do you think you can sing tonight?"

Betty studied Mickey's face, wondering if he could have done this. *Maybe he confronted Kat about running from the stage—of ruining the show and then things escalated from there?*

But as she looked into his red, tired eyes, she didn't see a killer's hidden guilt. She saw pain, radiating from his core. Pain from a guy who felt responsible for losing someone he loved—not by his own hand, but by a dozen things that brought Kat to the place of losing her life.

"I would sing if I could, Mick. But I'm not feeling very well—"

"Stomach hurt?"

She nodded.

"Body feeling weak?"

She nodded again.

"Sounds like you're coming down with something." He glanced at his watch. "Too bad, too. I was second-guessing my decision about your solo. I was going to ask you to do it tonight. You know, for the final number."

"Really?" Betty sat up. Her heart skipped a beat. *Do I really want to give this up? My last song under a German moon?*

"Sounds important," a familiar voice said.

Betty lifted her focus off Mickey's gaze and noticed Frank standing behind him.

"I think all the guys would like that." Frank stepped forward. "You should really consider it."

"No." Betty shook her head. "As much as I'd love to, I just don't think I'll be able to sing tonight."

Mickey nodded, and then he rose and patted her head. "I'll let the other girls know it'll be a duo."

Mickey walked off, and Frank neared, sitting down beside her. "What are you doing? I thought you were going to be ill tomorrow—for rehearsal."

"It won't work," she whispered. "Tonight's the last show. They did an autopsy in England and Kat didn't drown. She was dead before she went into the water. They're fearful that one of us will be next. They'll be shipping us back to England tomorrow. Tonight is the last show."

"Last show? You're leaving?" Frank's eyes widened.

"Yes." She reached out and stroked his cheek. "That's why it has to be tonight."

"Maybe I should just do it alone? Maybe it's not safe…," Frank said.

Betty jutted her chin. "I'm sneaking out of here with or without you. I sure hope it's with you because I'd hate to be roaming the countryside alone."

"You're stubborn." He placed his hand over hers, and then he turned his head and kissed her palm.

"Yes, I know."

"But you were also right about Kat. That must make you feel justified."

"No." Betty looked away. "It feels horrible." Then she lifted her eyes and met his gaze again. "It'll only feel right when we find out who did this—and we make sure that it doesn't happen again."

CHAPTER TWENTY-SEVEN

Frank could see his breath as he stood outside the back door of the Festspielhaus, waiting for Betty.

Am I doing the right thing? Am I putting her in danger? This might not have anything to do with Oskar at all. Then what?

He saw the door open, and he held his breath, waiting to see who emerged.

If we don't find anything tonight, then nothing's going to change the fact that Betty's leaving tomorrow. Then I'll just have to wait and see what the army does about investigating this.

His heart leapt in his chest when he saw her exit the building, and he scanned the area again to make sure no one was around. The jeeps—and the MPs watching over the vehicles—were parked in front. To avoid them, they could walk through the woods and find the trail, following it down the hill and past the pond, to Oscar's house.

Betty's eyes widened when she saw him, and she hurried toward him. She was dressed in her USO jacket and slacks, but Frank thought she looked just as beautiful as when she was dressed in her nice gowns and high-heeled shoes.

Dear God, please watch over her—

His prayer was interrupted when she opened her arms and threw herself into his hug.

"You're here." She sighed as if relieved.

"Yes, let's go before we're seen."

It wasn't until they made their way to the trail that he turned on his flashlight, looking to her. "Do you think anyone saw you?"

"No, I don't think so. Oskar was busy putting up sets. Howard and the other MPs moved to the side stage to watch the show. But I bet it's not going to be too long before they realize I'm gone."

Frank took her hand as they hurried forward. His feet pounded on the dirt trail, and he was sure they sounded like elephants running through the woods. Yet he wasn't worried about being quiet. He was more worried about getting to the house and checking it out before the concert ended. Then, depending on what they found there, they'd head back and hopefully search the Festspielhaus.

"Where's your camera?" Betty said, breathing hard as she jogged beside him.

Frank slowed his pace, but just slightly.

"Art has it. He's covering for me. I thought it would be obvious if there weren't any bulbs flashing in the auditorium."

"He didn't ask questions?"

"Nope. I told him you were leaving tomorrow and it was our last chance to be together. Art's a romantic—if that's what you call it. He nearly kicked me out of the booth."

They found the house without any trouble. It was a small cottage not a half-mile past Wahnfried.

TRICIA GOYER

Frank tried the handle on the door, but it was locked. He pushed harder with his shoulder.

Betty's hand was on his arm. "What if Oskar finds me gone? Do you think he'll figure it out? Come looking for me?"

"You know Oskar. He doesn't leave the opera house until the last person is gone," Frank said. "It's the middle of a show. There's no way he's gonna leave."

He finally forced the door open, and they slipped inside to a kitchen area. It was warm and amazingly clean. Frank shut the door. Obviously, Oskar cared for his own home as fastidiously as he cared for the opera house. They moved past the kitchen to the living room.

"Does it smell like chemicals to you?"

Frank sniffed the air. "I smell something, and gasoline too. Or at least I think that's what I smell."

"Maybe Oskar has something to do with the fuel thefts?"

"Could be, but what would he need that for? He builds stuff…" Frank looked at the table and bench in the room. They looked like props from some type of medieval set.

Betty touched his arm. "Speaking of that, do you think he stayed around the Festspielhaus during the war? I wonder why he didn't go away and fight? Sometimes he carries himself as if he's ancient, but he's not an old man. I'd guess he's only in his early forties."

Frank scanned the room, and his gaze stopped on the photographs hanging on the wall. The first one was of a man, woman, and two small boys. He approached them to get a better look.

Betty neared as well, running her finger along the wood of the frame. "Is that Oskar and his wife?"

"No, it doesn't look exactly like him. And the photograph is older. See its graininess? And look at their clothes." He pointed to the old-fashioned suit and Victorian dress. "I'd guess it's his parents. Maybe he's one of the boys in the photo."

"Yes, I think you're right." Betty pointed to the older boy. "I'd be able to tell that reserved smile anywhere.

They looked around some more, and Frank noticed there were many items related to opera—records, programs, and photos of Wagner. He moved down a narrow hall and found two doors. The first opened to a small, but neat, room. A wool coat hung from a peg on the wall. There were more photographs on the walls, mostly of beautiful women in stage costume—actresses Oskar had met from his work at the opera house, no doubt. *I wonder if it's hard for him? These people received fame, and he received no glory for his work. Yet without him the productions wouldn't have gone on.*

Frank looked under the bed and in the closet. He checked for loose floorboards, but he didn't see anything out of the ordinary. He rubbed his temples with his fingertips.

Maybe I'm completely off. Maybe I'm jumping to conclusions.

He walked back into the hall and saw Betty in the living room, looking inside a cupboard. She moved quietly and carefully.

Frank hurried to the second room and opened the door. He was about to take a step in when he paused. Most of the room was dusty, all except a pile of items near the door that looked as if they'd been put there recently. Despite the fact that the words were in German, Frank recognized the crates of explosives immediately.

How did he steal so much? It's not like someone could just walk around town with a crate like that. Frank guessed he had stolen it little by little, over time.

"Betty, I think you need to come and see this."

She hurried to the door, glanced inside. "What is that?"

"Explosives. And look." He picked up a floor plan for the Festspiel-haus. "It looks like a layout. I can't read all the words, but from these marks it looks as if Oskar has plans for bringing the building down."

Betty's eyes widened. "It is him. He's the one." She placed a hand over her heart. "But why?" Betty leaned against the wall, staring wide-eyed.

Frank scanned the room again. It appeared to be a child's room. There was a boy's toy gun. There were children's storybooks on a table and a child's drawing on the wall. There was also a larger photograph mounted and hanging in a frame. The photo was of a mentally handi-capped boy—a mongoloid—who looked to be about ten years old.

He moved to the dresser and discovered a death certificate lying on the top. "Oskar Stein. Born January 15, 1920. Died July 20, 1938, Hadamar, Germany. Cause of death says pneumonia," he read out loud.

"That doesn't make sense." Betty stepped closer. "Oskar is alive."

"Unless…" Frank hurried to the living room and took the photo off the wall, removing it from its frame. Betty joined him, watching.

Frank pulled the photo out and read the back. 1921. "Dierk 4, Oskar 1."

"Oskar—I mean Dierk—took on his dead brother's name? I don't understand. Can that be true?" Betty asked.

"I've heard of Hadamar," Frank said. "The Nazis would euthanize anyone they called 'unfit.' Children and adults who were mentally retarded were included. Mercy killings started even before the United States was in the war. They started with mental patients who were considered incurable—useless eaters. Some people complained, but mostly just those who lost loved ones. Nothing could be done, of course. Tens of thousands of people were dead before people even understood what was happening. Many people who lost family members were told they died of natural causes."

"How do you know this?"

"I met a man in England. He found a way to smuggle out his young daughter. She was mentally handicapped, and when he received orders that she was to go to a special hospital, he refused."

"And so Oskar took his brother's name? But why?"

"Maybe so he wouldn't be forgotten, or maybe so he could live two lives. One who would care for the Festspielhaus, and one who could destroy it."

"Destroy it?"

"I think I know what's going on. Maybe our friend Oskar had his own plot to blow up Hitler—the man responsible for his brother's death."

"You mean during the Bayreuth Festival?"

"Then or perhaps another time Hitler was around."

"But he's German. Didn't all the Germans love Hitler?"

"Maybe not, especially if Hitler was responsible for the death of someone he loved very much. Some of the military tried to assassinate the man; why not someone who'd lost a loved one at his order?"

"Or maybe the loss of more than one person." Betty sat on the couch. "Oskar told me once that his mother was deaf and that his parents moved away before the war. Maybe they left so the same thing wouldn't happen to her."

"That's possible. They most likely left to save his mother's life. Maybe after what happened to his brother…" Frank let his words fade. He could tell from Betty's face she understood.

"So he planned to blow up the opera house?" Betty bit her bottom lip. "It makes sense that he would want to end Hitler's life, but why destroy the opera house? He adores Wagner, and Wagner is the one who designed and built the Festspielhaus."

Frank pressed his hand to his forehead, trying to think. "You're right, and I don't have any idea what this has to do with Kat. It doesn't make any sense. If it weren't for the costume, I'd think we were heading in the wrong direction."

Betty gripped Frank's arm. "What if—what if he's still planning to destroy it? I mean Hitler is dead, but the opera house is still there. If Kat got lost in the opera house, maybe she came across something—something she wasn't supposed to." Betty stood and looked at the photo again then returned it to the frame.

"Can you think of a motive—of why he'd want to destroy it now?"

He watched as Betty strode around the room, and suddenly she looked at him, eyes wide, as if the pieces had begun fitting together in her mind.

"Look at these things that are important to him—the music, the sets, the productions, the glory. Things are so different now. Even though Oskar was going along with the changes—like repainting old sets or the new type of music—I know he didn't like it. In fact, maybe he was serious when he told me Wagner would never be played there again. Maybe he'd rather see it go up in flames than have to"—she swallowed hard—"to have the place sink so low because of American singers and dancers."

Fear stabbed Frank's heart like a frozen lance, slicing into his chest. "We need to get back there, Betty. We have to warn them. If tonight's the last night, it's also Oskar's last chance."

Frank ran back into the kitchen, with Betty trailing right behind him. It was only then he realized that they hadn't been alone in the house. Even though he'd closed the door when they'd arrived, it was partially open now.

Were we followed? By who?

Frank opened the door wide, and before he made it two steps onto the front walk, he got the answer. In the distance, a shadowy figure was racing back to the opera house.

It was Oskar—or whatever his name was.

CHAPTER TWENTY-EIGHT

Betty had never run so fast in her life. She'd sprinted up the hill, and even though she trailed behind Frank, she worked hard at keeping up.

"Betty, I don't know where Oskar went," he called back over his shoulder. "I'm going inside. Everyone needs to clear out!"

Betty exited the woods near the back entrance to the Festspielhaus. If it weren't for the small glimmer of light that flickered in the bottom corner of the building, she would have never known there was a door there. Heaven knew, she'd walked by it dozens of times going to and from practice and shows. Mostly hidden by bushes, the small door was painted the same color as the foundation stones.

"Frank, look," she called. Then she moved toward the partially open door.

She pointed, and Frank paused. He seemed torn between running in to tell everyone and following Betty.

"We have to warn everyone! We have to get them out." He headed to the back door. "Wait for me, Betty. Wait!" Then he disappeared inside.

Betty's heart raced. *There won't be time. There will be too many people to try to get out. We have to stop him.*

Betty slipped inside the small door. The music from the concert vibrated the walls around her. She recognized the music from Wally's big band number. The moonlight from outside filtered into the room, and she could barely make out a small table and chair. She peered into the room, almost expecting Oskar to be there. Her heart pounded so hard she was sure it was going to escape from her chest. She scanned the wall and, thanks to the moonlight filtering in the door, she saw a light switch near the door.

Betty sucked in a deep breath and then stepped forward. The door shut behind her and darkness enveloped her. Stretching forward, she reached for the switch. Her hand slammed into the concrete wall and something scraped her leg.

Rest in the Lord, and wait patiently for him: fret not thyself because of him who prospereth in his way, because of the man who bringeth wicked devices to pass.... The scripture verse replayed through her mind, but she received no comfort. The words meant something completely different when she was alone in a dark room chasing a madman—or at least she hoped she was alone.

"Oh, God, please, please. I need help." Before her prayer was even finished, her fingers brushed the switch. At the same time, she heard the door creaking behind her. She flipped the switch and bright light flooded the room. Then she turned, not knowing what to expect. It was Frank, standing in the doorway.

"Thank God." She ran to him.

"I can't believe you ran in here alone."

"I can't believe you didn't follow me."

"I saw Irene. I told her to clear the place out, and I told her to get the MPs searching the place."

As if on cue, the music stopped. A muffled voice—Mickey's—could be heard over the microphone, and while Betty couldn't make out his words, from the eruption of panicked voices and stomping feet, she was sure Irene had passed the word and the opera house was clearing out.

"Betty..."

She looked at Frank's face and saw him scanning the room. She'd been so focused on the sounds above her that she hadn't taken time to see what was there. It looked as if someone had gone crazy with an ax. There was a theater chair that had been chopped into a thousand pieces. Photos of Hitler hung on the wall, all of them with slashes and knife marks. Scattered on the ground were song sheets, photographs, and programs from numerous Nazi events. Frank's guess had been right. Oskar, or Dierk, had hated Hitler. She only hoped their second guess wasn't true—that Oskar was bent on destroying the Festspielhaus, even though Hitler was gone.

"Betty, you need to leave. The MPs are no doubt taking the others back to Wahnfried. Head to the house with them. It's not safe here. The MPs are supposed to be coming."

"No. They don't know Oskar. I don't know him that well either, but maybe if I find him, I can talk to him. Or you can talk to him—about the loss of your sister. Maybe he'll see that he's not the only one who's gone through that pain. More than that"—she moved down the hall, not waiting to hear Frank's arguments. "Two sets of eyes are better than one."

Betty hurried down the hall with Frank right on her heels. She scanned from side to side as she ran, looking for doors or alcoves where Oskar could hide.

"It's just like the hall upstairs. Identical almost."

The hall stopped at a set of stairs, and Betty ran to them. They led up to a trap door. Betty stepped aside and let Frank go ahead of her. He pushed on the trap door, and she could tell that he felt resistance. He pushed harder, opening a small gap, and reaching his fingers through, he touched something. "It's a rug, I think. Can you reach up and try to pull it off as I push?"

"I'll try." Betty reached through, grabbed the edge of the rug, and pulled it over as Frank lifted.

The trap door opened, and they peeked their heads out.

"We're in the hall on the other side of the dressing rooms." She watched as Frank climbed up the stairs, pushed the rug completely out of the way, and opened the trap door fully, letting it rest on the wall.

Frank looked around. "If Kat ran down this hall by accident, and she came across Oskar—doing something—then he could have been scared and reacted."

"I can't imagine him killing her." Betty thought of the man who'd always been there, at their beck and call, to help with whatever prop they needed. "Then again, if he wanted to blow up an opera house, maybe he's not as innocent as he seems."

She climbed the stairs after Frank. At the end of the hall, a door stood partially open.

Frank hurried ahead of her and pushed the door open. Then he flipped on the light. Betty followed him.

Inside, the large room had been set up like a set of a play. Furniture had been arranged. Costumes were hung. And there was something else.

Betty hurried forward to a table bearing a hypodermic syringe with a long needle. She'd seen syringes like that before, in a newsreel that showed the concentration camps. They were used to shoot poison directly into the hearts of those condemned to die. The newsreel had said they'd been used before the gas chambers had become common.

"Betty…"

She turned to the sound of Frank's voice. He was standing near the costumes, holding one up. It was a white silk gown with sleeves. Two other dresses just like it hung on the wall. "I think we know where Kat ended up. Where she spent her last moments. Is this similar to the dress she wore?"

"Yes." Betty pointed to the needle. "And I think I know how she died." She walked over and took the dress in her hands, feeling her chin quiver.

They heard footsteps behind them, and Frank drew his gun and turned.

Betty recognized one of the MPs who'd been backstage earlier, but she didn't know the older, red-haired man with him. Both men had their guns drawn.

"Officer Frey." Frank lowered his gun and placed it back in its holster. "You're back."

"I got news yesterday that Kat's death wasn't suicide after all. I came back up here to talk to a few people, including you." Officer Frey glanced around the room. He walked over to the table and saw the long needle, nodding his head. "But maybe I had the wrong guy in my sights. I've been known to be wrong before."

"We went to Oskar's house—"

Officer Frey held up his hand, silencing Frank. "You can tell me all the details later. But I have to say I'm not happy with how you handled it. You cleared out the place, Frank. The soldiers are up in arms. Everyone in town is no doubt panicked. Do you seriously believe your friend Oskar is going to blow this place up like Irene said? Don't you think murder is bad enough?"

"I do, Officer Frey. And we can either argue about it or try to find him. I suggest we don't stand around here for long." He moved to the door and then paused. Officer Frey hurried over and pointed his gun at the dress in Betty's hands. "That looks familiar."

Betty took a step forward. "Yes, this is the same type of dress Kat was wearing when she was found in the pond. It's different from the one that she wore during the concert."

"And how did you know what she was wearing? Were you there at the pond? Or maybe…" He hurried forward and pulled the garment from her hands. "Maybe you saw photos?" He leaned in close, his face only inches away from hers.

Think, Betty, think before you speak.

Betty stepped back. Then she turned to Frank and noticed his wide-eyed gaze.

"That doesn't matter now, does it?" Frank said. "We can talk through all the details later about how Oskar did it, but we also have reason to believe he has this placed wired with explosives. They could detonate any minute."

"Fine. We'll look around. This is our job—this is what we do. I sent for the demolition experts. They're on their way to check things out. If there are explosives, we'll find them."

"It's not *if* there's explosives," Betty said. "There are. We saw crates of them. That's what we found at Oskar's house. There were boxes, crates. I have no doubt that explosives will be found around this place."

Officer Frey stepped forward, and then he motioned for Frank and Betty to leave. "If you truly think this place might explode into flames, I wouldn't stick around. And bring that extra set of prints into HQ tomorrow, Frank. We wouldn't want anyone to find them and cause a fuss."

Betty saw the look on Frank's face relax.

"C'mon, Betty." Frank stretched his hand to her. "Our work here is done. Officer Frey will take care of everything." Frank turned back one more time. "I wouldn't linger around here too long, sir—just in case." They hurriedly moved to the back of the building and then ran outside. Far off in the distance, groups of soldiers waited, watching, talking. Betty scanned the clusters of people, but she didn't see any of her friends. Or Mickey.

"So what are we going to do, just wait around until it blows?" she asked.

"Hopefully the fact that Mickey made tonight the last show caught Oskar by surprise. Maybe he wasn't finished setting everything up.

Maybe that's why he never got Hitler—his evil motives outweighed his skill." Frank shrugged. "That's what he gets for trying to accomplish such a big goal alone."

"Or maybe he stopped his plans when Hitler died. Who knows how long those things have been in that room? Maybe he killed Kat for a different reason."

"C'mon, Betty. They're right. Let's not worry about this. The proper authorities have everything under control."

"They don't have Oskar." She felt a shudder travel up her spine. "Do you think he's still in there? Did you see him run inside?"

"No, actually I didn't. I lost him on the hill. I just assumed he went inside the Festspielhaus."

"Good. Maybe he ran off and is hiding in the woods. Maybe he never had any intentions of coming back and setting off explosives. I hope for the guys in there that's the case. I hope he never comes back."

Frank put an arm around her shoulders, as if assuring her he'd protect her. "I don't think he'll be showing his face any time soon. At least I hope he won't."

Betty was still trying to process all she'd learned in the last few hours when she noticed someone approaching.

"There you are." It was Billy, Irene's boyfriend. "The girls were asking about you. They were worried when they looked around backstage and you weren't there. Irene hoped that you went back to Wahnfried. They're scared that the same thing happened to you that happened to…"

"Happened to Kat? Is that what they're worried about?"

Billy nodded.

Betty turned to Frank. "We should hurry down there. Maybe we can get a ride. Those girls are scared of their own shadow."

"Yes, but you can't blame them with the ghost and all," Billy snickered.

"Ghost?" Frank asked.

"It's squirrels or something in the basement. Sometimes we could hear shuffling below us. Other times it sounded like footsteps," Betty explained. "Kat was horribly worried about it. She said they were ghosts of former Nazi officers."

"So that's where the Nazi officers used to stay?"

"Yes, it's the Wagner family home. All visiting dignitaries stayed there. Hitler too—"

Betty's words were interrupted by the sound of a woman's cry. "Frank! Frank!"

They turned and noticed a woman being dragged from the back door of the Festspielhaus.

"Do you know that woman?" she asked.

Frank didn't answer Betty. Instead, he rushed forward. "Magdalena," he called.

CHAPTER TWENTY-NINE

Betty looked at the dark-haired woman sitting on the chair across from her and Frank. After Magdalena had insisted that she needed to talk to Frank, they'd all gotten a ride to Frank's house from an MP. Betty had only gone along under one condition—if Billy would go to Wahnfried to tell the others that she was okay. She'd caused enough people to worry about her lately.

"We caught this one sneaking around," the MP had said. And it was only later, when Frank had guided the thin, shivering form to one of the MP's jeeps, that he explained to Betty that the woman was Art's friend.

Now Betty eyed her, remembering how Frank had told her that he knew someone who used to sing at the Festspielhaus when Wagner's works were performed. *Was this poor woman once a famous opera singer?* Betty's heart went out to her.

"I needed to talk to you. I told Art to ask you to meet. I went to Festspielhaus looking for you." Magdalena lowered her head. "I knew I can trust you—saw you in church."

"It was you? You wrote all the letters?"

The woman nodded.

"Did you leave that note at the church too?" Frank asked.

"Yes, the message was something Dierk's father say to him. I hoped you would ask him to translate."

"What was it?" Betty asked.

"*Fear lends wings.*" Frank turned to Betty. "Oscar—Dierk—told me it meant fear would make you do things that you think impossible in any other situation."

"When Dierk become afraid, his father told him he was stronger than he believe."

"Yes, but what is Oskar afraid of now?"

"Many things. But most maybe afraid of finding happiness when all he loves is gone. His family, music."

"Is that why he wanted to destroy the Festspielhaus? So he wouldn't find happiness in different people, in different music?"

"I do not know. Then if I know Dierk, I know he had big plans."

"You think there's something bigger than blowing up the opera house?" Frank rose and walked to the window, looking out, as if checking to make sure Oskar was not out there, listening, waiting.

Seeing him made Betty want to tell Magdalena that she'd heard enough. With each passing day there were more problems, more pain. She didn't know if she wanted to hear the rest.

When will it be over?

Maybe I should be happy we're supposed to leave tomorrow. Who wouldn't want to leave this madness behind?

But deep inside she didn't want to leave. She wanted to see this through. She'd left home without closure, and finding answers here seemed ten times more important.

"We have to figure out what Oskar was up to—where he went," Betty said.

"I do not believe Dierk wants something big," Magdalena said, her voice soft, as if she too feared Oskar lurked. "It is about being complete. In all things, Dierk finishes all he works on."

"I'm still not used to it when you say Dierk." Betty tucked her hair behind her ear. "Everyone in the USO thought his name was Oskar. How do you know so much about him? Did you work with him often?"

Magdalena wrapped her arms around her waist, as if trying to hold her emotions inside. Still, her shoulders quivered. "We were in love at one time. We saw each other for many years. We kept our relationship hidden. No one would understood."

"Because you were the star singer and…"

"And he was prop director, yes." Magdalena lifted her gaze and focused on Betty's face. "Then things changed. Hitler came to power. Hitler took everything away—all Dierk loved. It started with his brother, Oskar."

"Yes, we saw his photo. Was he mentally retarded?" Frank rejoined them at the table.

"Yes, but you would never know if you saw him with Dierk. He brought Oskar to the workshop. He was teaching him to bring tools and lift props. Then mercy killings start—but no one know what happening at time. The mentally retarded were taken to special homes. Our leaders promised to care for them. Dierk resisted, but then his parents thought this would be better. His mother was deaf and ill. She was having a hard time caring for Oskar. His father was older too, and Dierk had much to lose. Hitler was personal friends with Wagner family, and he gave money to Festspielhaus. Yearly festival bigger each year. He had no choice. Dierk agreed to let them send Oskar for care."

"And his parents?"

"When questions came about deaf, blind, elderly—Dierk's parents moved. He was alone. His whole self filled with hate."

"Were you still engaged at this time?" Betty reached over and took Frank's hand.

"Yes, months after his parents left, but Dierk heard about Oskar's death and was different. He was always thinking about Hitler, especially when Fuehrer was in Bayreuth—when Hitler sleeping just down road.

"One evening Dierk was very angry. I left his house after dinner, but something tells me stay close. I walked down road and hide in bushes and watch. Dierk left house, and I believe he go to Festspielhaus. No, he not stop, keep going. He walked to Wahnfried. I saw him go to back, and that is all I saw. Somehow I think he make it inside, and I think I will hear next day Hitler killed in sleep."

"Weren't the SS guards there?"

"Yes, by road, but Oskar gone around back of house. His father did construction, you know, just as on opera house. I am sure Oskar knows more about Wahnfried than Wagners. He loves opera house.

"Or loved it." Magdalena corrected herself. "I can know why he would wish to destroy the Festspielhaus. He hated Hitler but he loved Wagner. I know him. I watched him. I snuck in during practices. I tried to hide."

"It was you." Frank slapped his leg. "It makes sense now. I'm glad I wasn't seeing things."

"Yes, I watched performances, and I knew what he is thinking—better to destroy opera house than have such performances done on stage. First Hitler and then Americans—I know he believed place he loved be disgraced forever. I wrote letters because I almost know what he was thinking, and I worry."

"It was you," Frank exclaimed.

Betty wanted to interrupt, to ask about what letters they were talking about, but she knew it wasn't the most important thing right now.

"You know of my letters."

Frank nodded. "They were given to me. I was looking into them. And that last letter…" Frank let his voice trail off.

"I asked Art to give to you. He asked no questions. Giving them to offices did not help. I knew you help me. You love my God. I saw you praying. I knew I could trust you."

"But how did you know that Betty would be able to point out the dress?"

"I wait in woods outside Festspielhaus. I heard this was last performance. I want to talk to Oskar. To tell him maybe things change. That Wagner's operas come again." Her words caught in her throat. "I saw Oskar carry her. It was dark—in middle of night." Sobs interrupted Magdalena's words. "She—she was dead."

"And you saw the dress?" Betty asked. "And you knew I'd recognize it was the wrong one?"

Magdalena wiped her face and nodded. "Yes, it was opera dress."

"But why were you willing to reveal yourself by giving Art the letter?" Frank asked. "Surely you knew that eventually Art would have told me where the letter had come from. You were putting yourself at risk."

"I was more afraid for other death. Art told me you took photographs of Kat. I knew Songbird—she would know dress. I am afraid something was going to happen—soon."

"I don't understand."

"There are important dates. People understand Wagner and know this. Important dates, like when some Wagner's operas first performed."

"Like *Rienzi*?" Betty blurted out, pleased with herself for once again feeling part of the conversation.

"Yes."

"And when was that?" Frank gave Betty a curious look, as if impressed she'd figured that out.

"Was not performed in Bayreuth—but date was October 20, 1842," Magdalena said. "I know this because I performed in production one hundred years later." She sighed. "It not been performed at Bayreuth Festival. And some people think never to be."

"Betty and I heard a little about the opera—about how Rienzi tried to defeat the nobles and raise the power of the people. We know he doesn't succeed, but how does he die?"

"He burns."

Betty felt her heartbeat quicken, and then everything started fitting together in her mind. She rose from the sofa, kneeling before Magdalena. "What part did you play?"

"I do not understand why is important."

"Just tell me." Betty took Magdalena's hand.

"I play Messenger of Peace. I wore white silk gown. Same he put on woman."

"He's sacrificing all he loves," Betty blurted out. "The Festspiel-haus—and the woman he loved. In his twisted mind he placed Kat in your role." Betty focused on Magdalena's face. "The show was starting—his big plans. He didn't have you, but he had her. Kat was in the wrong place at the wrong time."

"But he not succeed destroy Festspielhaus." Magdalena looked to Frank.

"Maybe because everything happened too soon." Frank stroked his cheek. "October twentieth is still ten days away."

"But what if that was only one part of his plan? What if there was someplace else—smaller, closer that he could still destroy? Some place less complicated to blow up?" Betty stood and turned to Frank.

"We need to get to the Wahnfried." He reached a hand to her.

Betty felt tension tighten her neck, and she thought of her friends. Please, Lord, no—please protect them.

"But how? How will we get there?" Betty followed him outside. She glanced back and noticed Magdalena wasn't following. "Are you coming?" Betty asked, then she turned and could see the woman through the open door. Magdalena just sat, as if frozen in her seat.

"C'mon, Betty, we don't have time."

Betty followed him, climbing into the jeep. Then she watched as he reached down under the dashboard, fiddling with some wires. Ten seconds later, the engine roared to life.

"I never stole candy from the general store," Frank said, "but my sister did like to dare me a lot…"

He popped the vehicle into gear and steered into the street.

"Well, at least your vice came in handy," she said as they drove away.

* * * *

Betty was surprised when they approached the estate and didn't see any MPs by their jeeps.

"Where are the guards? The MPs?"

When they turned onto the driveway, she noticed one MP standing there, gun pointed. The worried look on his face softened when he noticed Betty.

"Are the performers inside?" she asked.

"Yes." The man nodded as he walked up to the jeep. "All the women, and the drummer too."

"And the rest of the guards?" Frank asked again.

"Oskar—the prop manager—arrived not too long ago and said there was another body in the pond. The MPs went to check it out."

"They left?"

"Oskar said he would watch over everyone inside—said he and Billy would be able to handle it."

"Oskar's inside?" Betty's hand covered her mouth, and she felt her shoulders tremble.

"Yes."

Frank pushed his finger into the MP's chest. "Go get Officer Frey now. He's at the Festspielhaus. Tell him to bring as much backup as he can."

Frank jumped out of the jeep and Betty followed. He paused, looking back at her as if weighing if she should come.

Betty jutted out her chin. "I'm going." Then she ran up the front steps and opened the door to the house before he could stop her. Frank pounded right behind her.

Betty took two steps in and paused. There, sitting next to the phonograph, was Oskar, but he wasn't listening to the record the young soldier had left. It sounded like the music she'd heard in newsreels and she guessed it must be Wagner's music.

"Oskar, what are you doing?" Frank asked, stepping forward.

The bottom cabinet to the phonograph was open and Betty saw explosives inside. *Had they been there the whole time?* Her knees weakened, and she reached a hand toward Frank. From the corner of her eye, she noticed Frank reaching for his gun.

"I would not do that, Mr. Witt." Oskar lifted his hand, and Betty saw he was holding something—she assumed some kind of trigger—with a wire that led to the explosives. "Put your pistol on the floor and then kick it my direction."

"Okay, Oskar. I trust you. I know you wouldn't want to hurt Betty. We are your friends." Frank put the gun on the floor and then kicked it toward Oskar. It was far enough that Frank couldn't reach it, but not close enough for Oskar to reach either. Betty's heart sank as it slid across the room.

"Where is everyone?" Betty asked, looking down the hall.

"They are locked up at the moment—in a special room I set up in the basement. The concentration camp down the road was not using their poisonous gas at the time, and I thought I would borrow some."

"Are they—they dead?" Betty's throat grew thick, tight.

"Not yet. I had a dilemma. To use the gas or the explosives. I was going to gas them first—a mercy killing really—until I heard the jeep pull up." He glared at Frank. "You foiled things again, Mr. Witt. I thought you were only supposed to be around to photograph big events, not stop them."

Betty shook her head. "I don't understand. Why are you doing this?"

"There was a boy of fifteen. He listened to an opera and he had an idea of ruling the world. In his madness…" Oskar's words caught in his throat. "My brother was my best friend. The most gentle person you can imagine." Tears rimmed his eyes.

"I'm so sorry about your loss. But Hitler is dead. The war is over."

"As long as this house stands, people will come. Not tomorrow or the next day, but they will come. They will stay here." Oskar's voice rose in volume. "They will walk these halls. They will come and hear the music at the Festspielhaus—darkness will be carried upon the notes. It will come upon them as it did Hitler. I cannot let this stand."

"It's too late. They've already discovered the explosives in the opera house," Frank lied. "There are men there right now taking them out. If you turn yourself in now…"

"No!"

"But the women," Betty said. "We only tried to do a good thing. If you kill them—you would be the same as Hitler. Dierk." She dared to use his name. "You will kill innocent people just like Hitler did. What do you think your brother Oskar would think about that?"

Dierk's eyes widened. His finger twitched on the trigger.

"I think it's more than that—more than what Oskar—Dierk—is saying." Frank looked to her. Then he looked to Dierk. "There's a story I heard, you see. It happened in 1908. Claude Monet had worked three years on some new paintings, and they were going to be exhibited in a huge gallery. Two nights before the show, they were previewed by friends, family members, and critics. Everyone said the pieces were Monet's best work. But when workers arrived the next day to prepare for the exhibit, they found three of the paintings had been slashed with a knife. Monet was heartbroken, and the art world in an uproar. No one understood how someone could be so calloused to destroy such beauty. Pleas rose in the papers for the criminal to turn himself in. The perpetrator, of course, didn't do that. Just one day away from the exhibition, everyone was worried the crime would happen again. Guards were posted outside the building, making it impossible for anyone to get in. That night, three more paintings were destroyed—again some of Monet's best work. The crime was committed by the guard who'd been posted inside the building. He was asked, 'You know what will happen, don't you?'

"'Yes, I'll be tried and most likely imprisoned for life,' the man answered.

"'Aren't you sad about losing your freedom?' they asked him.

"'Yes, I am.'

"'Then why would you commit such a crime?' they asked. 'Surely there isn't anyone in all of France who will have pity on you.'

"'My life is meaningless,' the man said. 'All my life I've met great men and women and seen them praised. I have no talents, but I wanted to do something to force people to notice me. To put my name in the papers.'

"He was hauled away to jail," Frank continued, "but not before he gave one last statement. 'Many people will remember Monet. They will praise him. But now they will also speak of the man who destroyed the work of a master. Losing my freedom is a small price to pay for immortality.'"

Betty looked at Frank, sure he'd lost his mind. *Oh great, I'm dealing with two crazy men now.*

"Are you saying that's me? That I'm bent on destroying Wahnfried and Festspielhaus for fame?" Dierk jutted his chin.

"No, for immortality. If you had succeeded, your name would have indeed lived on. Twenty years from now, no one will remember the man who kept the Festspielhaus in running order—through the Germans and the Americans—but they will remember the man who destroyed it—and destroyed Wahnfried, filled with American musicians and singers. Isn't that right?"

"How dare you!" Dierk stood. In his hand, the trigger trembled.

Betty heard something—the sound of wood being smashed. She looked to Frank, but his eyes remained focused on Oskar.

"Admit it! This has nothing to do with your brother. That is only an excuse!" Frank shouted.

"I do not need to admit anything. How dare you accuse me of such things. Besides, these women—singers you call them—these musicians, they deserve to die." He lifted his hand, as if preparing to release the trigger. "Using such a great stage for their—"

Frank darted forward.

"No—stop!" Betty cried. "Stop!"

A gunshot split the air, and Betty saw Frank dive for the trigger. At the same time she watched as Dierk fell into the chair. Frank grabbed for the man's hand and held it closed around the trigger.

"Betty, don't move!" a voice called from the kitchen area. Betty recognized that voice. She turned just as Officer Frey stepped from the back where the boarded-up door was, gun raised and pointed.

"You okay, Frank?" Officer Frey asked, approaching him.

Frank nodded, taking the trigger out of Oskar's hand, holding it. "I'll feel better when one of your experts can get here and disarm this thing. If it had released all the way, this whole place could have gone up. From what Betty heard at night, my guess is Oskar likely has the whole house wired."

Dierk slid to the floor, moaning. Officer Frey handcuffed his hands behind his back.

"I see the MP found you," Frank said, letting out a slow breath, attempting to calm his heart, despite the trigger in his hand.

"Yes," Officer Frey said. "As far as I was concerned, it was the third time you cried wolf. But since the other two times turned out to be accurate, I decided to respond to the call."

"You found explosives then? At the Festspielhaus?" Betty asked.

"There were rooms full of them. It looks like this man was stopped before he finished, but there was enough to send up some fireworks, that's for sure."

A jeep parked in front of the estate, and Betty looked out the window to see four more military police climb out.

"The others—they're in the basement." She turned to Officer Frey. "I think there's some type of door from the back leading down—or at least that's my guess from what Magdalena said. Oskar's plan would have worked if it wasn't for her."

"Another hero?" Officer Frey asked.

"Yes, she is. We'll introduce you to her later. And speaking of heros…" Betty hurried to Frank and stroked his cheek. "Are you okay?"

"I'm fine." Then he looked over to Officer Frey. "Go get the others. I'll be here when you're done. I promise. I'm not going anywhere until this is disarmed."

"Harmon, Johnson," Officer Frey said to two of the four MPs that entered, "get over here and haul this guy to the field hospital. We need him patched up enough to face trial. Smith, Adams," he said to the other two, "you come with me and get that door open to free those girls."

"Trial? Does that include a murder trial?" Betty asked.

Her question paused Officer Frey's steps. "For the murder of Katherine Wiseman. Between the secret rooms, Oskar's explosives, and the fact that Katherine was wearing one of Oskar's costumes, we have a good case. Then there's this." Officer Frey pulled a handkerchief out of his pocket. Gingerly unfolding it, he revealed a silver cigarette holder.

Betty nodded, tears filling her eyes. "That's Kat's too. Where did you find it?"

"In the room he'd set up. With the needle and poison used for lethal injections there too, we're almost positive we found the murder scene."

Betty's heart felt as if someone had bruised it. Her mind replayed Kat's last day. Hearing the news about Edward. Her worry about returning to the screen. Trying to perform. Running out.

"Kat no doubt had come upon Oskar—or upon some incriminating evidence—when she was lost," Betty said. "And Oskar couldn't let word get out."

"Yes, but think of it this way." Officer Frey approached and placed a hand on Betty's shoulder. "If that hadn't happened—if Kat hadn't died, Oskar might have pulled it off. She lost her life but saved thousands in the process. If Oskar's plan would have succeeded, the whole place would have gone up, with all the soldiers inside."

Betty nodded, looking to Frank through tear-filled eyes. "And sometimes knowing that—knowing the lives that were saved—makes it easier to handle our losses, doesn't it?"

* * * *

Betty looked up at the giant moon as she sat on the front porch of Wahnfried next to Frank. The explosives had been disarmed. Her friends had been found. Rescued. And now they were trying to calm themselves in their rooms. Even the MPs had settled down in their jeeps—expecting a quiet night. She finally had a chance to sit next to Frank and truly think through what had just happened.

"So you have to tell me." She leaned her head against his shoulder. "How did you figure out what Oskar was really up to—especially the part that all of his motives centered around his desire to be known—remembered?"

Frank ran his fingers through her hair. "I thought of it when I was in his house. There were those photos of famous singers and musicians. And I thought about how hard it would be for him to be behind the scenes all the time. Sometimes I feel that way—to a much lesser degree. The images I capture move people, but no one looks at the byline. There are all types of behind-the-scenes stuff. I'm okay with that, but obviously, Oskar wasn't. He took care of everything and made sure the productions could go on, but he never received his reward. He heard the applause, but it wasn't for him. He knew the opera stars, but to them he was a nobody."

She closed her eyes, enjoying the touch of Frank's fingers through her hair. For the first time, she realized how tired she was. "So how did you think to tell that story about Monet's paintings? That's awful, by the way. Poor man."

Frank chuckled, surprising Betty.

"I made it up, every word."

"What? Tell me you're joking!" She sat up and looked at him, noticing a sparkle of humor in his eyes.

"That's the truth, Betty. I made it up. The whole truth is that Monet destroyed the paintings himself. A few days before the exhibition, he went through and slashed them all with knives. He said they were rubbish. But according to the critics, they were his best work." Then he tapped the tip of her nose. "Artists, I hear, can be very temperamental."

"That's so sad." She leaned back against him again. "What a loss."

"I know. It's a shame. Sometimes we don't realize what we have until we destroy it."

"It sounds like you're not talking about Monet's paintings anymore?"

"No, Betty. I'm talking about us. I'm sorry I told you that I didn't care, and that I had used you."

"Frank, I could see how you felt every time you looked at me."

"Well, I want to be perfectly honest from now on, so there's something else I need to tell you. Something I've hidden from you. And I promise it's not a fraulein."

"You're making this sound serious."

"Well, anything I keep from you is serious, right? And it's important to me." He sighed. "What I've been trying to say is that those days when I didn't come around, I was actually taking classes—high school classes. Betty, the truth is I never finished. I was so eager to do my part in the war that I dropped out and joined. I didn't think much of it until the war was over. Then—well, then I really started thinking about it when I met you. A man needs to think about the future."

"Oh, Frank, is that what you've been worried about? Don't you see that I care for you—respect you—for who you are now?"

"So you don't think any less of me for being in high school?" he asked.

Betty grinned and stroked his face. "I've never met a high school boy like you before. Good thing there weren't any around Santa

Monica. I might have never have come over here to Germany—and found you. And I would have never experienced such a kiss, under a German moon."

"What kiss?"

"This one," she said, leaning up and pressing her lips to his.

EPILOGUE

There was standing room only at the Festspielhaus. Two months had passed since their last show. It had taken that long for the place to be cleared of all danger, and the GIs seemed ready for holiday entertainment.

Betty watched as Irene chased Billy around the stage in a short skit they'd dreamed up. They circled around the other musicians, to the edge of the stage and back, a real cat-and-mouse chase.

Then, in the middle of it, Billy paused and turned to Irene. "What do you want," he asked, "a chocolate bar?"

The soldier's roared with laughter, and Betty did too.

After that was over, Mickey announced the last number of the night, performed by Wally's band. They played a jazzy piece, and Betty reached over and grabbed Frank's hand, swinging their arms to the beat. Today, he'd told her before the show, Art had volunteered to get the photos, and Frank was just around to stand by her side and clap the loudest—something Betty actually enjoyed.

She couldn't help but study Frank's face more than she studied the show. After Dierk was jailed, Betty had written home and told her family about all the danger wrapped around her first week in

Bayreuth—but she spent even more time writing to tell them about the handsome soldier she'd met. Her mother's letters were now coming regularly, and Mother stated that Frank indeed sounded like someone worthy of Betty's heart.

Betty had been even more surprised to receive a letter from Frank's family. She smiled, remembering how Frank's mother had stated that if Frank waited too long to suggest marriage that Betty might consider asking *him*. Betty hoped it wouldn't come to that, but she had always dreamed of a Christmas wedding.

The jazz number ended, and Mickey headed out to wish everyone good night. He'd barely gotten started when the soldiers interrupted his words.

"Songbird, Songbird." A chant rose up, filling the large room with men's voices.

Betty turned to Frank. "What are they saying?"

"They're saying your name, darling. You better head out there. I don't think they're going to stop until they get another song."

"What should I sing?"

Frank smiled at her. "Do you think it matters?"

"No." Laughter spilled from her lips.

Betty moved onto the stage with quick steps, feeling her skirt swishing around her knees as she walked. Cheers rose up when the men saw her, and when she placed a finger over her lips they quieted down.

"Tonight I'm gonna sing a special song, for a special guy..."

"Me!" a GI in the back shouted.

"Me!" another said.

"Me too!" Shouts erupted around the room.

Betty rested a hand on her hip and looked toward the orchestra. "'It Had to Be You' please, Wally? For…"

She swept her arm, waving it in front of the whole audience. "For all these guys and especially for—" She turned and pointed to where Frank stood on the side stage—or rather where he had been standing. "You." Her brow furrowed, seeing he was no longer there.

The music started, and she no longer had a chance to worry where Frank went. She had an audience to entertain.

"It had to be you—" she sang.

Cheers erupted, and Betty tried to continue singing, but her words were interrupted by the noise. She paused and placed her hands on her hips, noticing that many of the guys were pointing behind her. Betty turned and gasped as she saw Frank there—a smiling Frank, dressed in a white suit and kneeling on one knee.

He held up his hand and in it a simple gold ring glimmered under the spotlights. The music continued playing, the crowd continued cheering. Betty could see Frank's lips moving and while she hoped he was saying what she thought he was saying, she couldn't hear his words.

She leaned down, moving her mouth close to his ear. "What did you say?"

He stood, grabbed her, and pulled her close. "Betty…"

She didn't think it was possible, but the cheers behind her grew even louder.

Frank leaned closer, nearly shouting into her ear. "Betty, will you marry me?"

Betty stepped back slightly and nodded. "Yes!" She wasn't sure if he heard her, but she was sure he understood, because he placed the ring on her finger. Then a smile filled Frank's face, and he swept her up, twirling her around in a circle.

Finally, she felt her feet touch the ground. Frank stepped back and then he turned her back to the crowd.

She knew she had a song to finish.

Betty took a deep breath and waited as Wally picked up where she'd left off.

"It had to be you…"

Heart-stopping suspense...
entwined with soul-searching romance...
set against a historical backdrop readers will love!

Summerside Press™ is pleased to announce the launch of our fresh line of romantic-suspense fiction—set amid the action-packed eras of the twentieth century. Watch for a total of six new Summerside Press™ historical romantic-suspense titles to release in 2010.

Now Available in Stores

Sons of Thunder
by Susan May Warren
ISBN 978-1-935416-67-8

Two brothers love her—but only one can have her heart. Sofia Frangos is torn between the love of hot-headed, passionate Markos, and his younger brother, quiet, intelligent Dino. Markos longs to honor his family, Dino wants to forget the tragedy that drove them from their Greek home to the shores of America. One brother offers the past she loves...the other, a future. Which "Son of Thunder" will she choose? From Chicago's sultry jazz-era clubs...to Europe's World War II battlefields...to a final showdown on a Greek island, the *Sons of Thunder* discover betrayal, sacrifice—and finally...redemption.

Coming Soon

Exciting New Romantic-Suspense Stories by These Great Authors—
Cara Putman...Susan Page Davis...Melanie Dobson...and MORE!